THE DUKE'S GUIDE TO FAKE COURTSHIP

JADE LEE

HISTORICAL

If you purchased this book without a cover you should be aware that this book is stolen property. It was reported as "unsold and destroyed" to the publisher, and neither the author nor the publisher has received any payment for this "stripped book."

Harlequin® HISTORICAL

ISBN-13: 978-1-335-53995-3

The Duke's Guide to Fake Courtship

Copyright © 2025 by Greyle Entertainment, LLC

All rights reserved. No part of this book may be used or reproduced in any manner whatsoever without written permission.

Without limiting the author's and publisher's exclusive rights, any unauthorized use of this publication to train generative artificial intelligence (AI) technologies is expressly prohibited.

This is a work of fiction. Names, characters, places and incidents are either the product of the author's imagination or are used fictitiously. Any resemblance to actual persons, living or dead, businesses, companies, events or locales is entirely coincidental.

For questions and comments about the quality of this book, please contact us at CustomerService@Harlequin.com.

TM and ® are trademarks of Harlequin Enterprises ULC.

Harlequin Enterprises ULC
22 Adelaide St. West, 41st Floor
Toronto, Ontario M5H 4E3, Canada
www.Harlequin.com

Printed in U.S.A.

Recycling programs for this product may not exist in your area.

Are you rea...

USA TOD...

Sisters Grace and Lucy were belatedly found in China by their long-lost father, the Earl of Wenshire. Taken back to England, and in need of advantageous matches, each is thrown into the world of London society, catty tea parties and extravagant balls. But Grace and Lucy were raised to fight for their happiness, and scary debutante mothers won't stop them!

When Grace is propositioned by Duke Declan to engage in a fake courtship in exchange for rejecting his cousin's proposal, their staged caresses and practiced dances begin to feel all too real in

The Duke's Guide to Fake Courtship

And look out for the book of her younger sister, Lucy, coming soon!

Author Note

Who doesn't love a fake courtship? It's one of my favorite tropes, and I got to really indulge with this book because it's not only one fake courtship! Just how many people are pretending to be in love? Hard to tell, honestly, because our characters aren't exactly sure what they want or how they feel. Isn't that the way love works? One moment we're being polite, exploring possibilities with a handsome earl, and then the next, everything changes. A duke shows up, meddling parents destroy our peace and we're trying to be honest about our feelings—but what exactly are they? There's love, intrigue and some very good spice in this tale. I hope you enjoy it as much as I did!

Jade Lee has been scripting love stories since she first picked up a set of paper dolls. Ball gowns and rakish lords were her first loves, which naturally led her to the world of regency romance. A *USA TODAY* and Amazon bestseller, she has a gift for creating lively worlds, witty dialogue and hot, sexy humor. She's earned an MFA in screenwriting from the University of Southern California, published seventy novels and won several industry awards including PRISM Best of the Best, RT Reviewers' Choice and *Fresh Fiction*'s Steamiest Read. Check out her devilishly clever historical romances at www.jadeleeauthor.com.

And lest you think *Bridgerton* is her only fav fandom, she's got a few other fancies. She adores shifters and writes about them as Kathy Lyons—visit www.kathylyons.com. But her biggest love is for her grandkids. They inspired her foray into picture books as Kat Chen—visit www.kat-chen.com.

The Duke's Guide to Fake Courtship is Jade Lee's debut title for Harlequin Historical.

Look out for more books from Jade Lee, coming soon.

For Soraya, my amazing editor.
This book would never have happened
or been as awesome without you.

Chapter One

Declan was a temperate man.

He did not consider that a virtue. It was an act of self-preservation against a father and uncle, a drunkard and a wastrel respectively. Not to mention nine previous generations of vicious arseholes who all carried the Byrning name. Once upon a time, that had been an asset. The Byrnings had helped tame England and had received titles and coin in reward. But now Declan lived in a civilised time where intemperate rages were frowned upon.

His mother had declared—when he was three years old—that he would be a temperate man or she would destroy him. He had done his best to comply. What boy didn't want to please his mother? And so no one knew the fury that seethed beneath his exterior.

Unfortunately, it was very close to the surface now. His mother was banging on his chamber door the morning after his birthday celebration and he was imagining violently ripping the door off its hinges and throwing it out of the window. Unfortunately, he knew even that show of temper would not deter her.

'Good God! Shut her up!' he growled into his pillow.

'Brisley is handling it, Your Grace,' said his valet, his words thankfully very muted.

'He won't last for long,' he retorted, because his mother was nothing if not determined.

So he forced himself upright and grabbed the restorative offered by his valet. Declan doubted that it would help, but it could hardly hurt. He choked it down, then forced himself into the wingback chair next to the shuttered window. A minute later, he opened the newspaper, as if he didn't wish himself at the bottom of the Thames.

Only then did he bid the man open his bedroom door.

'Good morning, Mother. Have you come to wish me a belated happy birthday?'

'I fail to see why one should celebrate the mere fact—'

'Of living another year,' he finished for her.

She said something to that effect every year. Fortunately, his father had been more jovial in that and every way, so there'd been happy birthdays throughout his thirty-one years. The former Duke had also been more violent and hateful, so the memories were a mixed bag. In any event, this had been the first birthday celebrated without his father, and that had made it a commemorative one.

'Don't interrupt me,' his mother snapped.

'Don't burst into my bedchamber or pound on my door.' He'd almost said his father's door, but of course it was his now. 'You don't live here, Mother.'

And she hadn't for several years. At present, she resided with her sister-in-law in a neat townhouse far removed from the London ducal residence.

'But I am still responsible for seeing to the seemly disposition of the family.'

Yes, she had taken on that mantle, hadn't she? She and his aunt had set themselves up as the moral authority over the entire extended family. And, given that they both held inordinate influence over polite society, she did have some power in that regard. But if she planned to chide him for celebrating his birthday, then she was—

'Cedric is in trouble,' she pronounced. 'You must stop him.' She pulled out a pocket watch from her reticule. 'You have until teatime.'

He frowned—a painful act—as he set the paper aside. This unseemly display was about his cousin?

'Where is he?' Last he'd heard, the man had travelled to China with the East India Company.

'You'll find him at the docks, on a boat called *The Integrity*. As if naming a thing is enough to give—'

'When did he arrive in London?'

And why hadn't the man contacted him? Declan certainly would have invited his cousin to his birthday celebration. The two had been at school together, and though not quite the same age—Declan was older by three years—were close enough to be friends.

'How should I know? He sent a note this morning, informing his mother of the details. He intends to bring some chit to tea today.' She shuddered. 'I shan't be there, of course. It would be inappropriate for me to overshadow my sister's tea just because she lives upon my indulgence. And besides, we have agreed that you will stop this nonsense immediately.'

Of course they had agreed. Never mind that Declan might have a different opinion. But, rather than address any of the many objectionable things she'd said, he decided to focus on the most important.

'Cedric is engaged?'

'Not officially, of course. That's what you have to stop!'

Good Lord, the woman's voice was a near shriek—and she was a woman who never raised her voice. He waited for her to continue while simultaneously hoping that she would expire upon the spot.

She did not do either. In the end, he had to prompt her.

'Why should I stop it?'

'Because the girl is miserably unsuitable. His mother and I have discussed this often. We have decided on the ladies who will serve the Earldom. This chit does not.'

Yes, he knew that the two women had developed lists of eligible girls for their sons. It was their favourite discussion and they never thought to involve their sons in any of their decisions.

'Who is this woman?'

'She's the illegitimate child of Lord Wenshire, and Cedric is bringing her to tea.' She made a face as if the man was bringing spoiled fish.

'Shouldn't you meet the woman before—?'

'Unsuitable!' she snapped.

He winced. 'Yes, I heard that.'

'Fix it.'

He waited a moment, staring at his mother's rigid face. He wondered for a long, self-indulgent moment what she would do if he refused. There were several hundred ways she could make his life unpleasant, but at the end of the day it would merely be uncomfortable. He was now the Duke, she the Dowager Duchess. Officially, he held all the power. He could refuse her at his whim.

But that was the response of a child, not an adult, and certainly not one of a duke. His cousin's choice of wife was significant, not simply because Cedric was a future earl. Cedric stood shoulder to shoulder with Declan as leaders of their respective branches of the family. A wife would influence the family for better or worse in very significant ways.

Declan owed it to everyone to meet the girl.

'Very well,' he said as he set aside the paper unread. 'I will go.'

His mother nodded with a self-satisfied smile. 'I knew you would rise to the occasion. I hope you see now how intemperance one night makes the next morning nearly unbearable.'

He gritted his teeth. Damn the woman for being right. Several caustic words burned on his tongue, but he swallowed them down. She was still his mother, not to mention a duchess, and therefore deserved some respect. Also, cutting into her for her overbearing, supercilious, condescending attitude would be like scolding a dog for having fur. It was simply who the woman was, and he had ceased tilting at windmills some time in his early adolescence.

He did arch his brows at her, in an attempt at ducal arrogance. 'I cannot dress with you here,' he said. 'And therefore I cannot depart for this boat.'

She sniffed, as if his words had an actual smell. 'First you will deal with your cousin, and then I should like you to attend Almack's this Thursday. There are several girls I have selected who will make excellent duchesses—after my instruction, of course. Select one this week and you can be well on your way to filling a nursery this time next year.'

He didn't bother interrupting her. The woman rarely stopped speaking even when interrupted. So he waited in stiff silence until she was silent. Then he gave her a single, hard word.

'No.'

'What—?'

'No.'

She rolled her eyes, then abruptly decided on a gentler approach. She settled herself in the chair opposite his and spoke calmly.

'Declan, think. If you are to avoid the legacy of your name, you need a wife who is calm, who doesn't invite rages, who is unimpeachable in character and lineage. There are precious few of those around. Indeed, I have inspected every one within a decade of your age.'

He shuddered to think of how that process had gone.

'Mother,' he said dryly, 'you will not be selecting my bride.'

'Well, of course not!' she snapped, her softer tone gone. 'I have just narrowed the field—'

'I will select my own bride. Soon. You will not dictate that. Do not even try.'

She tsked deep in her throat. And then her brows went up and she took on *that tone*. The one she'd used all through his childhood. The one that told him exactly what she was about to say now.

'You are too mercurial to make this decision. It is the Byrning legacy, you know. High temper, irrational actions. It will destroy you as it destroyed your father.'

It was true. It was the dark spectre that hung over his family. Not just his family tree, but his own flesh and blood.

His father's unbridled rage at a servant had caused his sister's death. His little sister had stepped into the fray to protect her nanny, only to receive a blow herself by accident. It had killed her. His father had become a drunkard that day, choosing to become insensate rather than succumb to the Byrning legacy again.

That had been his father's solution. And it hadn't worked.

The man had had many rages afterwards, but mostly he'd been too drunk to harm anyone. In the end, he'd stumbled into the Thames and drowned, leaving his son in charge of the Dukedom.

'I have not had a rage since my adolescence,' he reminded his mother. 'My faculties are well in hand. I will find a bride of my own choosing.'

He said the words, but in his heart he knew his mother was

right. All those qualities she listed were exactly the ones he needed. He must marry someone of even temperament and impeccable manners. She would help him remain calm and soothe over any missteps he might make along the way. And he would need to find her soon because he was an unwed duke who needed an heir.

And now, as he did every morning, he rededicated himself to staying rational, calm, and completely unaffected by emotion. And if he failed in that mission here was his mother, personally invested in keeping him in line.

'Do try to be logical,' his mother pressed. 'You need an heir while I am still young enough to ensure he is raised properly.' She leaned forward. 'So I can be sure the Byrning curse does not take root again.'

'It has not taken root in me!' he snapped.

She pursed her lips, then raised a single brow. That was all it took and once again he was a dirty boy with raised fists and a burning shame that his temper had once again made him go too far. Back then, he'd fight anyone who said a cross word to him. He'd found fights, he'd created fights, and he'd usually won them. Because he was heir to a dukedom and no one—even young boys—wanted to hurt him.

Time and constant admonishments from several people in his life had taught him to control his rage. He now buried his temper beneath logic and constant vigilance. He was not slipping now.

He took a long look at the mantel clock and arched a brow back at his mother. 'Do you want me to meet Cedric's bride or not?'

She clucked her tongue in disgust. She was not subject to the Byrning legacy of rage, but she certainly had her moments of annoyance. Her pinched face, however, did not move him.

'Very well,' she said as she pushed to her feet. 'We will deal with Cedric first.'

As if she would do anything now that she'd set him to the task.

'Then I expect you to choose a bride immediately afterwards.'

'Good day, Mother.'

After a long-suffering sigh, she spun on her heels and departed. Which meant Declan had no excuse to remain seated in the dark as he nursed his sore head.

Damn his father for dying. This really ought to be his problem.

With a sigh, Declan rang for his valet and prepared to meet a 'miserably unsuitable' woman.

Chapter Two

Declan arrived at *The Integrity* within the hour. Given the quiet and relative dark of his carriage, his mood had steadily improved. Nothing cheered him so much as being left alone. That ended, of course, the moment he stepped out into the teeming noise of the dock. And it was made worse as he struggled to find the ship itself.

By the time he strode up the gangplank he wanted nothing more than to get this task over with as quickly as possible. Which made the absolute absence of anyone on board a frustrating annoyance.

'Hello?' he called as he looked about.

He heard nothing. Or rather he heard a million voices around him, the cry of the gulls, and the splash of things hitting or being hit by water. Sadly, he could not identify any as coming from within the confines of this boat. Bloody hell—how did anyone understand anything amid this cacophony?

'On deck!' came a bellowing voice from below.

Declan jolted as he turned to see the muscular, moustachioed man climbing up from below deck. He was dressed casually, but his weathered face and the easy way he moved suggested he was at home on this ship. The command in his tone implied he was the captain. Declan was about to speak when he realised the man was squinting up into the sails as he shook his head.

'Half monkey, half bird,' he muttered—apparently to himself, because he seemed startled when he turned and saw Declan standing there. 'What ho?'

'Hello,' Declan said, though his gaze was going up, up, up into the sails, where he could just make out a figure springing lightly through the mass of ropes. Half monkey, half bird was right. As he watched, the sailor took an impossible leap, caught a rope, then swung around before another long jump. It was breathtaking. And possibly life-taking if the man missed.

But he never did.

'Good God,' Declan muttered, envy in his tone.

Once upon a time he'd wanted to be a captain on the high seas, answerable to no one, free to challenge the elements however he wanted, and able to wander the world on his own whim. It had been a boy's fantasy, of course. No future duke could risk himself that way, and only a child thought life aboard ship was easy. And yet watching the sailor fly through the riggings, he felt his heart soar. Such freedom!

'Crazy,' the captain muttered as he followed the sailor's movements. 'Some are born to this life; some find it. That one found it and has the devil's own determination to make it fit.'

Declan had no idea what that meant, but he had no desire to dispel his private fantasy. In his mind, that sailor had no cares except to run the riggings for fun.

He pulled off his hat as he addressed the captain. 'Good morning, sir. I'm looking for my cousin Cedric, Lord Domac. I was told—'

'Yes, yes, he's due. Said he'd be here an hour ago, but I knew better than to expect him.'

Wise. Cedric had never managed time well. Or money. What he did manage well were people. Something about Cedric's sunny smile, bright hair, and the mischievous glint in his eyes had the most stiff-necked duchess softening. That put him in direct contrast to Declan, who had always been sober, restrained, and aloof. Thanks to the Byrning legacy, that was the only way for him to be without striking terror in his mother's heart.

'If you're his cousin, then I'm guessing you're the young Duke. Pleased to meet you, Your Grace. I'm Captain Banakos. Lord Domac asked me to show you around.'

'You were expecting me?'

The man grinned. 'I was, Your Grace, though I didn't know it would be today. Lord Domac said you'd be coming to inspect things. Said you'd be determined to understand everything about the gal's dowry.'

And now Declan began to understand. His cousin wasn't marrying an unsuitable girl. He was trying to get the lady's dowry.

'Please, show me everything,' he said.

And see it, he did. Every inch of the stripped-down, well-managed vessel. Everything was in place, everything was clean, and the hold was impressively full of cargo that had yet to be transported to a nearby warehouse.

Captain Banakos was a delightful guide, with several good stories to relay, and Declan forgot his sore head, forgot his irritating mother, and thoroughly enjoyed himself.

Indeed, he'd taken off his boots and was partway up the mainmast barefoot when his cousin finally made an appearance.

'Aren't you too old for that?'

Declan was looking up into the rigging, but paused when

he recognised his cousin's voice. He noted as well the rough burr in it that indicated someone else likely had a sore head.

'Come on down, old man,' Cedric continued. 'It's too early to play monkey.'

Declan finally looked down. 'It's after noon, and you were expected several hours ago. Also, I'm only three years older than you.'

'That's old. Now, come down. I'd like to talk without craning my neck.'

Declan sighed. The air up here was clearer, and he'd discovered the unexpected thrill of challenging the sky by climbing. He hadn't got far, of course. Not yet. But he abruptly decided that he would someday. Unfortunately, now wasn't the moment. He needed to speak with Cedric, so he narrowed his eyes, planned his angle, and jumped.

He landed with a thud, the feel of the wood on his bare feet making him grin. He hadn't jumped like that since he was a boy. God, how he missed those days, when he hadn't been constantly aware of his violent legacy. When running and jumping had been fun and not an indication of generations of past misdeeds.

Meanwhile, Cedric was gazing up at the sailor still running about the rigging.

'Welcome back to England,' Declan said as he mentally closed the door on his boyhood dreams.

'Thanks. Isn't it your birthday today?' Cedric returned.

'Yesterday. And instead of birthday greetings the Duchess has ordered me to speak with you.'

'Has she?' Cedric drawled, his expression carefully blanked.

The poor man bore the moniker of 'The Inconsistent One', thanks to Declan's mother, so there was little love lost between the two. But rather than discuss that, he gestured around at the massive boat with a too-enthusiastic grin. 'Isn't she magnificent? Let me show you around.'

'I have been all over this boat already,' Declan said. 'And she's definitely seaworthy.'

It was the best compliment he could give to the efficient vessel. In truth, he liked it for being exactly what it needed to be, without luxuries, beautiful woodwork, or anything that would usually attract Cedric's attention.

'I know she's not much to look at, but she's exactly what she needs to be.'

Declan couldn't agree more, though he was surprised Cedric had echoed his thoughts. 'She's a fine ship,' he said in all honesty.

'And she's all mine.'

Had he married the girl already? Doubtful. His mother rarely got details like that wrong. What was more likely was that Cedric had yet to learn that wanting things and having things were entirely different. How like the young man to speak as if something were a fact when that was far from the truth.

'Truly?' he said.

Nothing more, but Cedric withered under Declan's stare.

'Um...well, it will be after the wedding.'

'Ah,' he said as Cedric ran his hand up and down the mainmast. 'About that...' he began.

But before he could go further, a voice interrupted from above.

'Beware below!'

Declan looked up, but Cedric was faster. He grabbed his cousin's arm and pulled him to the side rail. Then they watched in shock as the jumping sailor launched off the middle sail, flipped mid-air, then landed solidly on the deck. It was an impressive feat, and would have been a dangerous one if the ship had been full of people. Even relatively empty, the deck had coiled ropes and buckets all about. One slight miscalculation and the sailor would have a broken leg or worse.

Crazy! And yet Declan was impressed—especially as the leaper straightened up with an impish grin.

'I never get to do that when we're sailing,' said the boy.

At least Declan assumed it was a boy, given the grin, the diminutive stature, and the Asian slant to his features. Though Declan had met precious few Chinamen in his life—exactly two—he'd thought they all looked young, with features as refined as their porcelain. Smooth skin accentuated by dark slashes for brows and long, elegant fingers. This boy had the addition of a ready smile, a softly formed nose, and dark hair swept up into his sailor's cap.

'You're showing off!' Cedric said with a grin.

The boy laughed with a surprisingly musical treble, but Cedric hadn't finished.

'Did you have any problems getting here?'

'Took a hansom cab—as you suggested. But you're late.'

Cedric shrugged. 'You seem to have occupied yourself easily enough.'

'There's always something to do. I was checking the ropes. Rats are everywhere in London, and they'll eat the ropes if they're hungry.'

'There's too much good food in London,' Cedric scoffed. 'The rats will go for the better food and leave our boat alone.'

The sailor arched a brow but didn't speak. He didn't have to. Even Declan, who had spent little time on board a ship, knew that there were hungry rats everywhere, even in as wealthy a city as London. Especially in London.

'Very well,' Cedric continued. 'You can go back to it. We'll talk more in a bit, after I show my cousin around.'

The sailor grinned, then ducked away to climb the mizzenmast. The two men watched for a moment, and Declan was impressed by the young man's thoroughness as he ran his fingers over every inch of rope while clinging like a monkey to the rigging.

But, as fascinating as the boy was, Declan had a purpose here and it was time he got to it. He turned to his cousin, watching as Cedric continued to stare at the boy with a cat-with-the-cream smile.

'Cedric…' he began, but his cousin interrupted.

'I'm not going to listen. I've found a course, and I like it.'

Damnation, this was not going to be easy.

'You've found many courses over your life, and you have loved every single one.'

Cedric grimaced. 'That's part of being young.' He turned to frown at Declan. 'Weren't you the one always climbing trees, exploring caves, talking about sailing away to fame and fortune?'

'I was a boy.'

'And now we're both men who can choose our own paths. I've found a taste for sailing.'

'What if this passion burns out like all the others?'

Cedric looked him in the eye, straightening his shoulders as he faced Declan. It was the most adult expression he'd seen on his younger cousin's face.

'I have listened and learned. I'm not sailing the ship myself. I'm hiring people to do that.'

'You're the financial backing,' Declan said.

And though it wasn't a question, Cedric answered it anyway.

'Yes. And it will be profitable. I swear it.'

'But not with your own money. With your wife's money.'

Cedric waved that way. 'After the wedding, it will be mine.'

That was true enough, but the words still grated. What a poor lot for the woman who was attached like a barnacle to the real asset of her dowry.

'There are other ways to get money than trapping a young woman.'

His cousin snorted. 'Will you loan me the money?'

'How much?'

'Ten thousand pounds.'

Now it was Declan's turn to snort. 'Absolutely not.'

At least not without a great deal more study.

'Then she is the only way. My father has burned through everything else.'

Declan grimaced. Whereas Declan's father had been a violent drunk, Cedric's father was a vicious gambler. It was just another manifestation of the Byrning legacy. And, as with all gamblers, he won for a time, and then he didn't. At last reckoning the Earl had lost everything that wasn't entailed. Which had left Cedric to find a way to finance his own life and his sisters' dowries.

It wasn't the worst idea to marry for money. Just a cruel one.

'Who is this woman?' Declan pressed. 'The Duchess said she's illegitimate.'

Cedric scrunched his face up in a mockery of Declan's expression. 'She's been claimed by her father. More important, she has a lovely dowry. Recall, please, that I'm an adult and can marry the woman of my choice.'

'Within reason.'

Cedric was a future earl. He might not have as many restrictions as a duke, but he couldn't marry willy-nilly either.

'Marrying a by-blow for her dowry isn't reasonable.'

'On the contrary. It's exactly what my father did when he married my mother. And my grandfather. And his father before that. It's our family legacy as much as the gambling, and you know it.'

He did know it. He also knew that Cedric had once sworn never to marry for any reason except love. The man was a romantic. He'd fallen head over heels in love at least three times before he was sixteen. And yet here he was, openly admitting to being a fortune-hunter.

'You're the grandson of a duke, the son of an earl,' Declan said. 'There are scores of wealthy women you could marry. It need not be this woman. Your mother will be all too happy to introduce you to—'

'Empty-headed misses who bore me?'

'Do you love her? Is that it? You know that love is a fleeting indulgence—'

'I'm not a child, longing for a woman's touch.' Cedric gripped the rail, his expression unreadable. 'I need ten thousand pounds to buy this ship and a cargo. If you will not loan me the money...' He slanted a look at Declan.

'Absolutely not.'

'Then I shall get it through her.'

Declan crossed his arms, doing his best to understand his cousin's bizarre actions. 'Are you sure of her dowry?'

'Yes. It is being proffered by her father, Lord Wenshire.'

Declan frowned. He'd never heard of Lord Wenshire.

'He's Lord Whitley's youngest brother.'

'The eccentric?'

'The explorer. He made his fortune through the East India Company.'

Now he remembered—but he'd never heard of a daughter. 'And this woman is his child?'

'Yes.'

Declan leaned back against the railing, his gaze naturally

going to where the boy continued to inspect the ropes. It was merely a way to stall as he thought through the information.

'You're not infatuated with her? You are marrying her completely for her money?'

'I like her well enough.'

Society marriages had been built on less.

Declan started listing the facts, trying to sort through the issue. 'She is Lord Wenshire's daughter and dowered with ten thousand pounds.'

'She's dowered with this boat.'

Ah, now he understood. Still, he continued listing off her attributes. 'She was born illegitimate, but her father has acknowledged her and made her an heiress.'

'Yes.'

So why had the Duchess called the woman unsuitable?

'Our mothers think she's unacceptable. Is it really because she's a by-blow?'

Being born on the wrong side of the blanket was a black mark, but it wasn't an insurmountable one. Especially with a dowry worth ten thousand pounds.

'I cannot fathom their thought processes. I refuse to even try.'

Declan couldn't blame him for that. But what he couldn't understand was why his cousin had chosen a woman despised by his mother when there were so many others with good dowries?

'Out with it, Cedric. Why this girl? Surely there are dozens of well-dowered women your mother would celebrate. You can buy a boat then. Maybe not this one, but there are many others.'

His cousin arched a brow. 'You think so? Thanks to your mother, I have been dubbed "The Inconsistent One", and no wealthy woman wants that in a husband.' He crossed his arms. 'So, unless the family wants to loan me the money, I shall have to marry the girl I have chosen.'

'A by-blow foreigner?'

'Yes.'

'You are the son of an earl—'

'And the grandson of a duke. I know.'

'Why make things difficult? For her, if not for yourself. Do you know how hard it will be for any woman to go up against our mothers?'

His cousin tilted his head back as he looked up the mizzenmast. 'I require ten thousand pounds, Declan. If you care so much for the family name, then find me another way of getting the funds I require.'

He heard the finality in his cousin's voice. Or perhaps it wasn't finality as much as something a great deal darker. Blackmail.

'You are using this woman as a threat.' It wasn't a question. 'You will marry an unsuitable girl unless we pay to stop you.'

Cedric arched his brows in challenge. 'What is the family name worth? Surely ten thousand pounds—'

'Is a ridiculous sum. You cannot think we have that kind of cash simply sitting around.'

'She does. Or rather her father.'

'Don't be a fool. I will not give in to blackmail, and you are a cad to use a woman so cavalierly.' He shook his head. 'Cedric, what has happened to you? You are not a man to use a woman this cruelly. In fact, you once swore you would marry only for love.'

His cousin rounded on him, the movement quick. It wasn't violent, though Declan tensed at it, but the words certainly carried a threat.

'And when was that, dear cousin? When did we last know each other?' Venom dripped from every word.

Declan frowned. 'At school—'

'Yes. Ten years ago. When my father still had my sisters' dowries. When the most difficult thing we had to do was spend our winnings at cards.'

Cedric had gambled at cards. Declan had been too afraid of the Byrning legacy to pick up the habit.

'Then you disappeared to play in Italy.' Cedric spat the words.

'It was my Grand Tour,' Declan shot back.

And it certainly hadn't been fun. Not at the end.

'I don't care! You disappeared. My family money disappeared. And there I was, all alone, trying to find an answer.' He gestured expansively at the boat. 'And here it is. My answer.'

Declan shook his head, wondering where he had gone wrong with his cousin. How had that romantic boy turned into this angry, bitter man?

'I will not give you ten thousand pounds.'

'Maybe not,' Cedric said, with a too-casual shrug. 'Or maybe you will change your tune after tea this afternoon.'

Declan narrowed his eyes. 'What are you planning?'

Cedric smiled in a way altogether too calculating to be charming. 'Obviously you have met the lady early, but I shall introduce her to the rest of the family this afternoon.'

'I have met no one,' Declan snapped.

'My apologies,' his cousin said. 'Pray let me introduce you properly—but don't mention anything about our nuptials, will you? I haven't proposed yet.'

Well, that was something. The lady need not know she was a ploy being used to blackmail Cedric's family.

'You can be sure she won't learn it from me.'

He was here to stop the wedding, not push the relationship.

Cedric nodded, then put his fingers to his lips and let out a loud whistle. The boy who was now up on the middle sails looked towards them.

'Come here!' Cedric bellowed as he gestured.

The boy understood. He immediately began scrambling down the rigging, pausing at much too high a height before doing another one of those acrobatic flips to the deck. It made Declan's heart leap to his throat—half in envy, half in fear—but the sailor landed with natural grace before rushing over.

'Yes?'

Cedric laughed. 'Take off your cap. Let me introduce you properly.'

Shock was already rolling through Declan's system. His mind kept saying, *No, it isn't possible*. And yet, with his cousin, of course this was possible. And, indeed, things proceeded with horrifying clarity.

He saw Cedric grin as the boy whipped off his cap and a short crop of straight black hair tumbled down, held back by a crude tie. The boy—who wasn't a boy at all—smiled at him. Declan noted straight white teeth and a healthy glow after the exertion. He saw laughing eyes that might well be mocking his shock.

And he saw a beautiful woman in boy's clothes with bare feet and trim ankles.

'Declan, please allow me to introduce Grace Richards, Lord Wenshire's daughter.'

Chapter Three

Grace had been enjoying the freedom up in the sails too much to pay attention to the men's conversation. She knew she'd be summoned eventually. Lord Domac was always planning something, and this morning would be no different. But she knew her father looked favourably on the man, so she did her best to treat him generously. Plus, the gentleman had given her cab money for this early-morning trip to the boat, where she could once again run free amid the sails and her sister could hide below deck with the accounts.

She hoped the girl had stayed hidden from the men. It wasn't appropriate for a lady to be seen doing accounts. It wasn't appropriate for Grace to be running around the sails, but she and her sister did what was needed when they felt too confined.

Stays and etiquette lessons had their place. This morning had been about breathing freely one last time before the Season began.

But when Lord Domac had called she'd done her best to make an entrance. Cedric loved it when she acted like an acrobat in the sails, so she'd performed a backflip to the deck before doing her dramatic reveal as a woman.

In truth, she relished the slack-jawed shock on the taller

man's face. Men always underestimated her, and it was fun to see them surprised.

Though now that she was looking at the new gentleman's face, she had to admit that he hadn't reacted with as much shock as most men. Many grew furious at her reveal, so she tensed to run, but his movements were restrained. His brows rose, his mouth pressed tight. Rather than focus his anger on her, his glare skipped straight over her to land on Lord Domac.

Then it was gone. Two seconds later, he turned back to her with a warm smile and dipped his head in a formal greeting.

'A pleasure to meet you, Miss Richards. I am the Duke of Byrning, as my addled cousin neglected to say.'

'Stop being a prick,' Lord Domac groused. 'We're on board. We don't stand on ceremony here.'

The Duke arched his brows. 'Every woman deserves courtesy.'

That was a surprising attitude, and Grace pinkened in delight at his words, especially as he looked so steadily into her eyes. Normally men's gazes roved across her breasts or hips, looking for proof of her sex.

'My cousin is a stuffed popinjay,' Lord Domac said. 'He doesn't realise you prefer easy manners.'

Did she? She'd never met anyone who had used full manners with her. She'd seen from a distance as men bowed and demurred to other women, but never, ever had a man addressed her as if she deserved the full measure of his courtly manners. Not even Domac.

But this man did. He stood there in his gentleman's attire and gave her every courtesy. Even his bare feet didn't take away from the heavy impact of his regard. And so she gave him her best response.

'I am honoured to meet you, Your Grace.'

She curtsied as she'd been taught, though it probably looked ridiculous given that she wore a boy's clothing. Then she launched into the polite discourse her father had insisted she learn. First a comment on the weather, and then a question about the gentleman's interest.

'It's a sad wind today, I think. The boats are stuck without a breeze to lift their skirts. Have you an interest in sailing?'

Lord Domac grinned at her. 'You mean a breeze to lift their sails. Lifting skirts is something else entirely.'

Was he poking fun at her? He was the one who had taught her the phrase. 'Sails. My apology.'

Domac chuckled. 'Grace has learned most of her English from sailors and the like, but her father and I are teaching her how to go on.'

The Duke didn't even look at his cousin. Instead, he lifted his gaze to the slack sails. 'I know a little about boats and skirts, and the sails are definitely flat today. I am afraid my cousin has told me nothing about you. Were you born and raised in Canton?'

'I was.'

She could not be from anywhere else. Whites were only allowed in a small area of Canton. And half-whites, like herself, were lucky to be alive at all. Most were drowned at birth.

'Do you have much knowledge of China?'

Her father had told her that most would not know anything about her country. Indeed, they would not be able to find it on a map.

'More than most Englishmen,' he said, 'but nothing from someone who has lived there. I would love to learn more.'

She might have answered, but Lord Domac raised his hand to stop her. 'There is time enough to answer those questions at tea this afternoon. Grace has lived an extremely interesting life.'

The Duke's eyes narrowed, as if he was annoyed, but he didn't turn that rancour on Grace. Instead, he smiled at her. 'I look forward to learning all about it. Are you here for the Season, then? To find a husband?'

She was here because her only options in China were to become a nun or a prostitute. Lord Wenshire had offered her another option, and she'd grabbed it with both hands. But she couldn't say that now. Instead, she gestured towards London.

'My father wished me to see his homeland, and so I have indulged him.'

'You mean you have *obeyed* him,' Lord Domac corrected. 'As every good daughter does.'

She knew the difference between the two words and she had used the correct one. She had wanted to go to Africa, where she would be seen as foreign, but not a half-blood. In China, she was routinely cursed for her mixed blood. It would likely be the same here in England, since she was half English, half Chinese, but she had bowed to her father's wishes.

Rather than argue with Lord Domac, she continued to speak, working hard to act properly. 'My father came into my life only recently. He found me at a temple that is known to care for half-Chinese children. He claimed me as his own and offered to take me to England.'

'Extraordinary! And you went with him? Alone? Without even speaking English?'

'But she wasn't alone!' Lord Domac inserted. 'She has brought her sister along as well, and Lucy already knew English.'

Lucy had known *some* English, but it didn't matter. Neither of them had had a better option.

'Lucy isn't my sister through blood, but we were raised together. I couldn't imagine leaving China without her, so my father claimed us both.'

The Duke nodded slowly. 'Lord Wenshire is extremely generous.'

'Yes, he is,' she said, irritation making her voice hard.

Her father was indeed a generous man. The kind of person she couldn't believe truly existed, but months in his presence had shown her that he wanted the best for her and her sister. And it infuriated her whenever someone suggested otherwise.

He must have heard her tone because the Duke quickly dipped his head in apology. 'I meant no offence. Truly, I am simply impressed.'

She nodded, softening her own tone. 'I didn't believe it at first either,' she confessed. 'But he convinced me.'

The Duke's brows rose. 'I am desperate to hear more.'

'Which will happen at tea,' Lord Domac interrupted. He was always restless. 'Suffice it to say that Miss Richards is looking forward to an eventful Season.'

'Definitely,' she agreed.

Musicales, balls, and the theatre pulled at her curiosity. The way her father described them made her yearn to experience them. He made the Season sound like weeks spent in delight.

'Yes. Tea,' the Duke said, his voice dry as he shot a hard look at his cousin.

She had no idea what it meant, and no time to understand as he focused back on her.

'Do you attend with your father?'

'I don't know,' she said in full honesty. 'He does not often share his plans with me.'

Or his plans *for* her. He assumed that because she was new to English society, she had no idea how to manage herself. But she'd worked as a navigator on board a merchant ship for years. To think that she could not understand the niceties of appearing on time and dressing appropriately for this tea ceremony was an insult to her intelligence. But he was her parent, and she was here at his mercy. She would strive to hold back her temper.

'And does he know that you are here aboard ship this morning?' the Duke asked.

Although the man's tone was polite, Grace was accustomed to reading nuances in expression and tone. She read an implied criticism in the tightness of his face.

'Of course he does,' she said. 'I am on a morning outing with Lord Domac. My maid and my sister are below deck.' She straightened as his expression turned dark. 'I am completely safe here, and it is not your place to question my father's actions.'

Or her own.

It was a harsh response, but she'd learned young that men would take whatever authority over a woman they could. They might say they were protecting her, but it was merely a cover for their need to be in power. She had learned to strike back ruthlessly when a man sought to dictate to her, even in so small a thing as a dark look.

The Duke flushed, and his brows rose in an imperious expression equal to the haughtiest mandarin in China. 'I look to your *reputation*, Miss Richards. I do not blame *you*. I fear my cousin has been too lax with your safety.'

Her *reputation* was as a great navigator. If she weren't a woman, she'd have her choice of ships. Instead, she'd been run off the docks the moment she'd developed a woman's body and could no longer hide. So she'd gone back to the temple where she'd been raised, and that was where her father had found her. But she supposed the Duke referred to her English reputation.

Meanwhile, Lord Domac had focused on a different aspect of the conversation. 'You have brought Lucy here?'

'Yes. She needed the outing as much as I did.'

Lord Domac made a sound that she could not decipher. Half grunt, half amused chuckle. Then he rocked back on his heels and grinned. 'I believe we're done here. Grace, please fetch your sister and your maid. I have a carriage nearby and will take you back to your father's house so you can get ready for tea.'

She frowned. 'Tea isn't until four.'

Just how much time did he think it took to change her clothing?

'But you have lessons, do you not? Dancing, deportment.' He looked at the Duke. 'She's even learning a smattering of French.'

He sounded as if he was showing off a prize dog. 'We should trade phrases, Lord Domac. I will match my French to your Chinese.'

'But why would I need to learn Chinese when you are here?' he asked.

She could think of a thousand reasons why knowing a language was better than having an interpreter, but she didn't argue. Instead, she looked back at the sails. This was the first time she'd been able to breathe free since coming to London three weeks ago. She didn't want to rush back to corsets and dance lessons.

'There are a few more things I'd like to check in the riggings,' she lied. 'Can we wait a bit longer?'

Lord Domac groaned. 'There's nothing of interest up there.'

'Perhaps I could be of assistance,' the other man said. 'I would be happy to wait here until you are ready to leave. It will be entirely proper if your maid stays alongside.' He smiled as he looked at her. 'And I should enjoy getting to know you better.'

She was tempted. There was gentleness in his smile, despite his criticisms, and he was quick to apologise when he overstepped. That was something even Lord Domac never did. But she knew too little of Englishmen to trust her judgement regarding them. She knew her father approved of Lord Domac, so why would she risk alienating him in favour of this other, more interesting man?

Because she was always drawn to the new, the different, and the generally intriguing. She'd survived by being bold, and she liked this handsome man.

She gestured to his bare feet. 'Have you ever climbed up to a crow's nest?'

'Never,' he said as he tilted his head all the way back.

'It's a long climb and a fall would be deadly,' she said. 'But the view is the loveliest in London.'

His brows rose. No doubt he heard the challenge in her voice. 'How can I resist an invitation like that?'

He couldn't. No man could.

'I'll have to tie a rope about your chest. I will not be the cause of your mother's tears.'

He agreed with a nod and a grin. 'I put myself in your hands.'

Another surprise. Most men dismissed the need for a rope, their pride getting in the way of common sense. Clearly, this man was not a fool, and she respected him all the more for it.

Not so Lord Domac, who hooted his disdain.

'She'll have you trussed up like a Christmas goose. I've seen her do it before.' Then he punched his cousin in the shoulder. 'There's no wind today. The rigging's safer than your mother's stairway.'

That wasn't at all true. Climbing ropes was still difficult

if one wasn't used to it. And although this man looked fit, climbing was not a usual exercise for gentlemen.

Apparently he knew that, because he looked her in the eye. 'Do you tie me up as a joke? Or because it is necessary?'

'Necessary,' she answered honestly. Then she cast a look at Lord Domac. 'But I trussed *him* up like a fish in a net because it was fun.'

Lord Domac had joined their ship when they took port in India for the route back to England and had very quickly got bored. He had wanted to learn, and she had been happy to teach, but since her command of English had been weak, she had been forced to demonstrate rather than explain. That had involved wrapping ropes around him as they moved about the sails, especially at sea.

The Duke grinned as he shed his topcoat. 'Do as you see fit.'

'You won't get halfway,' his cousin taunted.

'How far did you get?'

'All the way up.'

Truth. But it had taken him several tries, and she'd had to wrap him until the ropes had practically carried him the whole way. She wasn't willing to do that again, just to salvage a man's pride. So while the Duke stepped over to the mainmast, she picked up a rope to steady him.

'This won't stop a fall on its own,' she warned. 'It's not a net. But it will slow your drop enough that you can catch hold yourself.'

He nodded as if he understood. She knew he didn't, but she liked the sparkle in his eyes. He was excited and, better yet, he was studying the ascent as he might a mathematical problem. She tied him in as best she could, and then secured the other end about her waist. If he fell badly, she would too, and then they would both die. But she'd done this several times before with other men. It was the only way to get new men up top. They couldn't let a woman get the best of them, so they went on when all reason told them to go down.

'Step where I step,' she said, 'and we'll both be fine.' Then she paused to raise her brows at Lord Domac. 'My sister is in the captain's quarters, looking at the accounts, if you'd like to speak with her. I'm sure she would enjoy seeing you.'

An understatement. For whatever reason, her sister had developed a keen interest in Lord Domac. If their father hadn't declared that Grace must marry first, Lucy—renamed from Lu-Jing—might very well be the one being shoved into stays and forced into tea ceremonies.

Lord Domac's eyes narrowed. 'She's below deck with the captain? *Alone*?'

'With our maid. We have made sure of the proprieties.'

He grunted—another one of those indecipherable sounds—then headed immediately below deck. That left her alone with the Duke.

'Are you ready?'

'I am.'

'Then so am I.'

She began to climb the ratline, which was another word for the rope ladder. Without question, this was one of her biggest joys. The climb to new heights, the kiss of clean air, and the sheer physical exertion that kept her blood surging. She loved it, and apparently the Duke had no problems with it either. At least for the lowest sails.

His breath became laboured after that, and she pulled him to the platform at the top of the upper main to rest. He landed with an exhalation of breath and an eager look around.

'No need to stop,' he said. 'I can keep going.'

'That's not what the captain is saying.'

'What?'

She gestured down towards the deck, where the captain was now standing at the base of the mizzenmast.

'That be far enough!' he bellowed. 'Bring 'im down.'

The Duke tilted his head, clearly listening, but then he looked back up. 'I don't hear anything, and you promised me the best view in London. You're not backing out on a promise, are you?'

'Never,' she said with a grin. 'But look down again. It's a fair way—'

'I know. I saw.' He grabbed hold of the next ratline. 'Are you too tired to climb up?'

He meant it. He wanted to climb. So she shrugged and scrambled up the next set of ropes. He laboured behind her, his breath steady, so she knew he wasn't afraid. At least not yet. As long as she didn't hear the short, tight breath of panic, she would keep going.

There were seven sails on the mainmast, and he scrambled up six of them without hesitation. She'd gone slower than usual for her, making sure to wrap an arm around each rung in the ladder in case he missed his step and she had to support his weight. He never failed, and for that she was pleased. Clearly this was a man used to physical exercise.

By the top of the sixth sail—the main royal—she forced them both to stop on the platform. Even without a strong breeze, the wobble of the ship made it a dipping and swaying plank of wood. Many sailors had lost a meal from this height. Lord Domac had lost his dinner two sails below.

'How do you feel?' she asked. 'Do you get seasick?'

'No,' he said as he looked all around him. 'There's wind here. I can't imagine what it's like in a storm.'

'Terrifying,' she said with a grin. The height was dizzying, and the mainmast never felt as solid as it did on deck.

He looked at her with an assessing gaze. 'You've done it, haven't you? I can't imagine.'

He was speaking honestly, so she honoured him by giving him the truth in return. 'A ship in a storm is frightening wherever you are. Up there…' she pointed to the crow's nest '…I was able to do some good.'

He narrowed his eyes at the barrel that sat atop another thin platform, still a sail's height above them. 'Doing what?'

'Watching for land. We were off course and needed some place to shelter.' She shrugged. 'I have good eyes.'

'And nerves of steel,' he returned. Then he proved that he also had a full measure of nerve by looking down without blanching. 'Have you seen people fall?'

'Yes.'

He looked up at her clipped word. 'I'm sorry.'

She wouldn't have thought that two words would ease her memories. She still had nightmares. But his sympathy was genuine, and she took comfort from it.

'Thank you,' she whispered.

He gave her a firm nod, then looked back up to the crow's nest. 'Can it fit two of us?'

'It will be tight,' she answered. Then she touched his arm. 'You have come further than your cousin on his first trip. There is no shame—'

'I want to go up.'

And to prove it, he began to climb even before she did.

She watched him go, her hold on the ropes as firm as she could make it. It was actually more dangerous for him to be above her. The added height would make it that much harder for her to stay on the ratline if he fell.

He didn't.

He made it to the crow's nest while she admired the strength of his body and the pure grace in the way he moved.

He wasn't a sailor, so he didn't have the flexibility of one. But he was strong, and sure, and never once did his breath shorten with panic. She couldn't even claim that for herself. The first time she'd climbed the ratlines her teeth had chattered from her terror.

He was even with the barrel-shaped crow's nest, and then climbed high enough to swing his feet into the barrel.

'Don't jump down hard,' she warned. 'The flooring isn't as strong as you think.'

He paused before jumping, looking down at her with wide eyes. 'I cannot tell if that's truth or jest.'

'Both,' she said with a wink. 'You're a big man who shouldn't be stomping around up there, but it will hold you.'

He didn't wait any longer before he jumped—lightly—into the nest. And she noted that, while he looked at the view with an awe-struck expression, he kept one hand on the rope and another on the mainmast.

She grinned as she scrambled up, but she'd underestimated his size. There was precious little room for her in the crow's nest, so she loitered above on the ropes.

'This is amazing,' he breathed as he looked all around. Then he glanced back at her. 'Do you know the sights of London?'

She shook her head, and he waved her in, moving back far enough that she could squeeze in beside him.

It was a delicate manoeuvre. She was not used to being touched by anyone, least of all a man she had just met, and yet there was a thrill in his heat and his hands. He let go of the rope and steadied her as she wriggled her way in. She felt his body as a large blanket of warmth, shrouding her from the wind, which was a good deal colder up top. But mostly she felt his breath in the expanse of his chest at her back, and the heat of it where it caressed her cheek. He must chew mint, she thought, for no man's breath smelled that sweet without it.

Then together they peered out over the masts of other boats to the tableau of London before them. And although she'd said she'd show him the best view from up here, he was the one to show her.

'That way is Southwark,' he said. Then he moved her around, pointing to the city. He named Westminster Abbey and the Tower of London. She couldn't see them clearly, but she didn't need to. What she felt was his body pressed against hers, the certainty with which he stood, and the pride he so obviously felt in his city. He grew so confident that he released his grip on the mainmast, bracing his feet wide as he tucked her against him. And she relaxed as she strained to see what he saw.

'I suppose this means nothing to you without your going there,' he mused.

'Then I shall be sure to visit the places you have named.'

He grinned at her. 'I shall take you,' he said. 'And you shall tell me how it compares to Canton. Does your land have such grand edifices?'

'Different ones,' she said. 'But still grand.'

'I wish I could see,' he said, and she heard a longing in his voice that she did not understand.

'It only takes a ship and some time.'

'It takes a great deal more than that,' he countered. 'As a duke, I have many responsibilities that keep me tied to England. You cannot imagine the complaints I would get if I left for so much as a week, much less the time it would take to sail to China.'

'You are fortunate to have a family who values you.'

As a woman of mixed race, she had discovered most people wanted her dead. She was beyond lucky to have found her father. Indeed, without him she might right now have been forced into prostitution for her daily bowl of rice. Instead, she stood with a handsome English mandarin while watching a seagull swoop past.

'What happened to your mother?' he asked, his voice low.

She jolted, feeling his breath against her cheek and the compassion in his words. It was a heady mixture when she was so used to harsh tones.

'I don't know,' she confessed. 'I was left not yet a day old on the temple steps.'

'You don't know?' he asked. 'But surely Lord Wenshire has discovered what happened to your mother.'

She flinched, panic surging into her throat. Damn it, only one day with a new person and she was already slipping.

'He searched before coming to the temple. The woman he loved—my mother—' she almost choked on the lie '—was murdered by her husband. She was his fifth concubine and very lonely. But even so he had the right to kill her when she became pregnant with another man's child. I was lucky that a servant took me to the temple.'

He nodded slowly. 'Why didn't you say that at first?'

Because it was a lie.

'My father told me to keep the details secret. China can be a harsh country, and he did not want people to think less of me because of my past.'

It was a feeble excuse, but he seemed to accept it. Or at least did not argue it.

'Your life must have been very harsh.'

Yes and no. She knew many people who had had it worse. Many who had died.

'I found a way to survive as a navigator. At least for a time.' Until her true gender had been discovered. 'And then my father found me. I was very, very lucky.'

'And I am even more impressed,' he said.

They said nothing then. They watched the birds and the bobbing ships. She surprised herself by relaxing into the moment. Their bodies were touching, and she ought to be afraid. She had never allowed a man this close before. Certainly not since developing breasts. And yet, she was not afraid.

She accustomed herself to the press of this man's body, to his scent away from the dock smells, and the safety of looking at a view without being wary of any danger. They were docked in a safe harbour, and he was not a man to fear. He was a man who made her skin tingle and her thoughts spin in new directions. She had spent a decade on boats, learning her trade. She knew what men said and did. But never had her curiosity been sparked so strongly. And never had her thoughts turned so intimate, so fast.

And while she was thinking all that, he glanced down at her and smiled such that the skin wrinkled around his eyes. Odd that she found that handsome.

'You are so comfortable here. Have you lived most of your life on a boat?'

'I am one of the best navigators in China,' she said proudly.

'How…?' He shifted uncomfortably as he searched for the words.

'How was it possible for a woman?'

He nodded. 'Yes.'

'I saw that every person must have a way to make money. Without a family, my choices were limited.'

Since she was a half-white orphan, her choices had been to sell her body or find skills that were valuable despite her mixed race and sex.

'I learned how to navigate from an old man who had done

the job before his eyes turned white. He introduced me to a captain who needed a smart navigator, even if she was a girl.'

'How old were you?'

'Eleven for my first sailing. But I worked hard and earned my place.'

His brows rose. 'I am impressed,' he said. 'To think of all the dangers you faced... Storms, pirates, brutal conditions...'

And her fellow sailors. Which was why she'd bound her breasts and kept to herself.

'I have fought for everything I've ever had,' she said. 'And I have had the protection of good men.'

If it hadn't been for the captain declaring her off-limits, she'd never have made it through her first voyage. Or any of the others.

She lifted her chin. 'I am lucky.'

'And a great deal more,' he said as his gaze travelled over her face. 'Cedric has excellent taste in women.'

She smiled, feeling the compliment warm her.

'But I do not think he has your best interests at heart.'

She arched a brow, already knowing this game. 'And you intend to save me?'

He mimicked her pose. 'Do you need someone to do so?'

She laughed and shook her head, knowing she lied. She had a vast array of skills, but she could not survive alone. Not without her father to support her or a ship's captain who would keep her safe while she worked. Or a husband to shelter her.

'I have come to England to be with my father and to see a new land.'

She kept her voice steady as she spoke, though inside she winced at the lie. She was here because it was the only safe way to escape China. It turned out that she would do a great deal to create a safe home for herself and her sister—

including leaving everything she'd ever known and lying to a very kind Englishman.

Meanwhile, the Duke had twisted enough in the crow's nest to look at her face. 'I came here today to dissuade my cousin from marrying a woman, only to realise she is an intriguing prize.'

He touched her face then. A slow caress of his thumb across her jaw. Fire sizzled in its wake, and her breath caught and held. Certainly she had experienced flirtation before, but this man had seen her worth faster than anyone else. He looked at her with admiration mixed with desire, and she wanted to leap into his fire just to feel the burn.

Madness. And yet she wanted it. Even more so when he leaned forward as if to kiss her. But she couldn't allow that to happen. It would be leaping into something she could not control, and that was dangerous territory—especially for a woman.

So she leaped free. A quick jump and a grab and she was swinging herself away from him for all that they were still tied together.

'Miss Richards?' he said as she pulled herself up and away. 'Is everything well?'

'Yes,' she said, horrified to realise that her breath was short with panic. It took her a moment to slow it down, to steady her heart, and to dry the slickness from her palms. 'Yes,' she repeated more strongly. 'We must go back down.'

It was a lie. There was no need to go down for more than an hour except boredom. But he didn't question her. Instead, he took one last look at the world around them before reaching up and pulling himself from the crow's nest.

She watched his strong arms, noted the size of his hands, and admired the ease with which he managed his body. No wonder he was an English mandarin. He exuded power with every movement.

Then he smiled at her, gesturing for her to begin the descent. Normally she would warn him to be extra careful. The descent was harder than the climb, always. But she didn't have the breath. And for the first time in years she felt awed by a man.

Chapter Four

Descending the mast was much harder for Declan. Before, his attention had been on climbing, climbing, climbing…but now his thoughts were on *her*. They ought to be centred on not plummeting to his death, but his mind returned to thinking about how different she was from any other women in his life.

He slipped twice. His toes didn't catch properly, his legs were wobbly from the unaccustomed work. Thankfully his arms held him upright and he was able to refocus his attention. But, damnation, it was impossible *not* to think about her.

She was a female sailor. That alone was startling. She had the physical strength for the work and the bravery, too, if her account was true. He shouldn't be surprised that a bold woman could become a valuable member of a ship's crew.

What shocked him was her sudden modesty. He hadn't climbed up here to become intimate with her, but there was no denying that once they'd been in the crow's nest her body had held a great deal of appeal. He loved the dark silk of her hair and the smooth sweetness of her face. She was exotic, and that had a special lure. She'd also looked him directly in the eyes when she'd spoken, she had listened to what he said, and when the tight quarters had pressed their bodies together he'd been shocked by the force of lust that gripped him.

But he was not a man to be ruled by his lust, so he'd kept his tone polite, he'd given her what little space had been available, and then he'd begun to see if she were amenable to his attention. A touch here, a whispered word there. All subtle, all respectful, and all received as she'd sunk back against him. He'd felt her heat, he'd felt her curves, and he'd started to think of ways to further their association.

Then it had all changed.

One moment he was leaning in for a kiss, and the very next moment she was jumping onto the ropes as if he were a rabid dog. So abrupt had been her movement that he'd looked for some sort of vermin at their feet. No rats except himself. And she'd looked pale enough that he'd feared she'd faint and fall to her death.

She had recovered, thank God, but she'd wasted no time escaping him. If they hadn't been tied together, she'd probably have leaped to the deck minutes ago.

That was not the reaction of a seasoned courtesan or a rough sailor. What had happened there resembled the response of a frightened virgin, and he could not reconcile Grace's appearance in coarse sailor's clothing with her modest reaction.

The dichotomy had him replaying their entire acquaintance in his head to see if he'd missed clues. And the puzzle had him missing his footing.

'Easy now, guv,' said the captain from only a few feet below. 'That's a long, hard haul ye did there. I'm right impressed.'

Declan righted himself and dropped heavily to the deck. The shock of the impact reverberated through his heels up to his spine, and he was appalled by the weakness in his legs from the exertion. He was even more startled to discover that he couldn't see Miss Richards anywhere. Nor did he see his cousin, though that was less surprising.

'Lord Domac left about fifteen minutes ago,' the captain said. 'Said he wasn't going to loiter here waiting.'

Of course not.

'And Miss Richards?'

'Gone below to change into her fancy dress. She can't go back to her father's house looking like a sailor, now, can she?'

Somehow she'd been fast enough to make it to the deck, untie herself from him, and then dash away—all before he'd made it fully down.

'She's a quick one, isn't she?' he asked.

'Has to be as a woman on a ship. Quick with a knife, too, and a well-placed kick.'

'Really?' Declan leaned back against the mainmast as he pulled on his stockings and shoes. 'What do you know about her? How long has she been sailing?'

'I only know what her father told me. She's his daughter from the first time he went to China as a young man. Didn't know he'd fathered her until a year ago. Then he spent months finding her.'

'And she was aboard a ship?'

The captain grunted. 'That's not where he found her. She's a good navigator—best I've seen—but she got into some trouble. I don't know exactly what. She told me the captain who'd protected her had died and… Well, sailors can be an unruly lot. I've got a good crew, but she still had to kick some sense into a few. My guess is, once her protector died she was hard pressed by the crew, and not in a good way. She ran back to the temple where she was raised. That's where her father found her an' talked her into coming here with him.'

That was an extraordinary tale. So extraordinary that Declan wasn't sure he believed it. But then again, he didn't know any women who could climb a mainmast either.

'She can really navigate a ship?'

'Reads a map like you an' me sees colours. Just looks and knows. Sees the stars and does the mathematics in her head.'

'Did you let her navigate for you?'

'She's a curious creature, always poking her head into everything, wanting to know what and why. She started playing a game with my man, seeing who could chart a course faster or better. It was her. Always her. When he got a fever she took over, easy as you please.'

Declan doubted anything for this woman had been easy, but he liked the notion of someone who constantly wanted to learn more about the world. He often suffered from an excess of curiosity, needing to explore beyond what his mother said a duke ought to know. Sometimes he defied her. Other times he gave in for the peace. And even though he knew his mother would damn him for his interest in Miss Grace Richards, he refused to be cowed.

He wanted to know everything about her. Most important, he wanted to know details that he could verify because she sounded more like someone in a tall tale of exaggeration than the flesh-and-blood girl who'd just run away from him in the crow's nest.

He was interrupted by her reappearance.

He'd been watching for her to emerge from below deck and should not have been surprised by what he saw. She wore a modest gown, walking boots, and her hair was arranged in a short, but respectable style. All very proper.

But he hadn't been thinking of her as a proper girl. She was the acrobatic sailor who had turned out to be female. Except now he was staring at a woman dressed as any lady of the *ton*. She walked in small, demure steps, her gaze was downcast, and her face appeared flushed with health. If it hadn't been for the straight, dark hair and the exotic cast to her features, he would have thought her someone else entirely.

She said nothing as she approached, and he stood there staring, dumbstruck by the change in her appearance. She pressed her lips tightly together as she waited and waited... for something.

'Miss Richards?' he said, her name both a question and a statement.

'Yes,' she answered.

Then she glanced awkwardly to the side, where her maid stood in polite silence. He caught the woman's encouraging nod before she spoke.

'Lord Domac has left,' she said bluntly. 'I need a way back to my father's house—'

'But of course. I will escort you,' he said, mentally kicking himself for being so stupid.

Hadn't he already offered to do that before? But he couldn't stop staring at her. Such a change from sailor to debutante, and yet she was beautiful in both outfits.

'Um...are you ready, then?'

'Do you have room for my sister as well? If not, we can take a hansom cab. I believe I have enough coins.'

'No need. There is plenty of room in my carriage.'

'Thank you, Your Grace.'

Then she turned to the hatch, where a young woman was slowly climbing up to the main deck. Her head was cast down, her hair was in an elaborate coif, and...

He blinked in surprise.

She was perhaps the most gorgeous creature he had ever seen.

'May I introduce my sister, Lucy Richards? Lucy, this is Lord Domac's cousin, His Grace the Duke of Byrning.'

'An honour to meet you,' the girl said as she dropped into a deep curtsey.

It was done beautifully, with fluidity and a coy glance upward in the way a courtesan might. She was undeniably lovely, and yet he found the mystery of her older sister much more intriguing.

'A pleasure to meet you, Miss Richards,' he said as he bowed over her hand. 'Are you ready to go?'

'Whatever you wish,' she said, her voice husky.

He frowned at the seductive note to her words, but her expression was demure as she straightened. Had he imagined it? He looked to the much more intriguing sister and saw a frown marring her otherwise smooth face. She, too, was wondering what the younger girl was doing and looked disturbed by the thought.

Excellent. He hoped that there would be some good guidance from her in the future—assuming the younger girl would listen. Meanwhile, he offered his arms to both ladies to escort them off the gangplank.

The elder Miss Richards stayed long enough to give her thanks to the captain, who returned her smile in full measure, and then all three began the awkward process of returning to the docks and finding his carriage.

He watched the older sister closely during all this, trying to mentally connect the woman in the crow's nest to this uncertain society woman. He caught flashes. Moments like when she forgot to keep her steps small and leaped over a mud puddle rather than sidestep it. Other times he saw the maid surreptitiously correcting her and watched as she obeyed with alacrity—though twice he caught sight of her pursed lips as she no doubt silently cursed the restriction.

And then—finally—they were in his carriage and headed towards her father's home. Now he could ask some of the questions that had been burning on his tongue. While all three women sat with folded hands, and their gazes trained through the window to the London streets, he could begin to indulge his curiosity. He counted himself fortunate that the older sister sat across from him, so he could see the open play of emotions across her face. It was less fortunate that the younger sister sat beside him, pressed too close against him.

'Is it common to educate women in China?' he asked.

The elder Miss Richards shrugged. It was an indelicate movement, and it earned her a sharp look from her maid. She stilled as she answered.

'I cannot answer that except to say I had tutors at the temple. The monks taught me very young to be respectful in my questions and to listen to the answers. That it was the only way to survive.'

He noted that she said 'survive' not *learn*, but he could not think of a polite way to press into that. Meanwhile, she turned the questions on him.

'What did you learn as a boy? What can you do?'

How to answer that? It was akin to asking him how he breathed. 'I attended boarding school, where I learned reading and writing. Mathematics, of course, and science.'

She waited for him to continue, her attention fixed upon him. When he spoke no more, she tilted her head. 'Languages? Just English, or—?'

'Latin, Greek, French... A smattering of others.'

Her eyes brightened. 'Can you teach me?'

'What?'

'I have heard about those countries—Greece and France.' She paused. 'Who speaks Latin?'

'No one,' he said with a laugh.

He tried to explain about Rome and the history of that civilisation. It was a complicated thing to discuss, especially as he quickly found holes in her understanding of English. But she remained animated in her interest. She listened carefully and asked questions, and he found delight in explaining what he could.

'There has been a great deal of conquering in this part of the world,' she said. 'Rome has come and gone while we have remained China. Always.'

That was an interesting idea, and he wanted to learn more, but there was no time. They had arrived at the small London home rented by her father.

Declan stepped out, reluctant to lose the intimacy of the carriage, but happy to extend his hand to her and her sister. The older woman grasped it with a strength that shouldn't surprise him. He knew how physically capable she was. But her demure dress continued to confuse him. He kept expecting her to act as a normal society woman when he knew differently.

Being with her was like unwrapping surprise after surprise, and he was intrigued in a way that had not happened with a woman in such a long time.

He escorted them both up the steps, then enquired if Lord Wenshire were at home. Sadly, the man was out, so Declan had no excuse to further his investigation into the pair. Instead, he lingered on the front step while both sisters curtsied to him.

'I should like to call on you again, if I may,' he said.

The older sister wrinkled her nose as she glanced at the maid. 'Is that allowed?'

He answered himself, rather than wait for the maid's response. 'It is,' he said, 'but I shall obtain permission from your father as well. Perhaps I will see you at tea?'

She nodded. 'This afternoon? You'll be there?'

'Nothing could keep me away.'

But first he had to have a very serious discussion with his banker. He was not a man to give in to blackmail, but he was already determined to keep this woman out of his cousin's clutches.

First of all, she didn't deserve to be abused by his cousin in this way. She was far more intriguing a person than his mother had suggested. Capable, attractive, and so different from anyone he'd ever met. She definitely deserved a better match than Cedric.

Sadly, it was the second concern that tipped the scales. As intriguing as she was, she was not capable of handling the life of a countess. He cast no aspersions on her. It was the simple truth that Cedric's wife would need to manage the *haut ton*. That required a knowledge of the English aristocracy which obviously she did not have.

Some things could be learned. But, as a foreigner, she would never be accepted and would constantly have to fight for the smallest amount of respect. It would be a terrible life, and Cedric was not one to retire quietly into the countryside, where his foreign wife might find some peace.

All in all, Miss Richards was exactly what his mother claimed: unacceptable.

The knowledge depressed him. He longed for a world where 'different' was celebrated. Everywhere he turned he heard the same ideas, the same sentiments repeated over and over again. Where were the fresh ideas? Where were the new perspectives?

Nowhere in his circle. People like his own mother made sure of that.

So that was the way of things and he would be a fool to disregard it. But the question of how to separate her from Cedric remained.

What exactly would Declan do to prevent the marriage?

Would he pay the ransom? That would be extraordinarily distasteful. Would he court the lady herself? Perhaps string her along long enough for her to realise Cedric's true nature? That, too, would be repugnant.

He would be no better than Cedric, pretending to court her without planning to wed her. Because he couldn't marry her either. If it was terrible to imagine her as a countess, how much worse would her life become if she were his duchess? She would be harassed and disparaged at every turn and, like Cedric, he could not leave London. He had responsibilities and political ambitions here.

Damn Cedric's irresponsible behaviour. And damn Declan's mother for dropping this disaster into his lap. There had to be a solution other than giving in to blackmail, and until he found it he would explore every option—even the most distasteful ones.

Chapter Five

Grace hopped into the carriage, her heart beating with excitement. Finally she was being allowed to mix with proper English company! She was to meet Lord Domac's parents—an earl and his countess—for tea. There would be other ladies and gentlemen there too, but with her father, Lord Domac, and the unsettling Duke of Byrning in attendance, she hoped that she would have enough friendly faces to do well.

And if that happened, then Father would allow her to attend her first ball!

She knew that plans were in place for her come-out. Her father's banker had a daughter ready for her come-out. Her name was Phoebe Gray, and she had wealth but no aristocratic heritage. It had been Mr Gray's suggestion that they come out together, and her father had thought it an excellent idea. They hoped to help one another launch into society that might or might not include the highest members of the *ton*.

But it all relied upon how well Grace performed this afternoon, and she was determined to make a good impression.

She only wished Lucy could come, too. The girl was almost painfully shy, and needed a lot of practice to make a good showing. But their father had insisted that, as the eldest, Grace was to enter society first. He had also pointed out—quietly, to Grace only—that Lucy needed more time to grow up. For all that she was a genius at sorting ledgers, she still seemed like a duckling wandering lost in the world.

So Grace sat in the carriage and struggled to contain her excitement. It was the first day of a new life for her, or so her father kept saying. And, even though she doubted it was true, his enthusiasm had slipped into her and now she quivered with anticipation. Unfortunately her father kept focusing on something else.

'You are a proper lady now. You cannot let anyone know you spent your morning half-dressed around gentlemen.'

'Two of them were there, Father. They know.'

'Pray that they say nothing. Let us hope they are gentlemen.'

By which he meant that he hoped they were circumspect men who would not shame a woman? Privately she thought the odds very small that any man would hold his tongue if her actions were truly as scandalous as her father suggested. But the whole thing made no sense to her. She had brought her maid, she had been dressed properly on the way to the boat and on her return. And once on the boat she had dressed appropriately to the location. Wasn't that what a sane person did? Dress and act appropriately wherever she found herself?

But apparently English rules were different, so she held her tongue. She looked down at her clasped hands and held her breath. Arguing never changed anything. It only made unpleasantness linger and she was in a mood to be happy.

'You remember what to do during tea?' her father asked.

'I have practised,' she said.

And she had. *Often.* Did he really think her so stupid as to not remember the English tea ceremony? It wasn't even a ceremony, just a shared drink and sometimes a bit of food. And yet he put so much importance on it.

'I pour tea, I drink tea, and maybe I converse.'

'You won't be pouring the tea. It's the conversation that is important.'

She nodded. He'd already said that a dozen times in the last hour. 'I shall do my very best.'

And then he did the one thing that had convinced her to risk everything on this mad trip to England with him. He softened his voice, he smiled at her, and he looked at her with such paternal love that her heart swelled.

And then he apologised.

'I'm sorry. I am pestering you to death. It is only my pride in you that makes me want to show you off. But even if all is a disaster today, then it will make no difference. We will find a new place to live, another city to conquer.'

Guilt ate at her stomach and she glanced at her hands. She knew her father was ill. Though he hid it during the day, he coughed often at night—sometimes badly. She hoped it would get better, but one never knew. He'd often said how he wanted to spend his last years in England, and so she'd come with him here and would do her best to make him happy because he had made her and Lucy safe.

'I need not find a husband,' she said, as she had a hundred times before. 'We can live together wherever you want.'

He clasped her hands in his and pulled them to his lips to press a dry kiss there. 'You and Lucy have filled my heart when I thought myself nothing more than a dried-up old husk. I want to see you both settled before I die.'

'We can be settled without husbands.'

'A woman cannot inherit. She cannot manage her own affairs without a man to sign the papers. It is the same in China—'

'I know.'

'So I must find a good man to take care of you and your children.'

She tightened her hands in her lap. 'You think Lord Domac is that man?'

Her father nodded. 'He will inherit an earldom. That is no small thing. He is impatient, as so many young men are, but I think he will mature into a fine man. If you care for him, I think he will take care of you.'

'I think he cares for my dowry, not me.'

'Nevertheless, I have faith in his sense of honour. He will respect you as a husband ought.'

She nodded. In truth, that was a great deal more than she had ever thought to have. In China, her mixed blood made her an outcast. If her father thought this was the best way to secure her future, then she would consider marrying Lord Domac. After all, she put no faith in love. She only wanted safety. If he proved he could give her that, then she would be happy to marry him. But since she had not yet seen any proof of that, she made no promise to her father.

They arrived at the London residence of Lord Domac's mother. Apparently the woman lived with her sister, the Duke's mother. Her husband the Earl lived elsewhere, as the marriage was not a happy one. This did not surprise her. Many wealthy Chinese couples lived as strangers. Nevertheless, Lord Domac had assured her that his father would be there today to appreciate her beauty.

Or perhaps to ascertain the truth of her dowry.

Whatever the reason, she resolved to make her father proud. So when they arrived she grinned as he tucked her arm against his sleeve. Then they climbed the steps and knocked.

The butler was polite, the drawing room very lovely, and the Countess was dressed in a fine dress that was not silk and yet appeared beautiful nonetheless, thanks to some well-placed embroidery. Having once tried her hand at stitching,

Grace knew how difficult the task was and appreciated the skill.

She and her father were introduced, and Grace made her curtsey. The Earl inspected her through his quizzing glass and the Countess looked at her as if she'd eaten something sour. Then, as one, they welcomed her father with polite phrases.

It was not an auspicious beginning, especially when the Earl rolled his eyes at his wife and headed for the door.

'I've seen enough and have an appointment. Good day.'

Then he grabbed his hat from the butler and departed.

Meanwhile, Grace looked about the room, seeing several plates of food in small cut bundles. But what stood out to her the most was Lord Domac as he lounged in a corner, a smirk on his handsome face.

'My lord,' she said. 'I did not see you there hidden behind the...the...' What was the name of the instrument? She couldn't remember. 'The music,' she said finally.

He grinned at her. 'It's the best seat in the house,' he said. 'I can watch everyone's expression from here.'

'Child,' the Countess said with a crisp tone. 'One cannot hide behind music. That instrument is a harpsichord. Harp. Si. Chord.'

Grace dipped her chin. 'Yes, my lady.'

'My daughter's name is Grace,' said her father, his voice cold. 'Or in this case Miss Richards.'

The Countess curled her lip. 'Of course. Miss Richards.'

Grace didn't know how to respond to that, so she kept her mouth shut and her head lowered. At any other time in her life she would have found a way to escape. Now she was glad Lucy wasn't here. The girl didn't need practice with this kind of disaster.

Internally, she sighed and accepted the inevitable. If Grace had one overriding strength, it was the ability to adjust when circumstances changed. She would do her best to mitigate the damage, but there was little more she could do.

Fortunately, the awkward moment ended as the knocker sounded again.

Lord Byrning? Her heart leaped at the thought, but the sound of female laughter filled the room. It was a very polite kind of laughter, quickly snuffed, and yet the sound lingered as three very lovely girls were introduced. They came with an older woman as chaperone, and every one of them was greeted with warmth by the Countess.

They were Miss Smythe, Miss Lockwood and Lady Jane, daughter of Lady Charton, who was their chaperone. Grace watched them carefully, so to emulate their mannerisms.

'Welcome, welcome!' the Countess enthused, then she shot a hard look at her son. 'Cedric, stop hiding in the corner. Come. Tell me you remember these lovely ladies?'

Lord Domac rose slowly to his feet. His smile was warm, and there was a languid kind of elegance to his bow. 'Of course I remember them. But pray, you cannot tell me that none of you caught husbands last season? I cannot credit it.'

'Why, sir,' said Miss Smythe, 'that is because you weren't there last Season.'

The other two girls giggled at that, and generally fidgeted where they stood. If Grace had been so wriggly at the temple, she would have been checked for fleas.

'Come in,' the Countess said as she gestured into the room. 'Let me introduce you to our other guest. Ladies, this is Miss Richards.'

'It is a pleasure to meet you,' she said, and she did a shortened curtsey because they were of equal social status to her.

'Oh... Oh, dear,' Miss Lockwood said as she pressed a

hand to her mouth. 'I'm afraid I can't fully understand her. What did she say?'

'Don't be a dolt,' Lady Jane cried. 'It was something polite, I'm sure. Wherever did you learn to speak English?' she asked.

'I learned from English sailors,' she said, doing her best to form the words clearly.

'*Sail*-ors,' said the Countess, correcting her pronunciation. Then she turned back to the women. 'How quaint.'

'Indeed,' echoed the girls as they wandered deeper into the room.

The three ladies and their chaperone immediately settled onto two settees while Grace remained standing. She hadn't been invited to sit and, frankly, the perfume the ladies used was making her nose itch. Her father smiled at her and gestured for her to sit in the chair where he'd been, but she knew better than to take an elder's seat, so she stood tall beside him.

There was a bouquet of flowers on a nearby table, and Miss Smythe complimented the arrangement. The Countess smiled, and then began a discussion of flowers that Grace had no ability to follow. She hadn't heard any of these words, much less associated them with a bloom. And then Miss Smythe, who was apparently regarded as a flower expert, began to address Grace.

'You should wear daisies in your hair, Miss Richards. They would stand out so beautifully against all that darkness.'

'Don't be so rude,' chided Lady Jane. 'Her hair isn't long enough to support flowers.' She looked over with a confused expression. 'Is it customary to cut one's hair in China?'

Best to answer in a general way, thought Grace. 'Every nationality cuts hair, else we would all be caught on tree branches.'

Her father chuckled. At least she had pleased him.

Lady Jane was not so easily amused. 'In England, we are taught not to walk into trees.'

The women laughed at that, while Grace steeled herself to endure. As unpleasant tasks went, this didn't merit a mention, but she was disappointed nevertheless. Perhaps if she engaged Lord Domac in conversation the women would leave her alone. Her father had told her that English men were allowed to marry without parental approval. She'd even include a compliment to his mother.

'Lady Hillburn, the flower designs on your gown are most unusual.' Grace looked at Lord Domac. 'English flower designs might interest my countrymen if they were stitched well on silk. Perhaps you could sell them in China.'

They had, after all, talked a great deal about what he thought would sell in Canton. Unusual flower designs would do well, she thought, at least until every artisan began copying them. But it was the best thought she had at the moment.

'Of all the silly ideas,' said the Countess. 'Flowers do not last long enough to travel to China.'

'Not the flowers themselves—' she began.

'Of course not!' Lady Jane laughed. 'But the designs. Embroidered on fabric. I'm sure they have nothing so elegant over there.'

Actually, the Chinese had elaborate art depicting all kinds of flowers. 'Your blooms are different,' Grace explained. 'And isn't different always interesting?'

Lord Domac chuckled. 'It's always intriguing,' he said, with a warm smile to her.

She smiled back, relishing the kindness in his face. At least until he turned to his mother. 'Painted fans, Mama. Perhaps we could export parcels of those to Canton. Make it all the rage over there.'

'What a clever idea, Cedric,' his mother said. 'I'm sure they have seen nothing so lovely as an English rose on wood.'

It was possible, Grace thought. She had not seen many English fans.

She turned to the women. 'Yours are so lovely. Would it be possible for me to look at one?' she asked.

'Oh!' Lady Jane said as she pressed her closed fan to her chest. 'I... Well, I suppose so.' She passed hers over and the other women were quick to join in.

Grace looked at each carefully, evaluating them as she thought a merchant in China might. She inspected the paint, the quality of the wood, and even the craftmanship in the dangling ribbon. And while she looked the conversation flowed around her, all of it insulting.

'I'm sure you've never seen anything so beautiful,' Lady Jane laughed. 'But I promise you this is a poor example. Something I use every day for making calls. I save my nicer ones—'

'For the balls, of course,' interrupted Miss Smythe. 'The white one you had at the Weckstein rout was stunning.'

'Do you recall how funny Miss Bradley was, accidentally getting it caught in her hair?'

'My goodness, how we all laughed. Now, have a care, Miss Richards, we wouldn't want you to get my fan tangled, would we?'

'Don't be silly. Her hair's too short for that.'

Grace let the conversation wash away. They were just being spiteful, she knew. Women in China had disdained her as well. So long as they hadn't tried to beat her, she'd counted the words as nothing.

What she couldn't ignore was the way her father's face fell with each horrid interaction. He kept tapping his foot in annoyance and shooting her apologetic looks. He did not want her to endure humiliation at these women's hands.

What he didn't realise was that their barbs barely registered. She was more interested in the idea of selling fans to China. That was, after all, what interested Lord Domac, and he was her only friend in this room.

In time, she finished her inspection and passed the fans back to the girls with her thanks.

'Well?' Lady Jane pressed. 'What did you think of them?'

'They're very lovely, of course,' she returned.

'Then they'll be popular in China!' Lady Jane crowed. 'I believe Lord Domac has landed upon a capital idea. Send fans to China!'

No, that wouldn't work at all—but Grace knew she couldn't say as much in front of these women. They would be insulted by her opinions. She maintained a wan smile as they began discussing which designs would work best, while Lord Domac listened with seeming fascination.

Though actually his attention wasn't on them, she noticed. It was on herself. And his face slowly lost its excitement as he read her expression.

'So not flowers,' he said finally, apparently ignoring everything the other women had said. 'Another design, perhaps? Something unique to England.'

'Perhaps—' Grace began, but before she could say more the door knocker sounded again.

Another visitor. Grace looked up with hope. She already knew where she stood with everyone here. Perhaps this newcomer would be more friendly and she could salvage something from this disastrous tea.

Like her, everyone turned to the door, waiting to see who entered. When a deep voice sounded in the hall, her heart soared and her entire body tightened. She had a simultaneous desire to run away from the man and to run towards him. In the end, she froze in indecision, her breath suspended as she stared at the doorway.

'The Duke of Byrning,' intoned the butler.

And there he was, looking as handsome in his gentlemanly attire as he had barefoot on the rigging, with the wind lifting his hair. He walked in with purpose, greeted his aunt with warmth, then nodded to his cousin. The women were all aflutter, each rising up to her feet to curtsey to the man. Thankfully, Grace was already on her feet, or she would have been left sitting there like an idiot. It took her father's not too subtle poke for her to remember to make her curtsey.

'Miss Richards,' he said. His voice seemed to wrap her in the same warmth as it had on the crow's nest. 'You look sensational.'

She felt her cheeks heat. Her father had said exactly the same thing, but every word from the Duke seemed to heat her to uncomfortable levels.

'I feel awkward in English clothing,' she admitted, 'but I am learning.'

'I would never guess.' Then he looked about. 'Has no one offered you a chair?' He turned and shot his aunt a hard glare. 'Pray, let me find one for you.'

'It is no matter,' she said, but it seemed he was determined.

Stepping out of the room, he directed the butler to bring a pair of chairs. A moment later two footmen appeared, each with a straight-backed chair. The Duke directed them easily, pointing to the narrow spot where she'd been standing. Her father had to push his chair to the side, and then the new chairs were squeezed in such that they became a single bench. The Duke gestured for her to sit, which she did as gracefully as she could manage, and then he took the chair beside her.

It was a great deal of movement and activity, and in the end he was sitting pressed so tightly beside her that it felt more intimate than it had in the crow's nest. She felt as if a deep breath would put her in his lap, and this time there was nowhere for her to run.

Even worse, she had absolutely no desire to move away.

Chapter Six

Declan liked his aunt as much as he liked all his older relatives. They were part of his life because they were family, and as the current duke he was responsible for their care. Certainly they had their own income and peccadillos, but once his father had passed he had become the head of the family. He would see to it that they did not disgrace their heritage, and indeed that they contributed to becoming the best England had to offer and not the worst.

So it was that he was quietly furious that no one had thought to offer Miss Richards a seat until he got there. It was unthinkable that she should be left to stand like a servant when all the others sat. Good manners required consideration for one's guests. Even if Napoleon himself had entered the room, he should be offered a chair while footmen went to gather the firing squad.

Unfortunately, he saw the embarrassment this had caused Miss Richards. Her cheeks had turned pink, her hands were clenched together, and her smile seemed frozen upon her face.

Thankfully, all was handled quickly enough and soon they were seated together so closely that he could measure the tempo of her breath by the pressure against his arm. And what a deliciously exciting feeling it was. What man *didn't* like being pressed up against a beautiful woman?

'Is everyone settled?' his aunt asked in hard tones. 'Shall I call for tea?'

Everyone murmured their delight at the idea, and his aunt rang a little bell in response. Declan didn't miss the envious looks the ladies shot Miss Richards, but he had no intention of indulging them. His focus was on making Grace more comfortable.

'I apologise for arriving so late and interrupting things. Tell me, what were you discussing?'

'Oh, my lord,' said Lady Jane, 'we were on the most fascinating topic. We were showing Miss Richards the extraordinary art in our fans.' She lifted hers up and snapped it open with a dramatic flick of her wrist.

'We're trying to think of a design that would be appealing to the Chinese. Then I'll export them and make a fortune,' Cedric said.

Declan glanced at Miss Richards' face, seeing the rigid way she smiled as she kept her eyes downcast. He might have mistaken it for a demure pose, but he felt the stiffness in her body growing tighter with every statement.

'What an interesting topic,' he said. 'Miss Richards, can you tell me what you find so different in our English fans?'

'They were talking about the meaning of the flowers,' she said. 'There is a whole language in them and I thought to learn it.'

'How very ambitious,' he said. 'I could never keep it straight.'

Miss Lockwood shifted towards him, her eyes alight with mischief. 'I was just about to teach her,' she said as she held out her fan and began pointing. 'This is a daffodil, and it means I am sending a message. This is an iris, suggesting preference. And here is a wild rose for passion.'

She tittered as she closed up her fan and pointed it directly at him with a flirtatious look.

Declan frowned, embarrassed for Miss Lockwood. She had named two of the flowers incorrectly, and he thought the meanings were wrong too. 'I believe I shall buy you a book, Miss Richards. One with the proper names of flowers and their meanings.' He leaned close. 'Don't try to memorise it now. Some things are best learned from a proper source.'

'What a very kind idea, my lord,' crowed Lady Jane. 'After all, it is important for all proper ladies to know the truth of these things.'

Then she raised her eyebrows and shot a glance at Miss Lockwood before rolling her eyes. It was her way of saying that she knew Miss Lockwood had her flowers all wrong, but she—a true lady—was better educated than to say so.

Honestly, it sickened him. The petty cruelty in this room had his blood heating to a dangerous degree. These women had a full world of conversational topics, but they could not resist poking at one another in the hopes of gaining favour with him. As if he'd care for any woman who would take pains to point out another's ignorance.

He turned away from her and allowed his attention to focus on Miss Richards. 'Surely the English are not the only ones to develop meanings from blossoms? What do the Chinese see in blooms?'

'The lotus flower is the most prized, of course. It rises from mud and blooms in perfection. It is called the seat of Buddha and it symbolises purity, long life, and honour.'

'How interesting—' he began, but his aunt tsked audibly.

'How very heathen to look at something that rises from the mud as a symbol of purity.'

Declan felt his teeth clench. His aunt had a difficult life, to be sure, but all she showed the world was bitterness—and he was tired of it.

'I find Miss Richards' knowledge extraordinary,' he said, with a pointed look at his aunt.

Unfortunately, her attention was focused on the butler as he appeared at the door with the tea tray.

'Here is the tea at last!' his aunt cried, effectively drowning him out. 'I declare that I am quite parched.'

Then she settled herself in front of the tray and began to pour for each person in turn. His aunt was a proper English lady, who had been taught the serving of tea in the schoolroom. She served him first, as he was the highest ranked person there, and correctly remembered his preference for milk. Then she continued about the room, her memory obviously serving her well as she poured for everyone save Miss Richards, who was addressed last.

The conversation continued and the ladies grew animated by the coming balls of the Season. Miss Richards did not participate, because obviously she didn't know any of the people discussed. Indeed, she was largely ignored by the company except for the occasional insult.

'Oh, Miss Richards, you wouldn't know this, but an earl is ranked higher than a viscount.'

'You must remember, Miss Richards, a waltz is a very exciting dance, but is not considered totally proper.'

He was moments away from the rude action of starting an entirely new conversation with her alone when Cedric beat him to the punch. Declan's cousin stood up under the pretence of selecting a sweetmeat in order to address her more closely.

'This must be terribly boring for you, Miss Richards. Perhaps let me divert your attention for a moment? I like the idea of exporting fans to China. Will you let me know if you think of a design that will appeal?' His gaze shot to Declan. 'That's what I need money for,' he said in an undertone. 'I want to sell goods to China and then bring back different things to sell in England. All our trade so far has been one-way, but the real profit is in going both directions.'

'A sound plan in theory—' Declan began, but Cedric was too caught up to listen.

'So…fans,' he said, facing Miss Richards. 'Could it be as simple as that? You'll be at lots of balls this Season, and you will see lots of different fans. Maybe a design will be intriguing to you.'

Miss Richards stiffened, and her face seemed to pale. 'I cannot speak to what the ladies of China would prefer, my lord. One would need to live inside the court to know.'

'But everyone likes novelty, yes? And English fans are different, yes?'

'Again, my lord, one would need access to the Imperial Court to know.'

Declan understood what she was saying, and knew it was the same here. Any man could bring his goods to England, but it wouldn't become popular unless a royal or an aristocrat declared it a delight. Without someone of influence in China praising English fans, Cedric would do as well tossing his fans into the ocean as he would in getting Chinese ladies to adopt them.

'What she means,' interrupted Cedric's mother, 'is that she's a nobody in China. She can't tell you what the ladies there want any more than my maid can.'

Miss Richards winced at that bold statement, as did her father, but she didn't contradict it either. And then his aunt passed her a cup of tea.

She hadn't asked for Miss Richards' preferences, and

indeed, one glance at the cup told him that his aunt had purposely curdled the milk with lemon. It was a petty embarrassment, one that demonstrated a cruel streak, especially as she quickly made herself a cup and sat back with a smug smile.

'To your health, everyone,' she said.

Then she took a sip from her own cup while her eyes remained fixed on Miss Richards. Would she take a drink from the rancid tea? Would she make a noise of disgust? Or would she leave the cup on the edge of the table so everyone saw that it was curdled?

Declan's fury became a painful thing. The Byrning legacy was eating him from the inside out. He kept his expression placid by force of will, but determined that his aunt would feel his wrath eventually. This was not appropriate behaviour for a countess, and so he would tell her in no uncertain terms. There was little else he could do—she lived on his mother's charity—but he would make his displeasure known. Just not now. That would be exposing his family's dirty laundry in public.

Instead, he decided to correct her subtly and see if she was appropriately shamed.

'My apology,' Declan said with a loud voice. 'I'm afraid I accidentally picked up your teacup, Miss Richards. It appears I'm quite addled.'

Then he pressed his own teacup and saucer into her hands, before reaching forward to grab her curdled tea. Miss Richards didn't say a word, but watched him with a startled expression. She knew what he had done, and it had shocked her.

Meanwhile, he shifted his gaze to his aunt as he prepared to drink the disgusting brew. Would she stop him? Would she allow him to taste such a thing?

'Oh, don't, Your Grace!' she cried as she set down her

teacup with an audible click. 'It's cold. I was slow in serving everyone, and yours was first.' She rang her little bell and when a footman appeared gestured to his tea. 'Take His Grace's cup away and bring more hot tea immediately.' Then she simpered. 'Really, it is so hard to get good servants these days. I'm mortified that I've served you cold tea.'

The other ladies rushed to reassure his aunt that they completely understood, thereby dropping them even further in his estimation. They shared tales of their displeasure with servants. They commiserated over how difficult it was to sack someone, but agreed that a lady understood how to do it with charm. And then, as if they had rehearsed it, they all turned to Miss Richards.

'Have you had that experience in China, Miss Richards?' asked Lady Jane. 'Servants who must be disciplined or who are simply too stupid to learn?'

They already knew the answer. Hadn't she just said that she had no entrée into the Imperial Court of China? As a bastard raised in a temple, Declan doubted she had experience with servants at all. But in this she surprised them all.

'Aboard ship there were always sailors who refused to take direction from a woman. I may have had the captain's trust as a navigator, but many men would not listen to my orders unless the captain relayed them. It was a constant problem.'

'I should imagine,' Declan said.

Meanwhile, Miss Smythe had abruptly leaned forward. 'You have worked as a navigator on board a ship?'

Miss Richards dipped her chin, her smile warming with pride. 'I have. I am very good at it.'

'But you're a *woman*!' In fairness to Miss Smythe, she didn't sound shocked so much as impressed. 'I cannot imagine anyone would listen to you. To any woman.'

'When I was younger, I hid my sex. Much easier to be a

young boy than a vulnerable girl. But as I grew older there were constant problems. I was fortunate to have the protection of a good captain, who made sure I was obeyed. And he had a solution for when I was not.'

Declan could not get over how difficult her life must have been. 'What was it?' he asked.

'What is always done. It was the captain's idea. I was too young to know what to do, but he taught me.'

Everyone looked around, confused.

Finally, it was her father who explained. 'If a sailor disobeys, he is flogged. It is the same on English ships.'

Lady Jane's lip curled in shock. 'You had men whipped? That sounds barbaric.'

'It sounds like necessary discipline to me,' Cedric said, nodding to Miss Richards as a way of showing his support. 'Ships can be lawless places.'

But Miss Richards shook her head. 'No, you misunderstand. The captain had men flogged many times, but I was still treated with disrespect.'

'What did you do?' Declan asked.

She looked into his eyes, her expression calm. 'I wielded the whip myself.'

Declan believed it. He had seen the proof of her muscles, felt the strength in her, and he had been in her company enough to know that she had hidden talents. He would not have guessed that she could flog a man, but that made more sense than that she would be anxious to learn flower language.

But the others did not have that advantage or perception. His aunt, in particular, pushed to her feet.

'Miss Richards,' she said in strident tones. 'In England, ladies do not lie. To think we would believe such a preposterous statement merely betrays your ignorance. I suggest you apologise immediately for your egregious actions.'

And here Grace must have finally reached her limit. She stood and, though she was not nearly as large a woman as his aunt, her composure radiated a confidence that he'd only seen in royalty.

'Should you like me to teach you how to do it?' Miss Richards asked. 'You think to belittle me, but you only damage yourselves.' She looked to the other ladies in the room. 'How can you accept being so small? Even your attacks are tiny, when you are capable of so much more than bad tea and ugly fans.'

The ladies gasped, his aunt louder than the rest, but did they understand what she was saying? Declan wondered. That she not only saw their slights, but counted them as less than nothing compared to what she had done with her life. She wasn't yet thirty and she had lived well beyond the bounds of anything these women considered possible.

In truth, he barely credited it. But far from being outraged, he was filled with admiration. Her sheer audacity impressed him, and her accomplishments were far beyond that.

'Would you care to ride with me in Hyde Park?' he asked abruptly. 'I should love to hear more.'

She blinked at him, and he watched as her expression turned uncertain. She didn't know the value of such an invitation, and had to look to her father for guidance. His aunt, however, didn't give her time for an answer as she voiced her outrage in the loudest voice.

'Your Grace! You cannot mean to foist such mendacity upon society!'

Mr Richards had found his feet, and he extended his arm to his daughter. 'Grace has not lied,' he said sternly. 'And I think we've had enough of your *polite society*.'

These last words were sneered, and well they should be. And now Declan was forced to apologise for his bitter aunt.

'Lord Wenshire, pray allow me to apologise for this terrible display. My aunt has been unwell, and I believe it has affected her temperament. I assure you, she and I will have words later.'

He shot his aunt a look that did nothing to assuage the fury in his blood.

His aunt's mouth fell open in shock. The other ladies gasped in horror, but he turned his back on them. They were no longer women to whom he wished to extend any courtesy. Meanwhile, he continued his apology.

'Pray, allow me to show your daughter that English society is not always so crass.'

'Declan!' his aunt snapped, her voice imperious. 'You are overcome with emotion.'

He froze, her words slipping like ice into his veins. Those were the exact words his mother had used whenever he'd grown the least bit upset about anything as a boy. A broken toy, a lame horse—all had been dismissed as Declan being overly emotional. And, given the legacy of his blood, it was the one thing that terrified him.

Was he overreacting to his aunt's horrendous display of bad manners? Damn her for making him second-guess himself. He took a moment to re-evaluate and decided—again— that she was in the wrong.

'Drink your tea, Aunt. I am finished speaking with you.'

She gasped in shock, her hand pressed to her breast. She had a weak heart, he knew. She often grew breathless when distressed. He wondered anew if he had gone too far, especially when she collapsed back down into her seat. Of course he knew that she might be faking that, but he also knew her condition was real. How awful if his display of temper ended up killing his aunt.

But it was too late to change that now. He turned back

to Miss Richards, though a part of him remained aware of his aunt's shortened breath. If she really did faint, he would call for a doctor.

She didn't.

'Miss Richards, I should also like you to join me at the theatre. With your father's permission, of course.'

No fool, the man dipped his chin in agreement. 'A wonderful idea. Grace has been hoping to see our theatre.'

'Then it is settled. A walk in Hyde Park tomorrow and the theatre the next day.'

Surprisingly, Grace shook her head. 'My come-out ball isn't until next week. I cannot go to the theatre beforehand.'

He nodded. 'Quite right. But we can walk tomorrow. Theatre as soon as you are out. And I shall expect an invitation to your ball.'

She dipped her chin. 'You honour me.'

He could do no less, given how abominably she'd been treated this afternoon.

'Perhaps your father would join us in Hyde Park tomorrow—but may I have the pleasure of escorting you home now?'

He lifted his arm for her, while her gaze hopped between him and her father. It was as if she couldn't understand a man extending such a courtesy to her. But in this her father helped.

He took her hand and placed it on Declan's arm. 'It's too far to walk home, but since it's a fine day you should enjoy a meander, yes? There's been so little time for me to show you the best of London. I'll have the carriage waiting nearby when you're finished.'

Now that she had her father's permission, Miss Richards nodded to him with the poise of a queen. 'I should enjoy a walk, Your Grace. If that is what you wish.'

And so began the most extraordinary discussion of his life as they walked out, without giving anyone else in the room so much as a backward glance.

Chapter Seven

Grace couldn't wait to get outside. London did not have the cleanest air, but it was better than the stuffiness inside. Not to mention the spiteful, small women right now exclaiming their outrage. She lifted her chin and ignored the catty whispers. After all, people had whispered, pointed or outright thrown things at her for her entire life. She had come too far to bend now.

She took her wrap from the haughty butler, but was forced to wait as the Duke looked around.

'Where is your maid?' he asked.

She frowned at him. 'We didn't bring her.'

It had been just her and her father in the carriage. Why would she need a servant's escort?

The Duke shook his head. 'Your father is too casual with your reputation.'

'I am not to walk abroad with my father?'

'No, Miss Richards. You are not to walk alone with me.'

Then he snapped his fingers at the butler, who bowed.

'Right away, Your Grace,' he intoned, before stepping over to whisper to a footman.

Grace watched the exchange with confusion, before turning her attention back to the Duke.

'I am not helpless,' she said.

She could fight, and she could run fast when the situation called for it. She was likely the most capable woman in this house, but she didn't say so—especially when the Duke shook his head.

'I protect your reputation, Miss Richards. Your person is safe with me.'

A moment later, a maid rushed up from below stairs, pulling on a cloak likely too heavy for the spring weather. She looked flushed, and her hands were raw, but her demeanour was cheerful enough.

'This is Millie, Your Grace,' said the butler. 'She is quiet and respectful.'

Those last words were aimed at the girl, as if she needed reminding how to act. The Duke nodded and turned to go, but Grace was not willing to dismiss anyone so quickly.

'We must have pulled you from a task. Do you need to return quickly?'

Millie's eyes widened in shock. 'Er...yes, miss. I were kneading the dough for tonight, but—'

Her words were cut off at the butler's imperious sniff. Then the man turned to the Duke. 'Millie is at your disposal for as long as you require,' he said loudly.

'Is someone else covering your tasks, then?' Grace pressed.

The girl dropped her gaze to the floor. 'You need not concern yourself with that, miss.'

Which meant, no. This walk was an added burden. But one look at the men's faces told Grace that her enquiry had infuriated the butler and confused the Duke. Additional discussion would not be looked upon favourably. The best she could do to mitigate the situation was to give the girl a gentle smile.

'We will not keep you away from your duties for long,' she said.

'Yes, miss. I will enjoy the respite. It is a fine—'

Her words were cut off again, this time by the snap of the butler's fingers.

Grace flashed an apologetic smile to the girl, then turned towards the door. She was momentarily confused when the Duke held out his arm, but she adapted quickly enough. She set her fingers on his forearm, as she had been taught, and they stepped out into the fine afternoon.

She didn't dare look behind her to see if Millie followed, but she could hear the girl's footsteps.

A few moments later, she spoke softly to the Duke. 'You are right. We should have brought my maid.'

He slanted her a glance. 'You are also right, but I don't think we agree on the reasons. You shouldn't worry about the girl's duties. That is Nagel's responsibility.'

'Nagel is the butler?'

'Yes. Generally, the butler manages the servants, along with the housekeeper.'

She nodded. She'd been taught as much. 'And does Nagel seem a forgiving kind of man? Does he understand what it takes to make bread, or that she will not have time to finish her other tasks?'

He was silent for a long moment. 'I have no idea what kind of man he is below stairs, though my aunt has praised his efficiency.'

She didn't respond. She knew what that meant in a Chinese household. A ruthless master often meant that the higher servants were equally ruthless, if not more so. She would have liked to believe that it was different in England. Her father treated his manservant well, and the maid who had been hired for herself and Lucy seemed kind enough. Indeed, Grace had learned nearly as much from her talkative maid as she had her tutors. But she could not speak to what happened in other households.

The Duke turned them to the right, his expression distracted. 'I will say something to Nagel to be sure that she is not ill-treated for this outing.'

He said the words, but she could tell from his tone that he thought it a needless action. And indeed, she agreed. If the butler were a tyrant, then a word from the Duke would make things worse rather than better. The only way to know would be to ask Millie what she would prefer.

She turned around to address the maid. 'Would that be helpful?' she asked. 'If the Duke were to say something to Mr Nagel? Or would it make things harder?'

The girl's mouth dropped open in shock. Indeed, so startled was she at being addressed that she couldn't seem to form any words, especially when the Duke himself turned to look at her.

'Well?' he enquired.

Thankfully, his tone wasn't abrupt, but she could tell the girl was nearly shaking in terror at being so addressed.

'Never mind,' Grace said, as she turned back. 'I think it best if we let things be.'

At least she hoped so. Millie didn't sport any obvious bruises, and she walked with a happy lift to her heels. If she were being mistreated, then it was well hidden.

They walked a few more steps before the Duke spoke again, his tone thoughtful. 'Is that common in China? Are servants usually…?' His voice trailed off as if he couldn't find the right words.

'Beaten? Raped? Terrified into submission?'

'Good God!' he gasped, clearly horrified. 'Is that how your underclass is treated?'

She turned to watch his reaction to her next words. 'Do

you suppose that never happens in England? If women are so safe, why do we need maids to go with us everywhere?'

He frowned, clearing his throat. 'Well, of course there are some instances. Horrible, terrible things. We most certainly don't condone it!'

'Neither is it condoned in China,' she said softly. 'But it happens nonetheless.'

He gaped at her. 'Were you—?' He swallowed. 'I mean—um...'

'No. I am whole.'

By which she meant she was still a virgin. However, she knew that for a discarded child such as her, she was the exception rather than the rule.

'The monks taught us how to fight. Even the girls.' Her lips twisted. 'Especially the girls.'

He nodded, though he still appeared flustered. 'I should not have asked. That was wrong of me.'

'Then you would have wondered—or assumed.'

He didn't respond to that, though she could tell he wanted to. Her father had wanted to ask as well, and it had taken many months of getting to know him aboard ship for them to become easy enough together to speak of it. Indeed, it had been Lord Domac who'd broached the question, thereby forcing the discussion between herself and her father.

'My parentage rests upon my face. Anyone who looks at me knows I am not of a blessed union. As such, I deserve less respect in China than even the lowest beggar of clear race.'

'That's despicable,' he said, his voice hard.

She glanced at him, startled at the vehemence in his tone.

It took him a moment to register her expression, and then his voice turned rueful. 'You seem shocked, Miss Richards. Do you think English men would treat you so shabbily?'

'Your aunt and her guests believe I am less than they.'

He snorted. 'My aunt and her guests believe *everyone* is less than they. It has nothing to do with your race.'

She arched her brows at him, and he flushed.

'Very well, you are right. It has a great deal to do with your race, and I am sorry for that. I had not thought that they could be so mean.'

She snorted, and then abruptly covered her mouth. She should not have expressed her doubt so openly. When he looked at her, his mouth agape, she tried to apologise. 'I meant no harm,' she said quickly. 'I do not know your customs. I should not venture an opinion.'

He sighed. 'I welcome your opinion, even when it is expressed inadvertently.'

Was that a kind way of referring to her snort?

'But believe me,' he pressed, 'some of the most despicable people I know are full-blooded Englishmen of high rank. And some of the kindest come from the lowest rungs of society. I do not think title or bloodline are accurate measures of one's humanity.'

That surprised her. How did a wealthy mandarin meet anyone—kind or not—from the lowest caste?

He shook his head. 'You are shocked?'

'I do not understand England well enough to be shocked. In China, the rich children are kept well away from the poor.'

He nodded. 'Many are here, but I was a wanderer.'

She was not surprised. She remembered the way he had ached to go up the mast, and the hunger in his eyes as he'd looked around in the crow's nest. Many in this world were content in their very tiny corner, but she had spent years on boats or by docks. She knew the yearning in some to explore. She wondered if his responsibilities as a duke prevented him from indulging his desires.

'Where did you go?' she asked.

He smiled. 'Everywhere I could. Our nannies were always busy.' He glanced at her. 'I have a younger brother and three younger sisters. And two who did not live long.' His tone dipped at that, but he did not seem to dwell on it. 'Whenever they were busy with the younger children, I escaped to my own amusements.'

'I cannot believe your servants were so careless.'

'I was lucky in that,' he said with a grin. 'And I was lucky to befriend our gamekeeper. He had a boy a little older than I, whom I worshipped.'

She smiled trying to envisage this large man as a young boy. 'Did you try to do everything he could?'

'I did. And I assumed that because I was the ducal heir I should do everything better than everyone else.' He shrugged. 'I couldn't, of course. And I learned to stuff away my pride when dealing with Jacky or any of his older siblings.' He looked off into the distance. 'It wasn't easy. I had no control over my rage.' His lips quirked. 'Fortunately, I wasn't large enough to cause any damage. They were well protected from me.'

'Were they unkind to you?'

'No. Not unkind, exactly, but it gave me the experience of being the youngest.'

'Did they have a mother?'

'God, yes.' His tone and his expression softened. 'She told the most amazing stories. Tales of poor beggars who needed a helping hand, old men whom nobody listened to but who knew great secrets.' His gaze was soft in memory. 'I never heard those stories from anyone else. Honestly, I think she made them up, but she could tell them so well we believed them. And when she was too tired to speak she got her husband to tell them. And her father as well, who came to live with them.' He shook his head. 'That whole family was a never-ending source of stories, and always with a moral pointed at someone.'

'At you?' she asked.

'Often. Usually the ones about pride and wilful ignorance.' He chuckled. 'But I was not the only one who needed a lesson or three.'

She could hear the humour in his voice, and knew he had enjoyed a happy childhood—at least when in the gamekeeper's cottage.

'The monks had many such tales as well,' she said.

'I should like to hear them.'

'Lucy remembers them more than I do. I always wanted to learn how to slay the demons myself. I didn't believe that someone mystical would do the slaying for me.'

'A practical mind, then?'

She nodded. 'And too restless to sit still.'

She looked at him, wishing he had joined them on the boat four months ago instead of Lord Domac. She would have preferred learning English from him. She would have enjoyed long nights staring at the stars with him. But it had been his cousin who'd stepped onto the boat in India, and his cousin who had befriended her father. And it was his cousin her father had formed a friendship with.

She kept her thoughts to herself. Her father had told her to be discerning with the gentlemen she met. He wanted her to evaluate them honestly. So she tried to separate her feelings—which were definitely confused—from the facts.

The Duke seemed to be a man of influence and intelligence without the rashness she feared in Lord Domac. But he also seemed to dislike her restless nature. Hadn't he chastised her for travelling without a maid? And he was constantly worried about her reputation. The man was excruciatingly aware of all the tiny rules of society that she could never remember. She had no idea if he was right or wrong in his assessment, and she disliked not understanding the rules.

Fortunately, he didn't seem to be angry when correcting her. What irritation did colour his voice seemed to be directed at other people. Nevertheless, she was wary. He lived under a myriad of rules that seemed to apply to every detail of his life. Why wasn't he screaming in frustration at their constant weight?

She turned away, wishing she were naturally quiet, like Lucy. Would she never find a place where she could be herself safely? Of all the people she had met, this man interested her the most. But he clearly did not approve of her, so she would have to think more about Lord Domac.

That made her heart twist in a way that startled her. She liked the Duke, but she had liked many different men in her life. Turning away from them had never made her chest tighten with regret. What made him so different that her body seemed to want to linger near him?

Meanwhile, the Duke had guided them around a corner to reveal a wide open space of green set in the middle of the city. And not just green. She heard the happy babble of water nearby, not to mention the laughter of children and the murmur of voices from nannies talking as they watched their charges.

'This is St James's Park,' he said. 'It's one of the lovelier places in London.'

'It is huge,' she said as she stepped forward. Because it was spring, the flowers were a gorgeous riot of colour. 'This is available to everyone?' she asked as she looked around.

There were no gates that she could see. Only people enjoying the beautiful day.

'Do you not have public parks in China?'

'Yes, but most gardens are enclosed. Private places enjoyed by the wealthy families who tend them.'

'Then I am pleased to bring you here.'

She lifted her face to the sky, wishing to pull off her hat to feel the wind in her hair. She supposed it was enough to feel the sun on her face, if only for a few moments.

He let her bask for a bit, before directing her along a path. 'There is something I want to show you,' he said. 'Down this way.'

She followed, her steps lighter. 'So much space...' she murmured.

'I suppose things can feel crowded aboard ship.'

'Very much so,' she responded. 'And even in the temple there were people everywhere.'

Someone had always been watching, and many would take any excuse to discipline the half-children.

'Do you miss it?'

'What?'

'The temple. The boat. This must feel very different to you.'

'Everything is different, and yet so much feels the same. The clothes and language are different, but one city feels the same as the next to me. So many people, all thinking about their own lives, all crowded together.' She looked around. 'But I am learning your customs.'

'Indeed, you are. I do not think I could be half so easy in another place as you are here.'

He overestimated how 'easy' she was, but she smiled to pretend he was correct. 'Have you travelled much?' she asked.

'I have. I took my Grand Tour of the continent several years ago. My tutor insisted I go, despite Napoleon's antics.' He shook his head. 'Looking back, it was not as safe a choice as we thought, but obviously I survived. I think I was lucky, rather than wise, and I do have very fond memories of Italy.'

She faced him, intrigued by his far-off look. 'What was it like?'

'I was a young man of title and wealth. It was all parties and new foods. Parties and lovely weather. Parties and unbearable heat and beautiful women.'

'I thought you went with a tutor.'

He chuckled. 'I did. But he was a tutor who enjoyed—'

'Parties?'

'Yes.' He focused again on her. 'But I have never been so far as China. Or even Africa. You must have seen so much.'

'I saw views from the boat, and I tasted strange foods, but I was rarely allowed to explore.'

'That must have chafed.'

'No,' she said. 'I preferred the safety of a place I knew, with people who would protect me. I loved hearing tales when the sailors returned, but I had no desire to risk myself by exploring.'

'Truly? I would guess that anyone who jumps the riggings like you do would want to test herself.'

'On land? As a lone girl? No.'

She had seen enough in China by the time she was ten to know that she would not be safe in a city she did not know. Not without the protection of wealthy men and strong servants. Better to stay on the ship and listen to tales from a place of safety. Life aboard ship had been dangerous enough. She had not needed to seek out more dangers just for their novelty.

'I envy your freedom to wander as you chose.'

He shrugged. 'As I said, it was not so prudent a choice. I was young and stupid, and we paid the price.'

His tone was bitter, but not closed, so she dared ask the question. 'What price?'

'My tutor was murdered. I was nearly so.'

She winced. 'I am sorry. Was it the French?'

She had learned from her father about the war with Napoleon.

'That would have been more honourable. No, it was footpads. I lost my purse, not my life. My tutor was cut. Not so bad a wound, or so we thought, but then infection set in. He died eight days later, and I had to manage my return to England when I hadn't the least idea how it was done. If we hadn't squandered so much on wine and women I would have done better. I learned very quickly that my title did not protect me from much of anything.'

She watched him closely as he spoke, seeing shadows in his eyes. He knew, then, what it was to live in danger.

'How long did it take you to return home?'

'Several months.' His lips twisted in a rueful expression. 'Not so long in the grand scheme of things, but I have never forgotten what it was like to be hungry or afraid.'

A difficult lesson, then, but she could see he was a better man for it.

Then, before she could say more, he looked up and gestured ahead. 'Ah, here we are. What do you think?'

Chapter Eight

Declan watched her face as they stepped out through a set of trees to see the Chinese Bridge in all its glory. Though the yellow and blue paint had faded over the last year, it was still a lovely sight. Not as pretty were the burned remains of the pagoda, but from this angle it didn't look so bad.

It took her a moment to take in the view, and though she didn't immediately gasp about the sight before her, she did smile. 'That's quite lovely,' she said politely.

'It was constructed for the Grand Jubilee last year. There was a seven-storey pagoda right there, but it caught fire during the fireworks display. It was a sad end to the celebration, but impressive at the time.'

'You were here?' she asked.

'My whole family came to celebrate with the royal house. There were so many people here it looked like a sea of bodies. They were even in the trees—which made it all the more frightening when the pagoda caught fire.'

'Were many people hurt?'

'Several.' They started walking, heading towards the bridge. 'But only two deaths, thankfully. The Queen was most distressed.'

'What were you celebrating?'

'A hundred years since the Hanovers ascended to the English throne.'

'A hundred years?'

Her eyes widened before she quickly looked away, and he knew she was hiding her thoughts.

'Are you surprised by that?' he asked. 'That England has had the same ruling family that long?'

She shook her head, biting her lip as she stared at the water.

It took a moment before he realised *why* she had been surprised.

'How long has your emperor's family ruled?'

She smiled. 'The Qing dynasty began nearly two hundred years ago. The Ming dynasty lasted nearly three hundred years before that.' She glanced around, as if she could see the King and Queen in the shrubbery. 'China has stood for thousands of years. Twenty dynasties in all. I had not realised how young your country is.'

His brows arched. 'The Hanovers aren't our first ruling family, you know. But I suppose…' He counted on his fingers. 'We are only six dynasties compared to your twenty, so you have us there.'

She shrugged. 'China is very old and very large, but I am looking forward to seeing all the best spots in London. You did promise to show me.'

'I did indeed.'

'Perhaps we could go at a time when my sister could join us. She has been cooped up inside for so long. She longs to get out.'

'It would be my honour,' he said slowly, 'but I don't believe she is out yet, is she?' She looked disappointed at this reminder, and he flashed her a quick smile. 'I know our customs are strange, but they are for your own protection.'

'I understand. The wealthy Chinese hide girls away, too.' Then her next words surprised him.

'They think it keeps them safe.'

She didn't sneer as she spoke, but he heard the implied criticism.

'Women should be cherished and protected,' he said.

She faced him, her expression rueful. 'I have never thought ignorance was useful. Indeed, it can be dangerous.'

'But you stayed hidden on the boat rather than explore new cities. You chose protection.'

She nodded. 'Some risks are not worth the reward. I had found safety aboard ship.'

'So you think I am wrong,' he said, 'to worry about your sister's reputation and your own?'

How startling that he found himself smiling at that. No one had dared disagree with him in so long.

'I have no experience of your customs. How can I judge if you are right or wrong?'

'But I can tell by your expression—'

'Do not ask me questions when you will not like my answer.'

Her voice was curt, and he could see how she had tensed as if to run.

Damnation, he was making a muddle of this. After his family had treated her so abominably, he'd wanted to show her that not everyone in England was rude. More than that, he longed to return to their easy camaraderie from the boat.

But how to reassure her without going too far? He was not accustomed to navigating these seas.

'Miss Richards...' he began, daring to touch her arm.

Not hard, and not in a way that would restrain her, but to keep their connection for a little longer. He brushed his hand across her upper arm, and that seemed to be enough to keep her nearby even as he let his hand drop away.

'You recall me telling you about the gamekeeper's wife? The one who told me story after story?'

'Yes.'

He winced at the stupidity of his own question. Of course she remembered their conversation. It had occurred five minutes ago.

'Well,' he continued, 'some things she did not put in fables. Some things she said, and then she enforced. Do you know what one of her favourite dictums was?'

'I do not know what a dictum is,' she responded.

'It is a rule to live by. She said it was my responsibility to listen to everyone's thoughts, no matter how ridiculous. To listen carefully and decide. Not listening, according to her, was the gravest sin of any man, but it was worse for powerful ones. It would be their downfall.'

She arched her brows, challenging him without even saying a word.

He chuckled in response. The woman would not give him an inch that he did not work for. Odd how he found that attractive.

'What that means is that I don't want you to hold back your thoughts from me. Others might not be so open, but I demand it from everyone in my circle.'

'Everyone?' she pressed. 'Even your mother?'

He snorted. 'She gives her opinion whether I ask for it or not.'

He lifted his arm, offering to escort her onto the bridge. Given that she had run ratlines in a storm, the gesture was ridiculous. She had no need for any man to guide her, and yet she smiled at his offer. It was as if no one had ever thought to be polite towards her and, given his aunt's treatment of her, perhaps that was true.

'So you wish to hear my unbound thoughts.' She said it as a statement, not a question.

'I am eager for it.'

She shot him an arch look. 'Then you cannot get angry when I do as you ask.'

'Of course not.' Then he challenged her. 'Will you extend me the same courtesy?'

'Of not getting angry?' She pursed her lips, clearly thinking. 'I cannot remember a time when I wasn't angry,' she murmured, as if startled by her own thoughts. 'But I am not angry with you.'

'I am pleased to hear it.'

That was an understatement. Inside, he was whooping for joy. He guessed that she did not say such things to many people.

'Very well,' she said as she made an expansive gesture towards the park. 'I think this is my favourite place in London.'

It was not the topic they had been on, but he allowed her the pretence.

'I think you have seen little of the city. London has many other beautiful spots.'

And he wanted to show them all to her.

They were walking now under the remains of the pagoda. It had been rebuilt a little, and repainted, but they could see the remains of the fire in the ragged edges of some of the wood. Paint could not cover everything.

She stopped beneath it and looked up. 'It must have been a sight.'

He glanced at her. 'Are you being polite? Surely real pagodas are much more impressive.'

She nodded. 'They are, but they are structures used for

worship. They need to be large. This must have been lovely as a decoration.'

She smiled at him, and he had the feeling that she was meeting him halfway.

'It is very pleasant now, even without the extra storeys.'

He grinned back at her. 'Do you know, I haven't the least idea what to ask you. I want to know everything, but what does one ask first when one wants to know everything?'

He must have surprised her, because she burst out in a delighted laugh. She immediately covered her mouth with her hand, clearly embarrassed, but he gently pulled it down.

'Do not hide something as wonderful as a laugh,' he said. 'I told you, I want to know everything about you.'

She faced him squarely then, her eyes dancing as she studied him. 'I believe I feel the same. Please, start at the beginning. What did you do as a child, before you went to your gamekeeper's cottage?'

'Ran around terrorising my nanny. I ran, I played, I was king of my castle. Or a little prince.'

She frowned. 'Do you have a castle?'

'I do, but it is old and crumbling away. No one lives there any more but mice and—'

'The gamekeeper?'

He shook his head. 'Goodness, no. My father pensioned him off years ago. He has a handsome cottage nearby, where he plays with his grandchildren and teaches them how to hunt and fish.'

He leaned back against the railing, looking at her. He was fascinated by the mixture of races in her face. Square English jaw topped by golden skin that probably never burned like his did. She had a strong nose, from her father, and a fascinating shape to her exotic eyes. He could stare at her all day, but that would mean he missed all her other fascinating attributes.

He'd never met anyone who challenged his thoughts about the most common things. Who else among his set would bother worrying about a servant's tasks? Not to mention live her extraordinary life.

'What did you do as a child?' he asked. 'And do not mince your words. I truly want to know.'

She looked away, her shoulders hunching slightly as she spoke. 'I spent my days stealing food, hiding wherever I could, and getting viciously angry when anyone caught me.'

'How often did they catch you?'

She shrugged. 'Very often. I was not very fast as a child, or very smart.' She looked up to the top of the pagoda, her gaze distant. 'But I was very, very lucky.'

He was surprised by that. 'I cannot imagine that you thought yourself lucky. Did you ever have a home?'

'The temple was my home.'

'Didn't they feed you there? Why would you steal food?'

She grinned. 'Because I was angry. I wanted a family. I wanted nice clothes. I wanted everything I did not have, so I tried to steal it.'

He shuddered at the idea. His parents had been difficult, but at least he'd had everything he'd ever wanted materially. 'You were caught.'

It wasn't a question. She'd already said as much.

'Often. But not everyone in the world is vicious. I was taken back again and again to the temple, where children like me were managed.'

'Like you?'

She pointed to her face. 'Those of mixed race.'

'I think it makes you look stunningly beautiful.'

It was no more than the truth, but she seemed shocked to

hear it. Enough that it took her another moment before she continued her story.

'There was one monk who made it his mission to raise us. No one wanted us, you see, and for a girl that meant the temple or prostitution.'

He nodded. 'I am glad you chose wisely.'

'I didn't choose,' she scoffed. 'I was hauled back there, locked in, and treated harshly until I learned to listen.'

He jolted at that, his mind reeling from the way she had been treated for no other reason than the fact that her parents had been from different lands. She'd had no choice in her birth, but even so she'd been reviled.

What kind of resilience would it take to survive something like that? And to come through it as this beautiful, composed woman?

His esteem for her rose.

'How are you not a bitter, angry shrew of a woman? I mean no disrespect, but my aunt has suffered nothing so severe, and yet she spews venom everywhere.'

Her expression shifted to a kind of resigned acceptance. 'I am angry. I am bitter. And yet if I remain in those feelings how will I appreciate this beautiful day? This beautiful park? Or the truth that I am dressed in fine clothing and have eaten good food.'

'Remarkable.'

'The monks taught me well.' She chuckled. 'Probably much like the wife of your gamekeeper and her lessons. I fought like a demon, but they were stronger and smarter than I.'

Amazing. He had not thought they had anything in common, and yet he could see her point. Someone had raised each of them, and that someone had not been a parent.

'What else did the monks teach you?'

'To fight. I liked those lessons. And to speak respectfully. But mostly I learned to listen.'

'To religious lessons?'

'I didn't listen very well to those.' Her voice was rueful. 'The one monk in particular who took care of me taught me how to listen to what people wanted from me. He said once I knew how to do that, then I could choose my path. I could choose whether I wanted to give it to them or not.'

Such a valuable skill.

'And are you good at it? At knowing what others want from you?'

She shrugged. 'Good enough to survive.' Then she looked around at the park surrounding them. 'Perhaps I can even thrive. That's what I want,' she said, her voice growing softer. 'Somewhere I can be safe to choose any path I want. To do whatever I want.'

'And what is that?' he pressed, fascinated as much by the shifting planes of her face as the emotions they revealed.

'I don't really know. There are so many things I want to try. My father wants me to paint. He says I have talent. And I've been reading books in English. It's slow, but I am learning. Lucy wants to manage the buying and selling of cargo. She learned a great deal from the captain.' She stretched out her arms. 'I just want to try everything.' Her arms dropped to her sides. 'But instead of doing that, I'm learning how to serve tea and dance.'

'You don't like those things?'

She seemed to pull herself inward, pressing her hands to her belly. 'I am doing what I need to.'

To survive. She didn't say the words, but he heard them nonetheless.

'Your father wants you to marry,' he said. It wasn't a question.

'He says Lord Domac would make a good husband.'

How gratifying to hear the deadness in her voice at that. He did not wish his cousin ill, but he couldn't stomach the idea that this extraordinary woman would be married merely for her dowry. She was worth so much more than a boat or a cargo. And his cousin was a fool not to see that.

She would be wasted on Cedric. She deserved so much better.

'Do you know what my cousin wants?'

She nodded. 'He wants to impress people. He told me once that he already has a title, and most people bow to that. But those who don't will bow to money.' She turned to him. 'So he wants a great deal of money.'

He nodded slowly as he straightened up from the railing. Then he offered her his arm and they began to stroll again. He didn't want to completely disparage his cousin. Cedric had some very good qualities, but he was immature. He'd always been impatient, looking for a quick reward. He and his father shared that vice, whereas Declan's problem was in a dark, explosive temper. It had destroyed his father's life and had come perilously close to ending his several times.

Thanks to the Byrning legacy, rage was his constant companion. He kept it under control now, but there had been times in his childhood when that hadn't been the case. Now, as always when he met someone interesting, he resolved anew never, ever to show Grace his temper. It had already lost him good friends and one possible wife. She'd seen him nearly come to blows with a political rival who had drummed up heinous lies about himself and his family. That was the experience that had taught him that lies and insults were commonplace. Their only purpose was to goad him into a violent reaction that would show him in a dreadful light.

He would not let his temper get the better of him again.

Which meant he had mastered his legacy.

Cedric needed more time to master his problem.

'Do you know what Cedric will do to gain that money?' he asked.

'He will marry me for my dowry. But Father says he will honour me as his wife.'

She did understand. He didn't know if that made things better or worse.

'Are you in love with him? Do you want to marry him?'

She shook her head, as if that was the silliest question. 'I want safety. If he is my safest path, then I will choose him.'

'And if he is not?'

She twisted to study his face. 'Can a woman be forced to wed in this country?'

He flinched at her words, hating it that she had to think about these things. It was not something he cared to think about ever—but that was his failing, not hers.

'Yes. Women can be forced. But I will not allow that to happen to you.'

She searched his eyes, her head tilted as if she studied the stars for direction. 'How will you do that?'

How will you keep me safe?

She hadn't spoken those words, but he heard the question nevertheless. Inside, he felt every part of him respond to the call. As if she were indeed a woman looking for a saviour, and he a knight of old, searching for a quest.

It was a silly thought, but he would swear he'd heard the trumpet sound.

'I am a duke, and the head of my family. My cousin is...' He shook his head. 'If you do not wish to marry Lord Domac, send word to me. I will see that you are not forced.'

'Do you think my father would force me?'

His eyes abruptly widened. 'I...um... I don't know your father well. Do you think he would?'

'I don't think so. He is not a violent man,' she said. 'But he has strong beliefs in how I should behave—including whom I marry.' Her lips curved. 'That I *should* marry.'

Declan nodded. 'A woman is safer in this world with a good husband.'

'That's what my father says.'

'You disagree?'

It seemed as if they were throwing leaves at one another, questions that had no true weight. After all, the world had its rules, whether or not they agreed with them. And yet he found he enjoyed this discussion. She seemed to like it as well. And together they both seemed well pleased.

'I want to choose my path,' she said. 'And I want very much to make a good choice not just for myself, but also for Lucy.'

He could hear her devotion to her sister in her tone, but also the longing of a woman who had never had control of her life. And yet for someone without resources, she had done amazing things with her life.

'You are the best navigator in China,' he said, his tone teasing. 'Surely you can successfully navigate the *haut ton*.'

She snorted, the sound very unladylike and yet so charming.

'When your aunt is guided by the position of the stars, then I shall have faith in my ability to steer clear of her.'

'A fair point,' he admitted.

'You know,' she said, her words teasing, 'I am not the only female sailor in China. I had the example of a woman far more powerful than I could ever be.'

'A female sailor?'

'More than a sailor Ching Shih captains a fleet of boats.'

He shook his head. 'I cannot imagine it.'

This story was likely a fairy tale, when he preferred the comfort of facts. But he could not deny the animation in her when she spoke the name. And what did he know? China was a very different place from England.

'I can see you at the forefront of a fleet of ships. You have the strength of will to do it.'

'Then you have more imagination than most. No one thought I could be a good navigator, but I am one of the very best.' She arched a brow at him. 'Will you listen to the tale of China's famous pirate captain Ching Shih?'

'I cannot think of anything I want to hear more.'

Chapter Nine

'Why would you tell him that story?' Lucy gaped at her sister, clearly confused by Grace's contradictory behaviour.

They sat in Lucy's bedroom as it was the closest to their father's. It allowed them to hear his cough without hovering beside his bed. They both wanted to know if the tonic they'd given him this afternoon had helped ease his dry hack. So far it hadn't, but perhaps the medicine took a while to work.

Either way, they were passing the time by discussing in detail everything that had happened that afternoon—much of which made no sense to Lucy.

'You told me that men do not like powerful women. You told me to be meek. So why would you tell the Duke about China's pirate queen?'

'He was interested,' Grace said with an apologetic shrug.

How did she explain that once she'd started talking with the Duke, it had been so hard for her to stop? He seemed to value her thoughts and her opinions. And he never did anything that made her feel threatened. Even better, he clearly wanted to protect her. That was a potent lure for her, and she had been unable to control her words. As for her thoughts—well, they had gone rampant with ideas she did not want to express.

He excited her body and her mind. And that was as dangerous as it was wonderful.

'What did he think?' Lucy pressed. 'Did he believe a woman can lead a fleet?'

'As it happens, the Irish claim a pirate queen named Granuaile, so it wasn't a great shock to him.'

Lucy shook her head, clearly not understanding the spell the Duke seemed to have thrown over Grace. 'You told him you *admire* Ching Shih. You cannot admire a powerful woman without him thinking you want to be one.'

It was true. Grace understood the risk. No man, be he English or Chinese, wanted a woman who would dominate him. But she didn't want to rule over the Duke. She just wanted to spend more time with him.

'He kept asking questions. I promised I would answer honestly.'

Her sister leaned back against the wall. They were whispering together, just as they'd always done in the temple. But in this moment Lucy could not control her tone.

'I don't understand,' she said with clear irritation. 'Did you tell him that Ching Shih is bloodthirsty?'

'I did. Or at least that the sailors believe it.'

'And that you admire her?'

'I admire her strength. She didn't collapse and die when her husband did. She has forged her own path.' Her brows narrowed at Lucy. 'You know how much I have clung to those tales.'

Of course she did. Lucy knew everything about Grace. The two of them had been paired together since their earliest memories in the temple. Grace had never been able to sit still unless she held Lucy. And Lucy had rarely stopped crying except when near Grace. Or so the monks had told them.

As they'd aged, they helped one another survive. Grace was always faster, stealing food for them both when the temple didn't have enough for everyone. Lucy was the quiet one, the shy one—the one who watched and understood much more than anyone guessed. She was also the one who could apply logic in private but completely crumpled when interacting in person. Thank heaven numbers didn't change when she grew flustered. If she hadn't been a half-person, she would have made a merchant a great wife. As it was, she'd been doomed to live as a nun in the temple, counting sacks of rice and rationing it out to hungry children.

It had been the tales of Ching Shih that had shown them both that women could be strong enough to make a new kind of life for themselves. The two of them had hung on the stories of the pirate queen's life. They'd inspired Grace to seek out a man to teach her how to be useful on a boat. And they'd encouraged Lucy to want more than life as a silent temple nun.

It had taken years, and the special providence of luck, but now she and Grace were here with a father, who cared for them both. None of this would be possible were it not for those tales of Ching Shih.

Lucy gripped Grace's fingers, squeezing them tightly. 'Men want docile women. You have told me that a thousand times!'

Grace twisted her fingers out of Lucy's grip. 'He loved my tales. He begged me to tell him more.'

'Men will beg at the feet of their mistresses, but they will not marry them. How many girls have we known who believed the promises of men?'

Grace sighed as she flopped backwards onto the bed. 'He is different from the others. He listened to me. He wanted to hear what I thought. No other man has shown me such respect. Even Father tells me what I want instead of hearing my words.'

Lucy crossed her arms. 'What have you told me about men who make you feel good?'

'That they are lying,' Grace answered. 'That only you know what you want.'

'Yes!'

'But he's not like that!' Grace abruptly rolled over, to look at her sister. 'He's a good man. He's not violent. He enjoys new things.' She dropped her chin on her palm. 'He wanted the experience of climbing the rigging, so he did it. He wants to learn about me because I am so different. That's why I had to tell him about Ching Shih. It's a tale that he has never heard before, about a woman he never imagined existed.'

'How does that help you?' Lucy pressed.

Grace looked away. 'Perhaps it makes me seem less strange.'

Lucy shook her head and dropped down beside Grace on the bed. 'All men enjoy new toys,' she said, echoing the monks, who had taught something similar. 'That path leads to suffering.'

Grace flopped onto her back again and stared at the ceiling, her words coming as if she were talking to herself. 'He seemed impressed by what I can do on the sails. And he believes that I am a good navigator.'

'Anyone who knows boats knows you're a great navigator.'

'Yes, but Lord Domac needed to be convinced. The Duke just believed me.'

'Or he didn't see any reason to argue about what isn't important to him.'

Grace sat up, her face flushed. 'He believes me. He doesn't treat me as a child when I say things. He listens!'

Didn't Lucy know how rare that was?

Lucy softened her expression. 'Do you love him?'

The words cut straight to Grace's heart. It was possible,

she supposed. If she allowed herself, she might fall in love with him. But to risk everything on a feeling was madness.

'Oh, *mei mei*...' Grace moaned, calling Lucy 'little sister' in the most tender way. 'Half-people like us don't find love. You know that. We must look for safety. For us and any children that may come.'

Lucy shook her head. 'I still want love. And I know that's naïve.' She spread her arms and spoke her words to the ceiling. 'I want a man to fall madly in love with me. I want his thoughts on me at all hours of the day and night. I want him to sing songs to me, give me sweet food and kiss me all night long.'

Grace couldn't quite stifle her sigh. 'You're dreaming of Lord Domac.'

It was half statement, half accusation. After all, she could see the truth in her sister's dreamy eyes.

'What happened between the two of you that you would build such a fantasy around him?'

'Nothing,' Lucy answered—but in a way that Grace knew she lied. Something had sparked this dream.

'I cannot help you if you lie to me.'

Her sister flushed a dark red. 'There *was* something that happened between us. Not like you think. It was this morning when you were in the sails with the Duke.'

Fear clutched her heart. Had Lord Domac attacked her sister? She quickly scanned her from head to toe. There was no injury that she could see. And she wasn't acting like a woman hurt.

Grace swallowed down her fear and spoke calmly. 'What happened?'

'We were talking. He was asking about our life together in the temple.'

'Everyone seems very interested in that,' Grace drawled.

She supposed it was because there were no Buddhists in England, or so her father had said.

'He wanted to know about our parents. About how your father found us.'

Ice slid down her veins. This was something she and Lucy had sworn never to discuss, even between themselves. And yet she could already see that her sister had talked. 'You told him the truth?' she said.

'I didn't mean to. It just… He was asking questions and—'

'You wanted to please him. So you told him.' She groaned. 'How could you?'

'I didn't mean to!'

'What did you say? Exactly?'

Her sister bit her lip, but then she told the tale. 'He wanted to know how your father found you. How he knew you were his daughter.'

Even knowing the tale that was coming, Grace flinched. Back then, she hadn't spoken English. She hadn't known the monks had lied to Lord Wenshire. She hadn't known they'd played him for a fool.

'Lord Domac has worked out that we three are not related by blood. He guessed and I confirmed. He said you don't look like him. And I don't look like either of you.'

Guilt twisted in her insides. 'We don't know the truth,' she said, trying to convince herself. 'I'm the right age to be his child. And we have never pretended you are Lord Wenshire's child. But to me you're my sister. I would not leave China without you.'

Lucy smiled and squeezed Grace's hand. 'I know. I wanted to go with you. I wanted a new life.'

They both had. They'd both known their future in China was bleak. But that didn't solve the immediate problem.

'So now Lord Domac knows what even Lord Wenshire does not. That I am not truly his daughter.'

By the time she had understood enough English to realise what had happened, it had been too late. She hadn't been able to tell Lord Wenshire that she wasn't his true daughter. They had already sailed away, and he had shown her such love that she hadn't been able to hurt him with the truth.

'Lord Domac won't tell. He has no reason to. He knows that revealing it would destroy you. It would destroy us both, and he doesn't want that.'

She hoped so. She did not want to hurt her adopted father. He was a kind man, desperate for a family, and she and Lucy were all too happy to have what had never been theirs. Together, they made a loving unit, and she did not want that to change.

'You cannot tell anyone else,' Grace stressed.

'I know!' Lucy sighed. 'I didn't mean to tell him, but I'm glad I did. We'll soon find out if he wants you or the boat.'

Grace threw up her hands. Hadn't they been over this? 'He wants the boat!'

'Then he is not the husband for you!'

Lucy abruptly sat up, folding her legs in front of her so she sat like a monk teaching his class.

'If you believe the Duke is safe, then he is your man. Which means you are giving up on Lord Domac.'

Grace could hear the hope in her sister's voice.

'You are too enamoured of Lord Domac. He does not love you.'

At least she prayed he didn't. He had made it clear that he intended to marry Grace. What a disaster that would be if there were real feelings between him and her sister.

Meanwhile, Lucy twisted her fingers in the blanket. 'He might…'

'We were with him for four months aboard ship. If he loved you, he would have approached you. He would have done something.' She narrowed her eyes at her sister. 'Did he?'

'No!'

Was that too vehement a denial? She couldn't tell.

'In any event,' Grace continued. 'Father thinks I should marry him. And we all believe he is safe.'

'Because we know what he wants.'

'Yes. The boat. And he will let me navigate the boat and I can live safely on it.'

'For how long?' pressed Lucy. 'How will you climb the ratlines when you are pregnant with his child?'

'Ching Shih did.'

'And will he kill to protect you? You have said that a boat is too small a place, that it is too difficult to hide when everyone knows you are a woman.'

She leaned forward, and Grace could see the sheen of tears in her sister's eyes.

'Remember your last voyage before you came back to the temple? You said the sailors had blamed you for the storms. They'd tried to kill you—their only navigator—because you were a woman. You said you could not risk that again.'

'And we sailed to England.'

'You don't want to sail any more. Admit it.'

Grace's eyes dropped, because they both knew it was true. A short voyage with a trustworthy crew would be all right. But a long voyage such as Lord Domac planned would be too dangerous for a woman to risk. Even his wife.

Now that her point had been made, Lucy turned the conversation back to the Duke. 'What do you think Lord Byrning wants?'

Grace pursed her lips. 'I told you. Novelty. He seems to delight in learning about new things.'

And she admired that. So few men ever wanted to learn new things simply for the joy of learning. But that character trait came with a flaw. The moment she ceased being new or different, he would look somewhere else.

She gripped her sister's fingers. 'He will not be interested in me once I have told him all my tales.'

'Maybe... Or maybe not. Father said the Duke has to take a wife because he must have children. It's an English rule. Perhaps you can measure out your tales? Keep him interested long enough to marry you.' She leaned forward, her words light. 'The Duke is very handsome, isn't he?'

Grace's lips curved in an embarrassed smile. 'There was a moment on the bridge when he stepped into the sun. *Mei mei*, he was surrounded by light as if heaven blessed him. I felt such heat inside me. Just being near him burned the air from my lungs. And every time he smiles I see that again. I *feel* that again.'

She would not confess that to any other person, but she and Lucy had been sharing secrets since their youngest days. These feelings the Duke created in her were so large she had to tell someone. She had to understand why she ached every time she thought of him.

'You are in love,' Lucy said.

Grace dropped back onto the bed, her disdain obvious. 'Love or not, I do not make decisions based on *feelings*.' She all but sneered the word.

Lucy was silent for a while, and then she spoke, her words gentle. 'I think you should marry the Duke. He is rich and powerful and he will keep you safe.'

Grace stared at the ceiling for a long time, trying to sort through all the emotions churning within her. But in the end one question lifted to the top. One question that must be answered first before anything else could be decided.

'Do you really think it is possible?' she asked. 'That we could marry so well? Us?'

They were both of mixed blood. Half-people. That made them undesirable in China. Could the English be so very different?

'I don't know,' Lucy answered. 'Maybe if they fall madly in love with us they will not think that we are half-people.'

'I do not think the Duke is a man to fall madly in love,' Grace said.

He was too even-tempered for that. Even angry—and he had certainly been furious with his aunt—he had kept his tone even and his mannerisms controlled. No, the Duke was not a man to be ruled by any emotions, even one as pretty as love.

Lucy settled down beside her sister. 'I think I should spend some time with the Duke. If it is only novelty he wants then he will look to me, because I'll be new and different. But…' She grinned as she met her sister eye to eye. 'If he still looks at you, then you will know he wants you.'

Or else she would know that his eye would always turn to the next new thing. She didn't want to guess what she would feel if the Duke began looking at Lucy instead of her. The very idea cut her deep inside.

Lucy would not let the subject drop. 'Do you think we can convince Father to let me join you in Hyde Park?' she asked. 'That will be proper.'

'Everyone will be looking at us. Two half-Chinese girls in Hyde Park.'

Lucy flinched. She never liked being the centre of attention. 'That will be awful.'

'Maybe. But you cannot hide away for ever.' Grace touched her arm. 'You need the practice in public, and I will be there to keep you safe.'

'Very well...' Lucy pretended to give in, even though she had been the one to suggest the outing in the first place. 'But I'm only going because you need someone to keep you from spouting nonsense about pirate queens.'

Grace snorted. 'He loved those tales!'

'Remember not to overwhelm him with strange stories. We want him to think that we are normal women. Women who can be good wives.'

'I will try,' Grace said, her voice low.

All her faults rolled through her head, the things the monks had said over and over until she heard the words in her sleep.

'But we both know that I am too restless to be a good wife. I am too much like a man. I am too loud—'

'Stop it!' Her sister hit her with her fist, but there was no power behind it. 'You will stop repeating those lies.'

'But—'

'We are half-people, *da jie*,' she said, using the loving term for big sister. 'We must be double in order to be whole. So you cannot be too much of anything. It is not logical.'

Grace slanted her sister a fond look. 'Well, if it is not logical, then it must be a lie.'

'Exactly.'

'Because the world—and most especially men—always act logically.'

'Just because men are flawed, it does not mean we must be.' Lucy lifted her chin. 'Stop worrying. We will learn more tomorrow, when we go to the park. And if the Duke doesn't immediately fall at your feet then I will be on hand to make sure he tumbles deeply in love.'

Grace groaned. 'Even you cannot be so foolish.'

'Try to believe, *da jie*. It is possible for both of us.'

Grace didn't say anything. She didn't want to crush her

sister's childish dreams. But in her head she repeated what she knew was the wisest course. She would make no decisions based on emotion. In that, she and the Duke were the same.

Which meant neither of them would ever tumble into love with the other.

Chapter Ten

Declan arrived on Miss Richards' doorstep in a surprisingly unsettled mood. He was known in public as an even-tempered man. His reputation in the family, of course, was as a violent, ungoverned child prone to temper tantrums. That had been true when he was a boy, but thanks to the care of the gamekeeper's wife, not to mention the constant reprimands from his mother, he believed he'd outgrown such things.

It still required constant vigilance.

God knew, he had no desire to horrify Miss Richards with an intemperate display. So this disquiet as he approached her home bore some examination lest it lead to becoming overly emotional.

He had decided on a clear, logical list of facts.

Item One—this morning he had awoken in clear disarray. One minute he'd eagerly anticipated this visit, and then the next he'd dreaded it akin to attending a funeral. Such mood swings hadn't happened to him since adolescence. This fact was labelled *troublesome*.

Item Two—since leaving Grace yesterday he had ruminated on the story of a Chinese pirate queen. He had hung on her words even as he'd doubted them, and now he eagerly anticipated their next moments together and equally wanted to discard the whole discussion as poppycock.

The Irish tale of Granuaile was just as fanciful, but he knew of several who believed it. Perhaps many cultures created tales of pirate queens exactly because they were so much fun to imagine. Of course, an abandoned girl child would seize upon tales of a powerful woman as a means of giving herself hope. Therefore he would not discredit her belief until he found proof that it was false.

This fact he labelled *acceptable*. She believed the tale, and whether it was true or not made no difference. She admired the pirate's strength and independence. These were qualities he also admired. Therefore, the matter was settled in his mind.

Item Three—last night he had thought about the shape of Grace's body as she moved, the way her breasts shaped the modest gown she'd worn, and how he'd looked at her mouth and visualised things he'd never wanted to do with other society ladies. Lust had slammed through him, desire mixed with a need so strong that he had given in to the fantasy while in his own bed. He'd shamelessly pleasured himself while dreaming of her. And when was the last time he'd done that? Not since he was a randy boy, discovering women for the first time.

He wanted Miss Grace Richards—that much was clear. And damned if that want wasn't coursing through his blood now, even as he mounted the steps towards her door.

This item he labelled as *distressing* because his mother was right. The girl was unsuitable for marriage to his cousin or to himself.

It wasn't simple snobbishness. His duchess would have to understand polite society and would need to help him politically. She must make good connections and soothe ruffled feathers. And she absolutely must be able to face down the spiteful, vicious women in society, of which his mother and aunt were only moderate examples.

Miss Richards might be able to swing from the ratlines in a storm, but she had no understanding of the cruelty that could be inflicted upon a woman in society. He had seen strong women destroyed by daily attacks. At its worst, it drove some women mad. At best, it drove the unschooled away. They often found their own society, while hidden somewhere in the countryside.

But *his* wife could not run away. His political life was in London, where he enjoyed a robust discussion of the direction of this country. He meant to lead it in this new century, not wait on the sidelines as men too old or too stupid tried to keep everything *the same*. As if change was a dirty word.

Therefore he refused to marry a woman only to have her disappear to the country. He wanted children, and he wanted to know them. That wouldn't happen if whomever he married lived elsewhere.

Which meant that, even though Miss Richards stirred his loins, she was not the wife for him. And yet he longed to be with her, to hear the tales of her life, to understand more of the world beyond England's shores. How much further could one go than China?

She fascinated him, and yet he could not have her. Which, naturally, left him in a far darker place than he liked. Logic and reason had left him with one measly 'acceptable' against very powerful 'troublesome' and 'distressing'. He did not like that. Not at all.

Which meant that by the time he'd climbed the steps to her house he was holding on to his placid expression of polite interest by the tiniest thread. And yet he would not miss this outing for the world.

He was greeted at the door by Lord Wenshire himself.

'Your Grace, please do come in. I'm afraid we haven't been in London long enough to get a proper butler.'

Declan's brows went up. Hadn't they been in London for weeks now? 'Do you need assistance with that? I'm sure my housekeeper could help you find someone appropriate.'

The man sighed. 'I would be very grateful. Our last three have not…' He shook his head. 'The candidates have not lasted long.'

Declan frowned. Good servants were hard to find, but surely there was someone who could meet their needs. 'I shall have my housekeeper contact you immediately.'

'If she could be with Grace, that would be most helpful. I have been trying to teach her how to manage a household, including hiring the servants, but it seems I haven't the knowledge either. Not much call for a butler when travelling the way I have been.'

'No, I suppose not.'

By all accounts Lord Wenshire had wandered the world with little more than a knife and his wallet. Though Declan supposed that was an exaggeration. The man had worked for the East India Company and made his fortune there. Surely that company had given him more than a knife?

'I should love to hear about your adventures,' he said.

'I should enjoy speaking about them with you, though they are not as exciting as you might imagine.'

He might have said more, but at that moment the two ladies appeared, and Declan lost all track of anything but their appearance. Or, more specifically, Grace's.

Who the hell had put her in that awful pastel gown?

In his mind, Grace burned the way she had appeared on the boat, when she'd guided him up to the crow's nest. Her skin had caught the light differently from any way he'd ever seen before, shown smooth with a golden tan. Her cheeks had been flushed from exertion, and she'd listened to his words about London as if memorising every word. And then she'd turned to him, her eyes alight and her mouth so sweet. Her hair had been tangled and she'd worn a sailor's garb, but she'd been beautiful.

He saw the same slope to her cheeks now, and the same curve to her delectable mouth, but this time her casually short hair had been pulled back into a ruthless bun. There were tendrils of hair about her face that were meant to curl and bounce by her cheeks. That was the style that all the girls wore, but on Grace it looked appalling. Her hair dragged like tattered strings, out of place and clearly annoying her, given how she kept trying to tuck the strands behind her ears.

And that was nothing compared to the pale, washed-out puce of her gown. She was ten times more vibrant than that awful colour, and yet it seemed the dress was wearing her rather than the other way around. Especially with the horrendously large bow at the front, which appeared larger than her breasts.

'Good afternoon, Miss Richards,' he said as he bowed over her hand. 'I'm so pleased to see you again,' he said honestly.

Then he turned to her sister and did the same.

At least the younger sister had a decent gown. Less fashionable, less decorated, it fell in simple lines without décor, and that made it less of an atrocity.

He would have to tell his housekeeper to help with the girls' wardrobe too, if possible.

Meanwhile, Lord Wenshire spoke up. 'I thought to invite Lucy to join us. It's a fine day and she has been cooped up inside for so long.'

'Of course—' he began, but was cut off at a firm bang of the knocker.

'Goodness, who could that be?' Lord Wenshire asked.

The moment the door opened to show Cedric standing there Declan knew he should have expected it. Of course his cousin wouldn't allow Declan to escort Grace alone. He would force himself in if only to establish his ownership of the girl. Or rather her dowry.

It was Declan's fault for making the invitation at that thrice-blasted tea.

'Lord Domac! What a surprise!' exclaimed Lord Wenshire. 'Have we forgotten an appointment?'

'Not at all, but I couldn't allow His Grace to have all the fun.' He stepped past Lord Wenshire to bow over the ladies' hands. 'Miss Richards,' he said to the younger daughter, as he clearly caressed the girl's hand. 'Grace,' he murmured as he bowed again. 'You look ravishing.'

Had there been extra warmth in his greeting to the younger girl? Declan couldn't be sure, but the question was in his mind. Meanwhile, Grace was blushing prettily at Cedric's compliment.

'Lord Domac, welcome to our home,' she said, clearly a little flustered.

'He forgets his manners,' Declan interrupted. 'He is to address you as Miss Richards. A gentleman does not use a lady's first name unless the pair are engaged. Which you are not.'

His voice was cold, his attitude worse.

What the devil was wrong with him? He knew a thousand better ways to correct his cousin than calling the man out in public. But seeing his cousin fawning over Miss Richards had set his teeth on edge. The man was playing her false, and that heated Declan's blood to a dangerous degree.

He needed to control himself, but Cedric had always known how to irritate his 'older and more boring' cousin. As children, it had caused the man untold delight to needle

Declan, until he lost control and punched back physically. Then Declan would be punished, and Cedric given special treats. It had been infuriating, but it had been the byplay of children—boys in particular—and Declan refused to give in to it now.

And yet despite his determination Declan felt his temper rise. And, damn it, Cedric knew, because his face shifted into a mischievous grin.

'Oh, goodness, I'm forgetting myself,' Cedric drawled.

Damn, the man could be charming.

'It was Miss Richards' beauty that overtook my wits.'

It was the size of her dowry that had overcome him, and the joy he had at tweaking Declan—but, again, that could not be spoken of out loud.

'Well, we must be off,' Declan declared. 'So sorry, cousin, but my carriage will only take four. I'm afraid you'll have to make your own way to Hyde Park.'

'Don't be ridiculous. You and I have squeezed in together in carriages before. We can handle it for the short ride to Hyde Park.'

Of course they could. But if he knew anything about his cousin, the man would 'squeeze in' next to Grace—probably between both ladies.

'Don't be silly,' Lord Wenshire said, his voice calm. 'I can follow on foot. It's not that far, and I've been aching for a little exercise. The city is so confining, and I'm used to a more active life.'

Good God, did the man know nothing about randy young men?

'Please, Lord Wenshire,' he said quickly, 'you take my carriage with your beautiful daughters. My cousin and I will meet you there.'

And on the way he would have some choice words with the man.

His hard tone left no room for argument, and the logistics were quickly managed. And then, as soon as the carriage had rumbled away, he rounded on Cedric with a tone that was a good deal frostier than he'd ever used before in his life.

'What the devil are you about, Cedric?'

'At last,' his cousin drawled. 'I have your attention.'

'Of course you have my attention. What bloody good does that do you? I'm furious, and you're gloating about God only knows what.'

Cedric snorted. 'I'm gloating? Good God, you are in your dotage. Let me make this clear.'

'About time!'

His cousin continued as if he hadn't been interrupted. 'Miss Richards is to be my wife, and you are trying to take her away merely because you can.'

Of all the idiot complaints!

'Cedric,' he said, with as much patience as he could muster. 'I'm doing nothing of the sort. Damn it, we aren't children. She isn't a toy to fight over. Haven't you outgrown this by now?'

Cedric threw up his hands in disgust. 'I'm not playing. I am warning you, cousin, do not stand in my way.'

Declan gaped at his cousin, seeing a hardness he'd never witnessed before. Far from being the irritating little boy Declan remembered, Cedric had matured into a man with dark intent.

'Cedric, what has happened? We used to be friends.'

When the boy hadn't been torturing him.

'Friends? We rubbed along well enough when we were at school. You with your stuffy old chums and I with the fun ones.'

Declan tried not to roll his eyes at that. *Stuffy. Irresponsible.* These were insults they'd thrown at each other as they'd passed in the school halls. Hadn't they grown past these things?

'But then you disappeared,' Cedric all but spat.

'I was on my Grand Tour.'

And what a long disaster that had been, though he realised now he'd never told his cousin the fullness of what had happened to him during that awful time.

'And what about afterwards?'

Declan frowned. 'What *about* afterwards?'

'When my father gambled away our money? When he lost my sisters' dowries on some bizarre investment. Where were you then, when I needed help stopping him?'

He had no idea.

'How was I supposed to stop your father? I couldn't control my own.'

'I came to you. I begged you for help.'

'You came to the House of Lords during a vote! I couldn't drop everything to see you.'

'You sent me away. You wouldn't hear a thing.'

'We met later. We had dinner and some very fine brandy.'

'You laughed at my ideas.'

Oh, good God, they were back to this! 'You hadn't done any research. You had no idea if the investments would work.'

'I did research it!'

'Not enough. Damn it—'

'My sisters have no dowries!'

Declan folded his arms across his chest. It was one of the ways he made sure he appeared stern when inside he was holding back a scream. Or a punch.

'You should be discussing this with your father.'

'He's back in the duns again and you know it.'

He did. The Dukedom had long since cut off any support to his uncle. The man was nothing but an endless pit of gambling losses.

Cedric lifted his chin. 'I need to get my sisters something for their dowries.'

'Then bring them to me. We'll all sit down and discuss plans. The Dukedom will provide for their dowries. It will not cover your blackmail.'

Cedric shook his head. 'Miss Richards is my plan.'

'Miss Richards is your blackmail. It's cruel, Cedric, and it's beneath you. You and I both know she's not up to the task of being your countess. The *haut ton* would crucify her.'

Cedric tilted his head and stared at him. There was a darkness in the man's eyes that made Declan step back. Something he had never seen in the younger man's eyes and hoped never to see again. And yet as they stood there the blackness only worsened.

'Cedric,' Declan said softly. 'We will find a way to get you a boat. You need not marry—'

'Will it come with a navigator like her? Will it come with her father's money? Do you know how much Lord Wenshire made in the East India Company?'

No. Declan had made discreet enquiries, of course, but even those who had worked with the man knew nothing about his income.

'I do not,' he said softly. 'And neither do you.'

Cedric lifted his chin. 'I know enough. He is wealthy and he loves his daughters.'

'You are taking advantage—'

'I am marrying a woman whom I will treat well. I will let her be a navigator on a boat she loves. I will let her travel back to her home, and she will make me a dragon's hoard of wealth. Then you will come to *me* for money, you will beg my forgiveness, and you will take your supercilious nose and stick it—'

'You are not engaged to her yet!' Rage filled Declan's tone. He felt it burn as hot and dark as Cedric's hatred. And it dripped from his words like acid. 'You don't love her, and don't want to marry her. You are using her to blackmail the family.'

'Is it working?'

'Of course not!'

Cedric laughed, and the sound was not pleasant. 'I think it is.'

And then he had the infuriating gall to start walking towards the park with a jaunty step and a merry whistle.

Declan stared at his cousin, lava in his veins as his rage burned darker and colder, settling into lines he scarce knew were forming. This was something he had never felt before, something that overwhelmed him, darkened him, and then hardened into feelings that were deep and ugly.

His cousin would not have Grace. He would not abuse a girl too naïve about English customs to know what she was doing. And if Cedric tried anything that ended up damaging Grace, he would know such pain as only a duke could inflict.

Chapter Eleven

'I knew this dress was wrong,' Grace said once the carriage started moving.

'Why ever would you say that?' her father asked, without even looking at the hideous bow of her gown. 'The modiste said it was the peak of fashion. And both His Grace and Lord Domac said you look lovely.'

Grace looked at her sister. 'He said he was pleased to see me. Lord Domac said I looked beautiful.'

By which she meant that the Duke was not a man to lie, whereas Lord Domac clearly was.

She watched as Lucy's eyes widened, and she nodded as if she understood. But her father was oblivious.

'There you go,' he said as he smiled warmly at her. 'You are in the height of fashion.'

She did not argue. What was the point? He would see what he wanted to see, and thankfully he saw them both through the eyes of love.

'Father,' she said as she took his hands, 'thank you for that, but you know you do not have a head for fashion.'

'Fashion is ridiculous all the world over, and there is no putting logic to it. I am merely pleased that you have garnered the attention of not one, but two exalted gentlemen. Just imagine what it will be like tomorrow night at your first ball.'

Her smile grew strained. If her gown today was as wrong as she believed it might be, then her ball gown would be a disaster. The modiste had been too busy to give them much attention and had pulled the gown from somewhere in the back of her shop. She'd said it was all the rage, and Grace had no ability to disagree. Now she wondered if the woman had palmed off a terrible gown upon a person who didn't know better.

There was no help for it, of course. She was wearing it now.

Meanwhile, her sister poked her in the side. 'The Duke looked very handsome, didn't he?'

Grace felt her face flush. The Duke always looked handsome, but he'd seemed tense to her. His movements had been tight, his jaw clenched. There was a fight brewing between him and his cousin, and she wondered what words were being spoken.

Lucy gave her a mischievous smile. 'Maybe you think Lord Domac outshone him.'

'I think Lord Domac has a flatterer's tongue. I never know what to believe when he speaks.'

'Don't be silly. All you have to do is look at his mouth. When his smile is tight, with a lot of teeth, he has not spoken the full truth. He never lies outright. But when his lips are parted and relaxed he is open and honest.'

Grace frowned, trying to remember Lord Domac's mouth. 'How was he when he talked about my dress?'

Lucy shrugged. 'I couldn't see.'

Which was no help at all. And it didn't matter anyway because their carriage came to a stop.

Their father stepped out first, and then turned to help them. It was only as she cleared the carriage that she got her first look at the madness that was Hyde Park at the fashionable hour.

Circling the park were a slow promenade of dozens of carriages. A row of palanquins would have moved faster than those plodding horses, with men and women preening from their seats. The colours were dizzying to see, not to mention the abundance of ribbons and feathers. Even some of the men wore fabrics in bright patterns that made it so she could only see the colours and not their faces. It was as if she stared at a parade of attire.

Perhaps her bow was not as much out of style as she'd thought.

But a more narrow-eyed look around told her that no woman wore a bow as large as hers. And, worse, none of the elaborate knots were at the front, preceding the body like the bow of a ship. Good Lord, she looked ridiculous.

'Oh, dear,' she said as she turned to her sister. 'I think the modiste was playing a joke on us.'

'Nonsense!' Her father laughed. 'Do you not see the feathers on that woman's head? Or whatever pattern that is on the gentleman there? Fashion is nonsense. You fit right in.'

She didn't think so. And the moment she saw a pair of girls eye her and burst out laughing she knew she had the right of it. She grabbed her sister's hand. 'Quick. Pull this wretched thing off me. Rip it if you have to.'

Her sister's eyes widened, but she quickly agreed—though the movement was awkward, given that they were still in view of everyone. Grace tried to shield herself in the carriage, but it could hardly be done in secret. Worse, there was a telltale ripping sound as the stitches were pulled.

Fortunately, the ribbon had been attached to the top of the gown, not as part of the seam. So long as she was careful, her gown would stay in place. She hoped…

'There,' her sister said as the knotted fabric fell away.

'Oh, dear!' came a masculine voice from the opposite side from the park. 'Did you rip your gown?'

It was Lord Domac, striding forward with a sunny smile on his face. Since Lucy was busy tossing the bow behind her into the carriage, Grace was left to face the man alone.

'Yes, I'm afraid I was clumsy and stepped on it,' she lied. Then she frowned, looking over Lord Domac's shoulder. 'Whatever happened to the Duke?'

'Oh, he'll be along in a minute. He's older, you know. One has to allow for his advanced age.'

Advanced age? That was a lie if ever there was one. She knew the Duke had climbed the rigging more easily than Lord Domac. And now that she looked closely at the future earl, she saw sweat darkening his shirt collar. More likely Lord Domac had run ahead while the Duke had maintained a sedate pace.

'Did you race one another here?' she asked.

'And I won!' he quipped happily.

Then she spied the Duke, sauntering up the street. His steps were long, his movement steady, but there was a tightness in his gait that she'd never seen before. She glanced to her sister, wondering if Lucy saw the same thing, but her sister was gazing up at Lord Domac with a worshipful air.

Damn! The girl's infatuation hadn't dimmed.

Grace stepped forward, coming between her sister and Lord Domac. 'There is the Duke,' she said, too loudly. 'Look at the way the sun shines on his hair. I've never seen such a thing before.'

Well, not since walking on the bridge in St James's Park with him.

Lord Domac snorted. 'Blond locks are commonplace here. It's really nothing special.'

Possibly not, but she liked it that the man kept his hair clean. It was one of the things that she appreciated on land—the fact that one could bathe more often than only whenever there was a storm.

'Never mind that,' Lord Domac said. 'Shall we begin our promenade? Unless,' he said after a pause, 'you wish to put that bow back on? I believe we could make it stay close to where it is meant to be.'

Or it might fall off at the most awful time.

Fortunately, another voice interrupted before she could form a response.

'I believe that the gown is much improved,' said the Duke as he joined them.

His voice was a low rumble that didn't startle her so much as shiver down her spine all the way to her toes. And why were they curling as if they had been touched?

She meant to say something. She even opened her mouth. But her mind was blank. He stood right beside her, his body large, his expression congenial, and his eyes…

Oh, dear.

There was something in his eyes. Something dark and heated. Something that made her tense even as it thrilled her. She was not a woman who ran towards danger. Indeed, she was the exact opposite. She was looking for a safe harbour from the world. And right now she really ought to be running away.

'Your Grace?' she said, her voice a bare whisper.

'Come,' he said as he held out his arm. 'I believe I promised you my escort.'

She knew she was supposed to set her fingers on his forearm. But he held his arm out to her as if it were a club. Was she to grab it and bludgeon someone?

She hesitated, uncertain of him in this mood. And in the middle of her hesitation, Lord Domac chortled.

'Sweet heaven, Declan. Stop being such an imperious prig. You're frightening the girl.'

Then he smiled his most charming smile and held out his arm for her. She knew it was his most charming look because they had practised exactly this kind of promenade on the boat from China. She hadn't had full command of English then, so she had memorised all his different expressions instead.

And now she was wondering if that meant his mouth was tight with teeth or parted and relaxed. She had no idea. And yet she couldn't quite bring herself to cling to the Duke. He was obviously in a strange mood.

So she did what she'd always done in China when she was unsure. She stayed on her own until she knew exactly who was offering what.

'If I can run the ratlines aboard ship, then I can surely walk without aid in a park. Yes?'

'Grace!' her father said, his tone exasperated. 'You are not to mention that.'

'My apology, Father,' she said quickly. Then she looked at her sister, who had not said one word since the men had arrived. 'Lucy, let us walk arm and arm, yes? I see several ladies doing that.'

'Oh, yes!' her sister said.

And so they began their walk, with herself and Lucy leading while the three men trailed behind. Grace and her sister whispered between each other, commenting on the clothing they saw as they smiled at everyone who looked their way. And indeed there were several people who looked directly at them. So many that Grace began to memorise the pattern of their every glance.

First their eyes widened in surprise, then there was a slow

pinch to their lips as their gazes hopped to the men, and then they leaned close to a companion, be it male or female. All too soon sneering laughter would erupt, and all the while Grace felt her belly tighten with dread. She knew mocking laughter when she heard it. And she knew disgust in every glance. After all, such was the reaction in China when anyone saw her half-white face.

'I do not think this was a wise idea,' she said in Chinese.

'Not if we were alone,' came her sister's response in the same language. 'But we are with powerful men. We must use it.'

'How?'

Her sister tensed, then whispered urgently. 'Pick your man now. Either the Duke or Lord Domac.'

'You cannot simply demand—'

'The Duke. I agree.'

Then she abruptly shoved Grace sideways, hard enough that Grace stumbled...straight into the Duke's arms.

Chapter Twelve

Declan was still struggling with his rage when Grace stumbled. He saw the way her body jerked, but had no time to do anything more than lift his hands before she careened into him. He kept himself upright, his hands gripping her waist, even as her head bumped hard against his chest.

She found her footing quickly once she'd gripped his arm. Indeed, he felt her muscles adjust as she straightened her slender frame.

'I am so sorry,' she breathed, her face inches from his own.

He stared at her, moved by her beauty despite the ugliness raging inside him. His hands spasmed, unwilling to release her, and then, to his shock, his index finger slipped through the thin seam of her gown. He had been holding her tightly, but a well-made gown would not have given way so easily. He touched warm flesh, his finger sinking into the space between two ribs. He shifted his finger just to be sure, and felt the seam give even more.

Then he saw her eyes widen as she too realised that her dress had ripped.

'Good God, Declan,' his cousin drawled. 'Cease manhandling the girl.' Then he took hold of Miss Richards' arm, his dark, thick hand wrapping like a stain around her skin.

'Don't touch her,' Declan said, his voice hard and menacing.

The sound of his own voice shocked him, but there was nothing he could do to stop the deadly threat in it.

His idiot cousin didn't hear it, of course. The man had always been oblivious to his own stupidity.

'Come away, Miss Richards,' his cousin continued. 'The Duke is a clumsy oaf. I should not like him to hurt your gown with his bumbling.'

'I am fine,' the woman said, her voice soft as she turned her eyes towards Cedric.

Of course she was fine—not that his cousin had asked about her welfare. No, he had addressed her gown, which Declan had, in fact, already damaged.

'Step away, Cedric,' Declan said.

His cousin had not released Grace's arm, and Declan's fury was pulsing on its leash. It was an irrational fury, burning through him as it sought a target.

'Let her go,' Declan repeated, doing everything in his tone and body to warn his cousin.

Cedric's expression darkened. 'You arrogant—'

Declan struck. A single fist straight to Cedric's jaw. His cousin's head snapped round but his neck did not break, thank God. It did nothing to ease the black lava in Declan's blood.

Cedric stumbled backwards, but didn't fall. All too soon his shoulders squared, and his fists were quickly raised.

'Stop this!' Lord Wenshire bellowed. 'This is London! You're English!'

The other Miss Richards cried out as well. She reached a hand out to Cedric, but thankfully was clever enough to keep out of the way.

Declan noted these things in the way of a man hearing a distant noise. His attention was focused on the red mark on Miss Richards' arm. Cedric had hurt her, and for that there would be retribution.

Some part of him recognised his rage. Some tiny piece of his mind registered that for all his smug assurance that he had the Byrning legacy under control, it was here now—in full control of him. And it had decided to strike down any soul who dared defy him. In this case, his own cousin. It would not just strike Cedric down, but destroy him in the most primal way.

He stepped into Cedric's reach, already knowing his cousin would take the bait. Cedric did, putting power into his blow, but no real skill.

Declan had spent years since Italy learning how to defend himself from footpads and worse. He blocked it easily, and then he struck again. Blow after blow while his cousin struggled. He didn't care, and he didn't hear. All he did was feel the impact of his fist on Cedric's flesh.

Rage. Hatred. How it burned.

Until someone else's elbow hit his face, jerking him around.

As he wheeled back his arm was pulled hard with his momentum, and brought abruptly up and behind his back. It was a shocking change, since he was sure there had been no other attacker at hand. Not someone who could hit that hard nor manoeuvre him so easily.

Then white-hot pain cut through his focus.

He tried to jerk away, but the grip on his arm didn't tighten. No, it shifted, raising his arm more painfully until he was stooped over from the agony. He tried any number of manoeuvres, but he already knew it was useless. He was caught fast. Whoever held him kept the pressure strong, while around him was…noise.

So much noise.

Voices. Gasps.

He blinked as he looked around. Hyde Park at the fashionable hour was filled with all the *haut ton*. And every lord, lady, and miss was staring at him in shock.

'Are you calm?' came a voice behind him.

Miss Grace Richards.

He took a heaving breath. Had he been panting? Blood still coursed hot in his body, but his mind began to clear. He looked down to see Cedric on the ground, his face a bloody mess as he sent Declan a seething glare.

'Cedric?'

The man didn't acknowledge the question. Instead, he straightened to his feet to stand tall before Declan.

'I told you to let go of her,' Declan growled.

'I didn't hurt her,' Cedric snarled. He was always one to bluster when faced with a difficult situation. 'You, on the other hand—'

'Miss Richards?' Declan interrupted, alarm shooting through him. Had he hurt her? Where was she?

'I am well,' came a quiet voice behind him. Not just behind him, but right at his shoulder.

'You are the one restraining me,' he said.

It wasn't a question. He could plainly see the other Miss Richards, and her father too, both watching him with guarded expressions.

'Are you calm enough to be released?' she asked.

Was he? In truth he wasn't exactly sure. Rage still seethed inside him, but he thought it was under control. He took another full breath, using it to slow the heavy thud of his heart. His shoulders were still tight, his jaw still clenched, and all the people staring at him did not help. Nevertheless, he nodded.

'I will not hit him again, provided he keeps his hands off you.'

He felt the angle of his arm ease and breathed a sigh of relief despite the throbbing pain.

Miss Richards stepped around to face him. 'Why did you attack your cousin?' she asked, her expression almost bland.

'He hurt you,' he said.

'I did not!' Cedric snapped. 'You did.'

Declan's gaze dropped to Miss Richard's forearm. He remembered Cedric's hand there, he remembered a red mark, but there wasn't one there now. Her skin was flushed, but unmarked. And the more he stared, the more her skin remained smooth and clear.

'He hurt you,' Declan repeated, but there was fear in his tone.

Had he imagined it?

He looked at Miss Richards' face. She was watching him with a steady, clear gaze.

'I have run the sails in a storm,' she said softly. 'I am stronger than I look.'

Of that, he had no doubt. He touched his throbbing jaw. She'd effectively stopped him, and even his own father had been unable to do that.

'Look at her dress, you idiot!' Cedric snarled. 'You did that.'

Declan quickly scanned her body. She stood straight, with no marks, no injuries. It was only her dress which... He flinched. Bloody hell, her dress had a gaping hole in the side where the seam had ripped.

He frowned as memory crystallised in his mind.

He'd put his fingers through her dress. Oh, God. What had he done to her reputation?

With quick movements, he stripped off his coat and extended it to her.

She frowned at it. 'I am not cold.'

'You are in dishabille,' he whispered.

How had this happened? Panic was beginning to thrum in his veins. He knew that shame would come in an overwhelming cascade soon. His only defence, and the only way to keep the legacy in check, was to regain his full faculties.

But, oh, the pain in realising that he had not only failed to control himself, but he had also lost his temper so viciously in front of her. In front of everyone. She was the one he'd most wanted to show the best of himself. Instead, she'd seen the worst.

God, he was a disaster.

And it wasn't over.

He had to recall himself to the present, so he strove for rationality.

He started by pulling in his memories. He recalled that she'd stumbled sideways. But she was more sure-footed than a cat, which meant she hadn't tripped. Her action had been deliberate. She'd meant to fall into his arms…she'd meant to have him catch her and rip her dress.

His eyes narrowed as he remembered. 'You did this on purpose,' he said. 'Why?'

The answer was obvious, wasn't it? He was a duke. She was an unwed miss. Many had done worse to trap him into marriage. But he couldn't believe it. And yet he couldn't make sense of the situation any other way.

'What?' she cried.

And yet he couldn't stop seeing it in his mind's eye. She'd jerked sideways, right into his arms. He'd grabbed her and her dress had torn—in front of everyone in the *haut ton*.

Meanwhile, her father cursed and shrugged out of his own coat. Knocking aside Declan's offering, he gently set his own coat around Grace's shoulders. Then he put her hand on her dress and spoke softly to her. 'You need to hold the seam together.'

She nodded, her gaze downcast as she gripped the side of her dress. Then she turned to her sister. 'Come along, Lucy,' she said, defeat in her tone. 'We should go home.'

'No,' Declan said as he straightened up to his full height. 'No, you and your father will ride with me in my carriage.' Then he glanced about at the assembled gawkers, spying the sister of one of his oldest friends. 'Lady Bowles, would you mind escorting Miss Lucy Richards back to her home?' He cast a dismissive look at his cousin. 'I believe my cousin is indisposed.'

His cousin was bloody, one eye already swelling. His nose didn't look broken, but it was hard to tell as the man pressed a handkerchief to his eye.

Meanwhile, the lady stepped forward, her expression equally guarded as she turned to the younger Miss Richards.

'Hello, dear,' she said kindly. 'Let's step away from all this. Men can be such children sometimes.'

The disgust was heavy in her tone and Declan felt his blood heat again. She was right. He'd thought he'd outgrown his legacy years ago. Hadn't he said as much to his mother that morning after his birthday when this whole thing had begun? And now he was once again a ten-year-old boy, with aching knuckles and a growing, crushing shame.

He fought it the way his father always had—by putting on a ducal air that was a hideous lie. 'Commentary is not necessary, my lady. I merely require your assistance.'

'Oh,' the lady retorted as she gently guided Miss Lucy Richards out of the park, 'commentary will most certainly be made and not only by me.'

She was right, of course. He could already see the scandal whipping through the *ton*. Every tongue here was wagging, even as the onlookers waited to see if there would be more spectacle.

'Cedric,' Lady Bowles called. 'Do come and escort us, will you?'

His cousin had been fingering his split lip, but after another dark look at Declan he stomped away. Which left Declan with Lord Wenshire and Grace.

Lord Wenshire arched a brow. 'I believe,' he said darkly, 'your carriage is this way.'

Yes, it was. As was his doom.

How the hell had this happened? How had he allowed Cedric to goad him again? How had he not changed from when he was twelve and they'd brawled over toy soldiers. But Grace was not a toy. She was a debutante. And he had torn her dress in full view of the *haut ton*.

Was he now honour-bound to offer marriage?

He shook his head, clenching and unclenching his fists as he trailed behind Miss Richards and her father. Good God, he couldn't think straight. He shouldn't have come here this day. He should have realised that he was in no mood to control his temper. He should have realised the moment Cedric appeared that he could not stay vigilant against his legacy. It was always there, ready to destroy him when he let down his guard.

Had he ruined Grace? Had he destroyed his cousin's face? Why had he allowed Cedric to get to him? Hadn't he learned by now? God, he should not have come this morning. Hadn't he said that he faced something both *troublesome* and *distressing*?

He was such an idiot!

And now he was honour-bound to marry Grace.

And why did that idea not bother him, when he had just this morning decided she was unsuitable?

Chapter Thirteen

Grace climbed into the carriage feeling acutely uncomfortable. She knew she ought to feel afraid, or even horrified by the Duke's outburst. Instead, she felt unaccountably attracted to him.

She understood violence. Indeed, aboard ship she'd seen a great deal of things that had rightly terrified her. Now she had seen the Duke's fighting skill, and his rage, and she knew how dangerous that was. She never, ever wanted to see such things again.

But for the first time in her life such rage had been focused in her *defence*. Moreover, the Duke had given warnings to his cousin. He had told him what to do in no uncertain terms. It was Lord Domac's idiocy that he had not recognised the signs and heeded them. In truth, some demon inside Cedric had goaded the Duke into the attack. Who was so stupid as to taunt an enraged beast?

That was Lord Domac's error. Hers was to look at the Duke and see a man, not an animal. She knew from experience that a man who sank into rages was a beast in a man's clothing. He was unpredictable and dangerous. Her best bet was to stay as far away from him as possible.

But he had *protected* her.

It didn't matter that she hadn't felt any danger. That she

was perfectly capable of defending herself from Lord Domac. The Duke had seen the way she'd been manhandled by his cousin and had issued his warning. Twice.

That was the act of a man, not a beast. It was only the rage that had overcome him that had brought him low.

And the Duke did look low. She was already seated beside her father in his carriage when he shouldered his way into the vehicle. His jaw was tight, his shoulders hunched, and when he lifted his gaze to look at her she saw guilt, pain, and anger, all warring for pre-eminence. One of them would dominate, and that would tell her if she faced a man or beast. Unreasonable anger would end their association, no matter how handsome he appeared.

Pain at that thought cut sharp and deep, but she had long since hardened herself against pain.

Guilt, however, could not be pushed away. That was something she understood. She had only to look at her father's kind face to feel her own twist of guilt. What was so special about her and Lucy that he had claimed them and not the others? A dozen other mixed-race children lived at the temple, but he had taken her and Lucy.

But she couldn't think about that now. Instead, she studied the Duke as he settled into his seat and looked down at his clenched fists.

A moment later, the carriage started moving. It was not a long drive to her home, so they had little time. Unfortunately she had no understanding of what the English required in a situation like this. That was until her father started speaking.

'What you have done has shamed us all,' her father said, his tone hard.

The Duke's head snapped up, his eyes blazing with fury. 'What *I* have done? It began when she purposely threw herself at me!'

Her father stiffened, nearly rising out of his seat. 'How dare you say such a thing? My daughter is honest!'

Grace winced. It had been deliberate, just not by her hand.

She touched her father's arm and looked the Duke in the eye. 'The Duke is correct. The fall was on purpose.'

Her father twisted to stare at her. 'You would not do such a thing,' he stated flatly. 'You have little interest in catching a man, even a duke. Why would you—'

'Your sister did it, didn't she?'

The Duke's tone was defeated. She could see that he'd replayed the action in his mind and deduced the truth.

Grace nodded. 'Yes.'

'She knew your dress would rip. Why is it made so badly?'

She arched a brow at him, wondering if he would deduce that answer as well. A moment later, she saw him grimace.

'Your modiste is terrible.'

'What did you think of that bow, Your Grace?' she asked.

'It was hideous. You realised that and tore it off.' He took a deep breath. 'And there was no time to restitch it.' He shook his head. 'I shall have Lady Bowles take you to her modiste.'

Her father snorted. 'That is all to the good, but what will we do now? You have ruined her reputation.'

'I… I am not fit to marry,' he said. 'Not until I can control this.' The Duke leaned back against the squabs, his expression completely defeated. 'I am aware that this is not your daughter's fault, but it is the truth nevertheless. I will not propose.'

Her heart sank, even as she completely agreed with him. 'I cannot marry a man with no control,' she said. She looked to her father, who was already shaking his head. 'You know this to be true. I will not tie myself to a man who endangers me.'

She watched as her father pressed his lips together, clearly unhappy with the way this conversation was going.

Meanwhile, she looked to the Duke. 'Can you explain yourself?' she asked. She held up her arm. 'You can see that I was not hurt.'

The Duke's gaze rested hard on her skin. 'He was gripping you tightly. I saw it. He could have hurt you.'

'Yes,' she agreed. 'But I do not bruise easily, and I have endured much worse.'

His tortured gaze went to hers. 'I shudder to imagine what you have been through. It is not how a woman should be treated.'

She admired him for that statement. She knew he meant it. And so many men wouldn't say it, much less mean it.

'Why do you feel this so deeply?'

One thing about living among people who spoke a different language was that she'd become adept at reading their bodies and faces, despite their words. She watched as the Duke fought his own nature to hide from her question. She saw him try to gather his haughty air around him like a cloak, but then toss it aside with a clench of his jaw. He wanted to answer her as much as he wanted to hide from it. But in the end honesty won out and he faced her squarely.

'You are too new to England to have heard of my family's legacy. It's what we receive with the Byrning title.'

Beside her, she felt her father stiffen.

'Oh, dear…' the man murmured.

'You remember, then?' the Duke asked.

'As a boy at school.' He shook his head. 'Your father had a temper, but so did many other boys.'

'So did my grandfather and his father. All the way back for hundreds of years.' He looked directly at her. 'We are not known as men who control our anger.'

'Did your ancestors burn things?'

'Whole villages of our enemies. It's a bloody past, in a time when kings rewarded such viciousness.'

She watched him as he spoke. There was no pride in his tone.

'Were your rages rewarded?' she asked. 'As a boy, were they encouraged?'

He shook his head. 'Indulged is the better word. When I was a boy. But Mrs Wood—the gamekeeper's wife—would not let me get away with them. She taught me that a man controls himself. A duke even more so.'

There was more to the tale. She could see it in the tense set of his shoulders and the way his gaze slid away whenever he tried to meet hers.

'You became enraged when you thought I was in danger,' she said.

'Yes.'

'Were you hurt by your father as a boy?'

He shook his head slowly. 'Even at his worst, my father knew I was his heir. He did not touch me.'

'Then someone else.' It was not a question.

'Many someone elses.'

This time his gaze went to the window, though she knew his thoughts were not on the view.

'I had a sister...' He swallowed. 'She tried to defend her nanny from one of my father's rages. She ran into his blow. He threw her against the wall. Her neck was broken.' He took a shuddering breath. 'It was quick, at least. My father became a drunkard that night. He never raised his fist again—at least not with any power.' He snorted. 'He grew angry. He stormed and bellowed. But mostly he drank himself insensate. I think he was relieved when death finally came for him.'

He had told her some of this before, but now she understood it so much better. His family legacy was one of rage, but he was trying to fight it. And it was Lord Domac's perversion to ignore it or perhaps to encourage the disaster.

'You are the Duke now,' her father intoned.

'Yes.'

'And you just beat your cousin in Hyde Park at the fashionable hour.'

He paled, but didn't disagree.

She didn't say that he had done it in her defence, or that his obvious misery touched her deeply.

'How long has it been since you were gripped by such a rage?' she asked.

He slumped backwards against the squabs. 'Since I was in Italy, when I was attacked by footpads. That wasn't rage so much as terror. The spells were common when I was a teen. My sister was dead, my father a drunkard, and everything had changed.' He shook his head. 'But I learned to control them. I swear—' He cut off his words. 'I thought I'd learned.' He looked to her arm. 'I thought he was hurting you.'

What did she say to that? To a man who had carefully controlled his worst nature until the moment he'd seen someone hurting her? Mistaken or not, he had believed her in danger and had allowed his inner beast to fight on her behalf.

How could she not be grateful for that? How could she damn him?

She knew that a man who rages might turn his violence towards her at any moment. She had seen sailors who used any excuse to explode. But he was not that kind of man. He hated this fury inside him. The only question was how well did he control it? And could she risk being in his presence long enough to find out?

The answer, of course, was no. Logic and self-preservation told her that violent men were not to be tolerated. They always turned. This was not a kind world, and at some point a situation would turn against him. Something would happen, someone would defeat him, and he would react with violence. Such was the nature of violent men.

But she could not discard a man who had defended her. So few ever had. And none without conditions. Her father defended her because such was the duty of a man to his child. He didn't know it was a lie. The ships' captains had kept her safe because she had been their only navigator. All had got something from her in exchange for their help.

The Duke, on the other hand, had defended her because he'd thought her wronged.

After a lifetime of standing—afraid—on her own, the idea of having such a defender was a powerful temptation. And one that she was loath to give up.

'We should not marry,' she said, and the words were for herself, not him. She needed the ability to escape if necessary, and she could not do that if they were wed.

Her father disagreed. 'But what about your reputation? You are to be launched tomorrow night!'

She had no answer. This was his country, his customs.

'I shall court her,' the Duke said.

'What?' her father gasped. 'You have just said you will not marry her.'

'I shall let it be known that she has refused me. That she was shocked by my outburst.'

That was true, but she had not been shocked by his violence. Only by his defence of her and her attraction to him.

'Will that serve?' her father pressed.

'It will. I shall make my interest known. I will take the blame for my outburst solely upon myself.'

'As well you should,' said her father.

'And that should make her attractive to everyone else.'

She frowned. 'How?'

'Because I am an unwed duke. I will not attend any outing that does not have you included in it. And every society matron will want me there.'

He was so confident in his attractiveness. Usually, she would doubt such arrogance. Men often overestimated their influence over women. But she couldn't deny his appeal, so she nodded.

'I will allow you to court me,' she said, marvelling at her own arrogance.

If he wanted to pursue her, then she could do nothing to stop him. Except this wasn't a true pursuit, was it? He would only pretend to court her because it was the best he could do without marrying her.

He nodded, clearly satisfied.

Her father, of course, wasn't nearly as content, but he gave in with a grumble. 'Very well,' he said. 'Then you should take her out for her first dance tomorrow.'

'And then the first waltz,' the Duke agreed.

'There must be at least one other outing.'

'I have already offered to take her to the theatre.'

'Yes. And perhaps Vauxhall?'

Her father was pushing. He clearly wanted these things for her.

'It would be my pleasure,' the Duke responded.

The two men shook hands, as if she had no part in the discussion. She stared at them both, seeing satisfaction in their faces. Then, to her shock, the Duke turned to her. Leaning forward, he grasped her fingers and pressed a kiss to the back of her hand.

'Truly, Miss Richards, I apologise for the disaster of today's meeting. It is my hope that you can forgive me today's lapse and that we can begin anew. I swear to show myself a better man if you will allow it.'

He waited for her answer, her hand still clasped in his.

Heaven, what could she say to that? Her heart was beating triple time, her muscles were tensed as if to run, but where would she go? Out through the door or into his arms? He made her feel such contradictory things.

And still he waited for her answer.

The carriage stopped and the footman opened the door, but he did not move. He held her hand, he looked into her eyes, and he waited for her response.

'I will allow it,' she finally said, but what exactly had she just agreed to do? To dance with him? To attend the theatre with him as well as a pleasure garden? Or to let him tease her emotions in ways that had never tempted her before? Until she bit by bit opened herself to him?

That sounded like the height of folly.

And yet she had already agreed.

Chapter Fourteen

Declan didn't have much time. After his disastrous brawl in Hyde Park, he had to face the political consequences. No one in Parliament wanted a member of the Whigs making public displays of any kind, and they were understandably horrified by his actions.

He spent the rest of the evening and the next day soothing feathers and debating ways to make life better for the whole country. It was exhausting, but necessary. And if he'd thought he would get a moment's reprieve once he returned home, he soon discovered his error. He was met there by his solicitor, who had a ridiculously long list of legal matters to address regarding the ducal estates. And again he found himself reassuring the man that he wasn't impetuous or brash, despite the fact that he had recently been seen decking his cousin in Hyde Park.

The Byrning legacy was not taking over his personality. Everyone could remain calm. That was what he kept saying while privately he prayed it was true.

Damn it, he needed a wife. Someone who could help him calm his political allies, reassure his solicitor that he hadn't lost his mind, and generally share the burden of all his tasks. A foreign woman—be she Chinese, French, or from the moon—could not move through his world with ease. Not without extensive training, and maybe even not then.

It was a simple practicality: he needed help. And it was traditional: he was of an age to marry. It was the reality of life as a duke.

Meanwhile, the clock in his library ticked along like a reminder of the world rushing ahead whether he was prepared for it or not. He finished up as quickly as possible with his solicitor, cognizant that he still had a pile of urgent correspondence on his desk.

The man had just left when Declan was interrupted again.

'Just like your father!' a voice exclaimed as the door to his library burst open.

Declan tensed, but he didn't look up from the letter from his steward. He had yet to find a way to manage his mother's tendency to burst in on him whenever she felt the urge. To date, his best strategy had been to ignore her until she paid some homage to the niceties of his title.

'And now you're drinking just like him, too!' she exclaimed as she pointed to the glass of brandy on his desk.

Behind her, his butler came rushing in, face red with apology. 'Your Grace, I stepped away for a moment. She has a key, and I was not—'

Declan held up his hand. 'Mother,' he drawled, 'you do not live here. Please surrender the key.'

'Oh, good God, you're being ridiculous. I am a duchess and you are my son. I will not—'

'Mother, you will surrender the key or I will ban you from my presence.'

'Now you're being dramatic,' she huffed.

At that, he turned to face his mother directly and slowly pushed to his feet to face her. 'Mother, I recently beat Cedric bloody in Hyde Park. This is not the time to test me.'

'Don't I know it!' she cried. 'Everyone is agog—'

'Key! Now!'

The two words exploded out of him, bellowed and cold. He saw his mother shrink back, her eyes widening with fear, and he cursed himself for being a damned beast. Her gaze dropped to his glass of brandy. He hadn't taken a single sip, but she stared at it as if it were the devil's own piss.

'Do not become him,' she whispered.

'I'm not.'

'The cuts on your knuckles say different. Not to mention every Christmas when you were young and beat up poor Cedric. I thought you had gained some measure of control, but now I see—'

With a grunt of disgust, he grabbed the brandy and threw it into the fire. The glass and the alcohol exploded with a satisfying cacophony, but it did nothing to ease the turmoil inside him. His mother was right. How many times had she told him that his temper would destroy him? How many times had she punished him for the least outburst?

Countless. And all of it for naught because he was thirty-one years old and still beating up his young cousin. What the hell was wrong with him? Was he doomed to be controlled by a legacy he couldn't escape? The agony of that thought nearly broke him.

Meanwhile, his mother would not relent, though she took a different tack.

'Declan, my dear, I am concerned about you,' she said, her voice taking on a soothing quality that he couldn't help but warm to. There had been times in his childhood when she had been a doting parent. He had learned in adulthood that it was simply a character she adopted when she needed it. His mother did not have it in her to be truly motherly.

'Do not say another word until you set the key on my desk.'

'But—'

'I will not tell you again.'

He waited in indifference for her response. She would either comply or not. If she complied, he would win. If she did not, he would throw her out and be done with her for this minute. Either way, it was a welcome distraction from the shame of his actions in Hyde Park.

He heard the key drop onto his desk.

'There,' she said haughtily.

He straightened and turned back to face her.

But before he could speak, she waved vaguely at the ornate key. 'I have several more, you know. This is a game your father and I played ad nauseum.' She donned the exact arrogant expression she'd worn for her portrait. 'I am the Duchess of Byrning, and I have a right to be here as much as I choose to be.'

'You are the Dowager Duchess—'

'Until such time as you marry I have a right to be here.' She waved her finger at him. 'Everyone expects it. You might as well get used to it. Even the servants cannot stop me.'

That was the best reason to marry that he had ever heard. But in the meantime he would have all the locks changed.

'Mother, you must learn the limits of your influence. Barging in on me at your whim shrinks my respect for your intelligence.'

'Well!' she said as she sat down. 'I believe the one who's intelligence is lacking is you. How could you hit your cousin in front of everybody? It boggles the mind.'

'He was hurting her.'

'Who? That Chinese girl? Well, that's between them, isn't it? If they're engaged and all that.'

'They're not engaged!'

'Thank heaven for that. Was this afternoon's display your

attempt to dissuade him? Was that what you were doing? If so, then I applaud your reason, but I don't think it was effective. According to his mother, Cedric is as determined as ever to marry the chit.'

'He doesn't want to marry her. He wants her dowry.'

She snorted. 'Obviously! How does brawling in Hyde Park change anything?'

It didn't.

'I'm going to court her.'

'Who?'

Declan ground his teeth together but managed to answer civilly enough. 'Miss Richards.'

'How will that help anything?'

'For one, it will save her reputation. She was shocked by my temper—'

'As is everyone, though I suppose few are surprised.'

'She refused my offer of marriage.'

No fool, his mother stared at him long and hard. Then she shook her head slowly. 'You did not offer for her.'

It was a statement, not a question. And he was unable to lie directly to his mother's face.

'I… I did not. But that doesn't matter. This saves her reputation.'

'And makes her quite popular, I assume?'

'Yes.'

'Giving her someone else to fall in love with besides Cedric.'

He looked down into the fire, wishing now for the brandy that had just exploded. 'She does not seem especially enamoured of him. Or me.'

'That is her mistake and our good fortune. I assume you are to dance with her tonight?'

Of course his mother knew about her come-out ball.

'Yes,' he answered.

'Very well. Do the bare minimum and then send every possible gentleman over to her. Someone will turn her head quickly enough.'

Declan grimaced. 'I doubt she can be easily swayed. She seems…' *Capable, intelligent, remarkably composed...* 'A discerning sort of woman.'

His mother looked to him and shook her head. 'All young girls can be swayed. It merely takes the right application of pressure. Never mind,' she said as she pushed to her feet. 'I'll take care of it. Just play your part and no more.'

Part of him wanted to let his mother leave. Why poke the bear when she was already on her way out? But he knew from experience that he had to set down rules clearly or she would trample them.

'Mother,' he said coolly.

She stopped with one foot out the door. 'What is it now?'

'You are to do nothing to discredit Miss Richards or her family. Consider the lady untouchable.'

'Don't be ridiculous. She's the epitome of touchable. Her father's barely in society and she's a by-blow of mixed race. No one wants her here, and no one respectable will marry her. The sooner she gets that message, the better for everyone.'

Declan folded his arms. It kept him from choking her.

'She has done nothing wrong. You will not smear her.'

His mother threw up her hands in disgust. 'I begin to regret bringing you in on this business. She is *inappropriate*.' Her words were stated with diction as hard as glass.

'I am making her appropriate.'

'Not unless you marry her.'

He arched his brows. 'Do you doubt me?'

'Never,' his mother said. 'You've always been a man of your word. Unless you get angry or start drinking, that is.'

And there it was, the reason he let her run roughshod over him and the truth of why he never put her in her place or truly banished her for her tart tongue.

She was right.

Until he got his temper under control he was a lying fool, swearing to something one moment, then breaking his word the next time something upset him. That was how his father had been until his death. And that was how Declan had been in his teens and early twenties. It wasn't until after his Grand Tour that he had reconsidered his life.

And now that he'd pummelled his cousin, in full view of the *ton*, she had reason to doubt him again. If he tossed her aside now, when she was speaking the truth, then he would be no better than his father who'd been destroyed by the Byrning legacy. He needed to keep his mother's sharp tongue nearby, but he also needed her to be clear about the boundaries.

God, he needed a wife soon. One who knew how to manage his mother while keeping Declan calm. Naturally Miss Richards floated through his mind, but she was neither appropriate nor soothing. Indeed, when in her presence he felt hot and alive in all the best ways. But that made his temper short, and that led to...

Beating up Cedric in Hyde Park.

No, as much as he might wish it, Miss Richards would not make him an appropriate wife. God, how that thought hurt. But at least he could help her in other ways. He would make her acceptable and maybe she would find a man far removed from Cedric's greed or Declan's rage.

'You will leave Miss Richards alone,' he said flatly.

'Or what?' His mother threw up her hands in disgust. 'Honestly, it's almost endearing how you keep laying down the rules. Leave the key. Don't bother the girl. I am the Duchess of Byrning. I shall do exactly as I wish. And you will have to accept it because that is what a son does for his mother.'

He folded his arms. 'I do control your purse, Mother.'

Her expression darkened into her cold face, the one that had terrified him as a child. 'And you swore to me that as long as I kept my expenses reasonable you would never restrict my purse. Are my expenses over limit?'

'No.'

'Indeed, I think I'm well below my allotment this season.'

She was probably right. She kept better track of her finances than he did.

'Do you intend to go back on your word?'

'No,' he said again.

He couldn't in good conscience take her money away. It had been a stupid move to try to threaten her purse. But failing that he had no way to control her.

'Then I believe the matter is settled.'

'No, Mother, it is not. You will push and push until I must do something drastic that neither of us want.'

She waved a negligent hand at him, supremely confident in her ability to manipulate others to her will. 'Just do as you have promised. Pretend to court the girl while I throw handsome young men in her direction. Between the two of us she will be happily married to some nobody within a few weeks. Then she can retire to the country and have all the mixed-race brats she wants.'

She smiled at him.

'See? I can compromise. I shall do nothing to harm her.' She abruptly frowned as the grandfather clock in the hall clanged the time. 'Goodness, now we're both going to be late. I'll see myself out. And you must go and get dressed. Something restrained, to reassure everyone that you've not gone mad.'

She shook her head, speaking to herself as she pulled on her gloves.

'Why ever did I marry a Byrning? Violent beasts, every one of them. And they never change.'

Declan felt his throat close at her words. It was all he could do to remain upright and placid as she spun on her heel and left. But the moment the front door closed behind her, he collapsed into his chair.

Was it true? He looked at the space on the wall that had once held a portrait of his father. He'd ordered it removed the minute he'd ascended the ducal throne. But that didn't free him of the image of his father, of his grandfather, of all the Byrnings before him, who had been driven by their own vicious tempers.

Was he fated to be just like them, no matter what he told himself? If he married the wrong woman would he accidentally kill his own child in a temper? No, no, no! He didn't believe he was capable of that. But the scrapes on his knuckles said he was doomed.

Damn it, why did he have to have strong feelings for Miss Grace Richards? She interested him as none other, but obviously that made the rage burn hotter. She did not quiet him. She challenged him, aroused him, and made everything feel more alive.

He couldn't marry her. He shouldn't even be near her. But circumstances had forced his hand. And now he had to bathe before doing the pretty with her.

Odd how that thought brought a smile to his face. Looking at him now, no one would ever imagine the horror that lay just beneath his skin.

Well, no one but Cedric and his mother. Not to mention Miss Richards and her father. Plus anyone else who had seen him in Hyde Park.

Chapter Fifteen

Grace couldn't stop feeling the fabric of her dress. She had never worn anything so fine. It was *silk*. Certainly, she had seen great ladies in China in such attire, but never had she thought she'd be one of them. And here she was, far away from home, attired in silk that whispered delightfully across her skin.

'You look stunning,' her father said.

Her sister had said the same, as had their maid. But none of their breathless words could match the giddy unreality of the situation.

She was wearing silk. She was going to a ball. She was going to dance while gentlemen courted her. *Her!* A half-person worth nothing in China, a crazy navigator who had pretended to be a boy, and the mixed-race child of a kind old man who looked at her as if she had the moon and the stars in her hair.

'I cannot believe this is me,' she whispered as she continued to finger the fabric of her dress.

It was simple yellow silk with flowers embroidered upon the bodice. This gown was well made and came from Lady Bowle's own modiste.

'I cannot believe I am walking my daughter into a *haut ton* ball,' her father murmured. 'It is funny how a man doesn't think of these things until it's nearly too late.'

She reached out and squeezed his hand, feeling the icy

cold of his fingers. Her father wasn't healthy, though he hid it well. Out of respect, she kept quiet as she watched his face for signs of illness as she would watch the night sky for the path forward. She saw nothing but his usual kind expression and his sallow skin. If only his cough would ease, then he would sleep at night and be healthy again. But, failing that, she would do her best to make him proud tonight.

It wouldn't work. She would not be well received tonight. Half-breed children never were. But in this moment, in the dark carriage with her father, she was well content.

'You have given me more than I ever dreamed possible,' she said.

'You have given me more than I ever thought I could have,' he said back.

And then they were there, arriving early to her come-out ball.

It wasn't her night alone. She was to share the event with Miss Phoebe Gray. The girl was young, sweet, but had no claim to an aristocratic heritage. Her father was rich, but her only hope of a successful match into the highest level of society was if someone like Grace, whose father was of the aristocracy, joined her come-out. The hope was that together they'd draw enough of the *haut ton* for them both to catch someone's attention.

Grace wasn't supposed to know this, of course. Her father wanted her to be giddy about her come-out, so he pretended that everyone would accept them as wholeheartedly as he had. But living in fantasy had never worked for her or her sister, and so they had both questioned the servants until they'd understood what was happening.

Still, they allowed him the pretence, and... Well, she would wear silk and attend a ball.

Grace was smiling as the door to the rented ballroom was

thrown open and Miss Phoebe Gray waved her in. 'I'm so glad it is warmer now,' the girl said by way of greeting. 'We can open the French doors at the back. People can walk on the lawn. Isn't it perfect? Everything is going to be so perfect!'

Grace smiled. It was impossible not to in the face of such sweet exuberance.

'And you look gorgeous in yellow!' Phoebe continued. 'I could never do yellow. It makes me look like a badly made candle with a head for a wick.'

Phoebe slapped her hands to her sides and opened her eyes wide. If that made her look like a candle, Grace didn't see it, but it didn't matter. The girl was off onto another topic almost immediately.

'I've checked everything three times. The flowers are lovely. Have you seen them?'

'Only the roses in your hair,' Grace answered. 'They match your dress perfectly.'

Pink roses, pink gown and pink cheeks on a sweet face. Add in her blue eyes and golden hair, and the girl was English perfection made into a woman.

'You look perfect,' she said, wishing she knew better English words to describe the girl.

Phoebe giggled. 'I'm so nervous I'm afraid I'm going to burst into pieces!'

'Settle down, dear,' came a man's fond voice. It was Phoebe's father. The banker wore a genial expression as he bowed over Grace's hand. 'Allow them to take off their coats.'

'Of course. So sorry,' Phoebe said. The moment that was done, she grabbed Grace's hands and tugged her inside. 'There are yellow roses for you, too. Come and see! My maid is a whiz at adding flowers to gowns and hair and everything!'

Grace smiled and allowed herself to be pulled along, while

behind her the gentlemen greeted one another. Phoebe continued to talk, her excitement infectious, and Grace let herself be swept up in the wonder of it all. Tonight she was the daughter of a wealthy aristocrat, no matter what the truth might be. And tonight she would enjoy herself no matter what.

She dutifully praised the food, the decorations and the musicians. She allowed Phoebe's maid to put a yellow rose in her hair. And then she and Phoebe stood in their places in the receiving line to greet their guests.

And there were a great many guests.

Unfortunately, there weren't many *titled* guests.

It would appear that the aristocrats had no interest in lowering themselves to attend the come-out ball of the daughter of a banker and a foreign girl with a titled father. It hardly mattered to Grace, but she could see that her father was disappointed in the turn-out, as was Phoebe. Despite the many people who came through the door, the girl's eyes seemed to dim with every Mr So-and-So or Mrs Whoever who greeted her.

Every so often Phoebe would whisper to her.

'I thought Lord Someone-or-Other would come. He was ever so nice to me in Hyde Park.'

Or, 'Maybe Lady This-or-That isn't feeling well tonight. I thought she'd come, but I haven't seen her.'

Grace had no answer to such things. She didn't understand who was more important than someone else. But she recognised disappointment when the girl's smile faltered and her shoulders drooped.

As the arriving guests dwindled, Grace squeezed Phoebe's hand. 'We are two beautiful girls having a party in our honour. So many people are alone and hungry. If we cannot be happy tonight, then we are the miserable ones who will never know joy.'

She wasn't sure she'd said her words clearly. She was trying to paraphrase a sentiment taught at the temple. But her meaning must have been clear because Phoebe slowly nodded.

'You are right, of course,' Phoebe said as she lifted her chin. 'This is our night, and no one can take my happiness from me.' Then she grabbed Grace's hand and tugged her away. 'Let's get some lemonade before the dancing begins. I'm parched.'

Grace was gulping down lemonade when *he* walked in. She'd known he was coming, of course, but she hadn't expected him to make the kind of entrance he did. Late, and yet supremely confident as he was announced. Handsome, of course, but in the English way. Tall, and dressed in austere black with a cravat of perfect white, a large, brilliant blue sapphire set in the centre.

She was not one to be enamoured of English attire. At least not what the women wore. But the English gentlemen emphasised a lean elegance that she appreciated. And the Duke took her breath away. He stood a hand's breadth taller than the other men, he carried himself with unhurried power, and he took the time to greet his hosts with respect, including an apology for his tardiness.

'Oh, my God!' Phoebe gasped. 'You said he was coming but I didn't *believe* you! Are you finished drinking? Hurry! We must greet him! But we can't run. Don't run!'

Grace wasn't running. Indeed, Phoebe appeared to be talking to herself as she rushed forward, then abruptly moderated her pace. Ten seconds later she was in her spot in the receiving line and going into a very deep curtsey. The Duke hadn't even turned her way yet, but she dropped down as if her legs couldn't hold her up.

'My goodness,' the Duke said, amusement crinkling the corners of his eyes. 'What loveliness has appeared before me? Please, Miss Gray, let me see your gorgeous face.'

Phoebe rose, her cheeks pink and her eyes sparkling. 'A pleasure to greet you, Your Grace. I'm so, so happy you could attend.'

'The pleasure is all mine,' he returned as he kissed her hand.

And then, at last, he turned to greet Grace.

She didn't know what she expected when he saw her. Hopefully as warm a greeting as the one he had given Phoebe. Her focus was on quieting her own racing heart. But the moment he turned to her all other thought fled. She watched his expression change as his gaze softened and his brows rose. Where there had been amusement, she now saw heat. His eyes flickered, taking in the whole of her, but that lasted less than a moment. For the most part he stood there, apparently transfixed, while she watched him and wondered if she measured up.

She hadn't been nervous before, but as he stared, her heart trembled. What had she done wrong?

'Miss Richards,' he finally managed, clearing his throat as he spoke.

'Your Grace.' She dropped into a curtsey, as she had been taught, but he quickly tugged her upright.

'I did not think you could be any lovelier,' he said. 'I thought I was prepared to see you dressed…' He shook his head. 'I have never seen a more beautiful woman. And I have seen many.'

His words were mere flattery, of course. She knew better than to be taken in by overblown words. But they did not seem overblown. Everything in his face and body seemed earnest. And she could not help the flush of heat that filled her body. Did he really think her the most beautiful woman he'd ever seen?

'Your Grace,' she whispered again, not knowing what else she could say.

Thankfully her father saved her.

'You have arrived just in time,' he said loudly. 'I'm afraid my old bones aren't up to dancing any more. Would you mind taking my place for the opening dance?'

This had been planned in the carriage yesterday afternoon, but hearing it played out like this, Grace knew it sounded as if it were a surprise happenstance. And it felt as if it were the most startling thing as the Duke raised her hand to his lips.

'It would be my very great honour,' he said, before he pressed his mouth to the back of her hand.

Damn, damn, damn, why must she wear these stupid gloves? She wanted to feel his mouth on her skin. She wanted to know the calluses on his fingertips without the blunting fabric between them. She wanted to touch the man—and that thought was as shocking to her as it was thrilling.

Never in her life had she wanted to touch a man as she did right then. Indeed, it was as if all her body ached for a caress.

She heard the musicians readying.

She heard Phoebe's father chuckle as he came to Phoebe's side.

And she heard her own heartbeat loud in her ears.

Great heaven, what was happening to her? She tried to pull herself together. She forced some semblance of a smile as the Duke took her hand in his. And she managed, somehow, to walk to the centre of the ballroom.

Her father spoke first, of course. He uttered words of

greeting, echoed by Phoebe's father. And then, with great fanfare, Grace and the Duke began to dance. Phoebe and her father were also part of the set. All this had been decided beforehand. And Grace knew the steps. She'd practised them! But she'd never done them with the Duke before. She'd never held his hand as he drew her close, nor stepped around him as if flirting without touching. She'd never done anything like this with him, and...and...

And it was *wonderful*!

Her heart trembled, her breath stuttered, and nothing mattered except for the way he looked at her. He held her hand and her feet moved exactly as they ought. He smiled at her and her heart sang. And then their steps drew them close, and he whispered the most glorious words to her.

'This is just the beginning.'

Chapter Sixteen

Declan smiled, hoping to ease the anxiety on Grace's face. Clearly she knew that her debut was already a failure. Except for him, none of the *ton* were here. They wouldn't deign to attend the come-out of an illegitimate woman of mixed heritage and the daughter of a banker. He doubted that Grace truly cared, but he could see her worry for Miss Gray.

That was why he'd whispered to her that this was just the beginning. He'd known girls who had contemplated suicide after a bad launch. Every debutante needed to understand that the come-out ball was just the beginning of a long and hopefully glorious life. Surely Grace knew that elite society was only a small fraction of the wide world?

Thankfully, she seemed to understand. The dazed look in her eyes had cleared, her smile had strengthened, and she moved with increasing poise on the dance floor. She was athletic, so the movements of the dance were not difficult for her. She'd obviously had lessons and knew where to go when. But the more he looked at her, the more she seemed to come into her own.

He was no poet, able to express how beautiful she was while she blossomed in his arms. But one moment she was placing her feet where they belonged with obvious intent. Then the next moment she was *dancing*. The girl who'd begun the set had become a woman, who moved for the sheer delight of the music and the night.

He could not credit himself with her change, much though he wanted to. But he could thank God that he was here to witness her delight.

She was even daring to cast him a flirtatious look now and again. Obviously, she was not a practised courtesan. Her coy regard was not that assured. But she showed flashes of daring when her eyes, her hips or some slight lift of her shoulder tempted him to touch her.

And with each glance he dared to draw her closer. How he wanted to take her to places best reserved for fantasies that could not be indulged in the middle of the ballroom. But, oh, he thought about them. Imagined them in graphic detail. And he delighted in the shocking lust he felt for her.

When was the last time he'd felt such a pull to a woman? *Never.* And the realisation of what he felt was as wonderful a sensation as it was frustrating. Because of course she was off-limits, except in the very proscribed manner of the dance.

In. out. A bow. A spin. And through it all a desire to kiss her until he was senseless with hunger. Worse, he could see the desire in her. Every time their gazes connected, their hands touched or her lips curved as if just for him he knew she felt it, too. She wanted him. Despite what she'd seen him do in Hyde Park and how horribly his family had treated her. Despite everything, she desired him, and he was both humbled and deeply aroused by that thought.

'Excuse me, old chum, I wonder if I might impose for an introduction?'

A male voice interrupted his thoughts. And it wasn't until the broad shoulders of an old schoolmate jostled him aside that Declan realised the dance had stopped.

'What?' he said, forcing his thoughts to beat back his lust.

'Never mind him,' the voice continued. 'Declan and I are old schoolfriends. No doubt he's addled by your beauty. Propriety demands that he do the honours, but since he's been struck dumb I shall introduce myself. Lord Cubitt, at your service. Might I have the pleasure of the next dance? Or the next one you have free?'

Grace smiled, her expression uncertain. Apparently, Lord Cubitt was prepared for such a reaction, and quickly charmed his way around it.

'Pray, don't be afraid. You may tell me that your dance card is full. I shall be crushed, of course, but will survive somehow.'

He'd survive on the food offered during supper, because his title was completely impoverished. Still, he was a charming fellow, with a respectable title, and so Declan forced himself to do the pretty.

'Lord Cubitt will not step on your toes, Miss Richards. Indeed, he is accounted quite a good *dance* partner.'

Had he emphasised the word *dance*? Did she understand that he was not a marriage prospect? He could only hope.

Meanwhile, Grace nodded, flashing a sweet smile at the bounder. 'I believe you have no need to sulk, my lord. I do indeed have space on my dance card. As does Phoebe, I think.'

'She will be my next request,' the man said as he grinned and scrawled his name.

As Lord Cubitt did his work, Declan chanced to glance up. Good God, where had all these men come from? A steady stream of bucks, bounders and jack-a-napes were sauntering through the doors. Enough that Grace's father and Phoebe's parents were scrambling to greet them all.

Why ever were this lot here? Had the gaming hells and brothels closed for the night?

'There, that's done,' said Lord Cubitt. 'But lest I think I

can keep you all to myself, I have a few more friends who are desperate for an introduction.'

What? Declan's eyes widened as he saw a queue of gentlemen lining up, all vying for an introduction and a slot on Grace's dance card. Good God, it was as if all the reprobates in London had decided to come and court her.

Then, to his shock, he realised that was *exactly* the case. Every fortune-hunter in London was here, paying homage to Grace. And she, damn it, had no idea who she was allowing to touch her arm, to write their names on her dance card, to demand every single one of her waltzes.

Hell! He was supposed to have the first waltz. Her father had already agreed to it. But he had been too overcome with desire to think of writing down his name, and now... Her card was full while he stood there like an idiot.

Where was her father? Where were Phoebe's parents? They were supposed to protect the girls from reprobates. But of course her father didn't know who was who in London, and Phoebe's mother was at the door, keeping the worst ruffians from coming in. After all, none of these men had a proper invitation. Indeed, he now saw that both fathers were at the French doors at the back, preventing God only knew who from entering.

Damn it! Someone needed to help at the front entrance or Mrs Gray would be overwhelmed.

Bloody hell. He'd have to go.

He glanced back at Grace. The worst she might suffer was if a man took liberties with her on the dance floor. Mrs Gray, on the other hand, might very well be hurt as a few of the bigger men tried to muscle their way in.

'I'll be back,' he said into Grace's ear. 'Don't go outside with any of them!'

Then he ducked away before he could hear her response, crossing in quick strides to the ballroom door.

'Mrs Gray,' he said in his darkest tones, 'may I be of assistance?'

'Your Grace,' the lady said, clearly relieved. 'Thank you. These *gentlemen*...' her tone cast doubt upon the term '...do not have an invitation, and yet they seem to think they can simply descend—'

'Aw, milady, we mean no disrespect,' countered an infamous card sharp who existed on the fringe of polite society. 'We were asked to give Miss Richards a boost, so to speak. Just a dance—'

Declan interrupted, his tone hard. 'Miss Richards does not need "a boost" in a dance or otherwise. Pray be gone.' He reached out to slam the door shut, but was stopped by none other than his own cousin.

'They don't have an invitation,' Cedric said, 'but I do. My deepest apologies, Mrs Gray, for my tardiness.'

He stepped forward, neatly shoving the others back, while Declan winced at the dark purple bruises on the man's face. There was paste covering the worst of them, but the injuries were there for all to see.

'Cedric—' Declan began, though God knew how he was going to apologise for what he'd done.

It didn't matter. His cousin was addressing the other men crowding forward.

'Go on, now,' he said. 'I hear there's a new girl at The Rose Garden. Pray give her my regards and she might bestow a kiss upon you for the association.'

Only his cousin would barter a tart's kisses as a way to quiet an altercation. Though, to be fair, it was effective. Crass, for sure, but effective. The unwanted gentlemen left with a tip of their hats and a grin.

Meanwhile, Mrs Gray had greeted his cousin with a relieved smile. 'Thank you for your assistance, my lord.' Then she looked behind her at the dance set now forming. 'Though I'm afraid the bulk of the fortune-hunters got through the door before I could stop them.'

'Yes...' Cedric drawled. 'I can see that.'

Declan shot him a hard look. 'Was this your doing?'

'Mine? Good God, no! Do you think I want more competition for her hand? You're bad enough. Thank God you're old and boring, otherwise I'd never stand a chance.'

'I'm barely three years your senior,' Declan growled, his gaze on the men now surrounding Grace.

'And yet you act a dozen years older or more.'

'You cannot fault me just because you want to remain in your adolescence.'

'Oh, yes, I can, cousin. I absolutely can.'

Declan ground his teeth together, annoyed with himself. This was unseemly of them, sniping at each other in front of Mrs Gray. So, rather than respond, Declan bowed to the lady.

'If you would excuse us, Mrs Gray? I would like a word with my cousin.'

'Of course,' the woman answered, her worried gaze still scanning the newcomers. 'I should find Phoebe...'

'Yes,' Declan agreed. 'I think that would be wise.'

He waited while the lady hurried away before he turned to his cousin. But before he could speak Cedric forestalled him, holding up a hand as if to block a punch.

'I have no interest in anything you say,' said Cedric, and then pointedly ignored his cousin as he looked for Grace. 'I believe I shall go and claim my dance.'

'Her card's full already. I'm out, too.'

Declan didn't touch his cousin. He knew better. The man

was just as likely to punch him as to treat him with restraint. And could Declan really blame him?

Cedric stopped moving, clearly frustrated. 'What the hell is all this? Every fortune-hunter in England…'

His voice trailed away as he came to the same conclusion Declan had. They looked at one another and spoke the word at the same time.

'Mother.'

Meaning both their mothers together. And hadn't the Dowager Duchess declared this very thing not two hours ago? Her speed and thoroughness were daunting.

Cedric sighed, turning his bruised face towards Declan. 'You should just give me the ten thousand pounds, and then we can both be done with this charade.'

'Never.'

'You owe me.'

Declan winced. He did, but not ten thousand pounds' worth. 'I'm sorry, Cedric. I shouldn't have gone off like that, and I am genuinely remorseful. But you're not going to use my failing to destroy my family's coffers.'

'I'm part of your family.'

'Nevertheless.'

He could hear Cedric grinding his teeth together and, given the swelling along his jaw, knew that must hurt.

'A loan, then,' his cousin finally said.

Declan gave his cousin a long look. Damnation, he was actually considering it. Ten thousand pounds and this whole mess would be done. He could stop pretending to pursue Grace, his cousin would go away, and…

'No. What you are doing to Miss Richards is criminal.'

His cousin scoffed. 'Criminal? I intend to marry her. You, on the other hand, are simply toying with her.'

'You want her dowry, nothing more.'

Cedric didn't need to respond except with a raised brow. It was considered normal for a man to marry for a dowry. It was downright commonplace. Though one would think a future earl might have more self-respect.

'Leave her alone, Cedric,' Declan growled.

'No.'

'There are dozens of other fortunes around. Try Miss Gray.'

Though from the crowd of men around her, Phoebe's dance card was likely full as well.

'No.'

And there it was. Far from being a lost lamb, ignored by the *ton*, Miss Richards was now the most sought-after woman in London. And, far from dissuading his cousin, he had made Cedric dig his heels in even further.

It was exactly as Declan had planned, and yet, his body physically rebelled at the idea of Cedric or anyone else having Miss Richards. He was nauseous—and furious. It was all he could do to stand there, watching her dance with those blighters, without decking every single one.

If the sight of Cedric touching Grace had brought him to violence in Hyde Park, how would he handle seeing her wed someone else?

Chapter Seventeen

Grace had never been the focus of so much flattery. At first it had given her a sweet flush of joy. She had never been called beautiful so many times. But before long the compliments had begun to get repetitive. Then they had become ridiculous. And then, when even the most overblown compliment had served only to tighten her lips in annoyance, gentlemen had begun calling her the Ice Queen, who destroyed their confidence with a single frown.

She should have been disgusted, but they were so ridiculous that she hadn't been able to help laughing. And the moment she'd begun to laugh, they'd had her.

Everyone had gone to new heights of silliness for her smile. Gentlemen had pretended to fall prostrate at her feet with every giggle. And when even the most serious had declared they lived or died on her barest glance, she'd felt the attention go to her head.

How easily she fell as the flattery filled her to bursting. And why did it give her an extra measure of glee when every one of her laughs elicited a dark glower from the Duke? What cause had he to glare at her as men vied for her attention? Why did he cross his arms as if chastising a recalcitrant child when she was nothing of the sort?

She had survived on the streets of Canton and in the sometimes more frightening bowels of a merchant ship on the China Sea. This was fun. And he could go to Diyu if he would steal this evening's entertainment from her.

So she danced and she laughed. And when even Lord Domac—despite his bruised face—found a way to be charming during the supper buffet, she felt herself lighten for the first time in years. She was safe, warm, and well fed. She had men bowing over her hand and making themselves pleasing to her. And if only her father would smile everything would be perfect in her world, no matter what the Duke thought.

But her father was not well. The supper buffet was closing when she saw him stumble. Several gentlemen helped him to a seat. Her father had been celebrated almost as much as she, but she saw his pallor and knew that he was too tired to remain at the ball past midnight.

Within moments, she had made it to his side. 'Father, I think it is late enough,' she said as she clasped his frail hand. 'We should go home now.'

'What? And miss your triumph? We couldn't possibly.'

Did he truly think it was a triumph to have men vying for the chance to spend her dowry? Or did he think her too stupid to know why these grasping men were suddenly at her feet?

'This is no triumph if you are ill.'

'I am merely tired, my dear.'

He was more than tired, but she would not shame him by pointing that out.

Instead, Lord Domac offered a suggestion.

'Pray seek your bed, my lord. I shall see your daughter safely home.'

'You will do no such thing,' said a cold voice. It was the Duke, of course. 'She is not safe—'

'Have a care, cousin,' Lord Domac interrupted, his voice threatening.

The Duke looked as if he would argue, but then he swallowed. 'Her reputation will not be safe without her father. Perhaps it would be best if they both went home.'

Grace agreed, but her father would not budge. 'I will not cut short your fun,' he said as he squeezed her hand. 'The next set will begin soon. I shall simply wait—'

'No, Father,' Grace said. 'I shall spend the night with Phoebe. She will want to discuss every aspect of the evening. My reputation will be safe and my...my fun will be extended with my dear friend.'

This was the only compromise her stubborn father might accept, and indeed he finally agreed, once Phoebe's father was apprised of the situation.

With that matter handled, she watched as the Duke called for her father's carriage and saw the elderly man safely away.

But all that took time, and while she trusted her father with the Duke, she did not trust Phoebe with all the attention being showered upon her. If Grace felt herself caught up in the flattery, how much harder would it be for a sheltered girl? Especially since Phoebe was considered an eligible heiress despite her lack of aristocratic heritage.

Where was the girl?

The musicians had begun tuning their instruments for the final set, and Phoebe was nowhere to be found.

'Oh, no,' she murmured. 'Has anyone seen where Phoebe has gone?'

'Likely the ladies' retiring room,' one gentleman said.

'Goodness, no,' said another. 'She is probably taking some air outside. Shall we go and look?'

Go outside with them after the Duke had specifically warned her not to? Absolutely not.

'Where is her mother?'

'Never mind that,' intoned another gentleman. 'The set

will form soon, and I have been waiting an eternity to have you in my arms.'

'And you will be waiting a great deal longer if we do not find Phoebe.'

Thankfully Lord Domac understood her concerns. 'I'll go outside,' he said quietly. 'You look in the ladies' retiring room.'

She nodded and headed to the ladies' room. As it was late in the evening, the retiring room looked like a disaster. There were torn bits of fabric discarded in the corner, several tired maids stitching gowns or redoing hair, and a bevy of ladies talking in excited whispers. They all looked up when she came in, their expressions ranging from disdain to sweetness, depending on the woman.

Grace barely had time to acknowledge them all. Indeed, she'd only met them for ten seconds each in the receiving line.

'Hello,' she said calmly. 'Has anyone seen Phoebe?'

None had an answer.

And then one girl's head jerked up. 'That's the musicians! The last set is forming!'

With a gasp, everyone jumped from their places throughout the room and gave quick pats to their attire before scrambling out through the door. Grace had to leap sideways to avoid being trampled.

Once all the guests had departed, Grace took one last look around before turning to leave, but she was stopped by an older maid with a pinched expression.

'Miss,' the woman said in a low voice. 'Miss...' Then she pointed to a screen that shielded the room from the chamber pot.

Oh. But why would Phoebe need the chamber pot for so long? Unless... Oh, dear.

Grace carefully peered behind the screen. There stood Phoebe with a torn dress, a maid quietly stitching up her skirt and her face streaked with tears. Of all the things Grace had been imagining, this was the worst.

'Phoebe,' Grace whispered. 'Are you all right?'

The girl's head snapped up, her gaze sharpening from distracted to terrified. 'Don't let anyone see me,' she rasped.

'I am alone,' Grace responded as she stepped fully behind the curtain. 'What has happened?'

'I didn't want to go outside,' Phoebe said. 'I know better. I didn't want to.'

Grace felt her blood go cold. She had experience with this. Not personal experience, but she had sat with other girls, not all of them biracial like her. She knew the best thing to do was to hold the girl's hand and wait for the full story. Or enough of it that she would know what to do next.

Except Phoebe wasn't speaking.

She gripped Grace's hand and stared fixedly at the floor.

'How badly are you hurt?' Grace finally asked.

'It's nothing.'

'It's never nothing.'

Phoebe held up her arms. Her gloves were off, and her arms appeared scrubbed raw. Clearly she had tried to wash off the bruises that were dark on her pale skin.

'I kicked him and ran. But he...' She shook her head. 'He'd already torn my dress, and now there are dirt stains on the back.'

She pointed to where a dark, wet spot showed. Grace didn't see any dirt, but it didn't matter. The girl's absence from the ball and her torn dress would tell a tale to anyone who cared to look.

'You are not hurt in...in any other way?'

Phoebe shook her head. 'I don't think he expected me to fight.'

'I'm very glad you did. You should be proud of yourself.'

'It doesn't matter. My reputation is ruined,' she said on a choked-off sob. 'He said that I was ruined and that I would have to marry him now.'

'Is your father that cruel? Does he have no care for your feelings?'

It was an honest question. Many girls had suffered more at the hands of their fathers than from any suitor.

'What? No! My father will—'

'Will be very pleased that you fought.' Grace squeezed Pheobe's hands. 'Tell me who this man was.'

'What? No! I—' She dropped her face into her hands. 'It's over. I just want to forget it ever happened.'

How many times had Grace heard those exact words? All sorts of people had come to the temple for help, for safety, for counsel. If they were injured, the half-Chinese girls were often sent in to tend them. And in that capacity Grace had heard many awful tales. Women who were hurt simply wanted it to be over, but that could never be.

'You will never forget, Phoebe, as long as you live. Best face it now.' She lifted the girl's chin, being as delicate as possible but keeping her resolve clear. 'What is the man's name?'

'I didn't want to go outside with him. He was so much stronger than me, and I didn't want to make a scene. Not at our come-out ball.'

'Of course you didn't. But I need to know—'

'Lord Jasper, miss,' said the maid. She was another older woman, with a worn face and tired eyes, but her chin lifted as she spoke in a clear voice. 'I've already whispered it about to them that will listen. Stay away from him.'

'Thank you,' Grace said to the maid. 'You will take care of her?'

'Yes, miss. Ain't the first time I've had to mend a gown at a ball for all the wrong reasons.'

Well, that was truly horrible. Fortunately, in this case, there was something Grace could do. Something that had burned in her soul from the very first moment she'd come upon a girl crying while hiding. Never before had she the strength to do anything about it. Never before had she been able to strike back at men who thought they were untouchable. But she was not a weak, sheltered girl like Phoebe. Neither was she a shunned biracial child in a temple. She was an adult woman now, and she had learned a few tricks of her own.

She pressed a kiss to Phoebe's cheek. 'It doesn't feel like it now, but you'll be all right. You'll see. Your father loves you and would never see you hurt. You know it as well as I.'

There was fear in Phoebe's eyes. Probably worry that she had disappointed her father. Hopefully, the man would be the parent Phoebe needed. If not... Well, then that too was something girls often had to live with.

But Lord Jasper was an entirely different matter.

Grace stepped out from behind the curtain, then boldly left the retiring room. A few steps took her back inside the ballroom, where the ball was continuing as if nothing had happened. And along the walls, loitering in clumps, were the men who had come without invitation to the party.

She scanned the room quickly, looking for the Duke or Lord Domac, but neither was in view. Very well, then. It was up to her. And by the fury growing in her blood this was something she longed to do.

She crossed to the musicians. 'Stop playing. Now.'

It took a moment for them to comply. The music faltered

and then stopped. And then the dancers stumbled to a halt, all looking to where she stood before the players.

She stepped forward, pleased when the guests separated before her.

'Where is Lord Jasper?' she called.

No one answered. No one, that was, except Phoebe's mother, who rushed forward with a harsh whisper. 'Grace, this is unseemly. You must stop this—'

'Go to the retiring room. See to your daughter.'

The lady's mouth dropped open, her eyes widening with shock. Without another word, she rushed away.

Meanwhile, Grace turned back to the room at large. 'Come, come, Lord Jasper. I am the reason for this event. Myself and Phoebe. Surely you can present yourself to me, even though you had no invitation to attend.'

'I was invited by another lady,' drawled a man as he gestured vaguely to a bevy of girls in the corner. 'And was most welcomed once I arrived.'

'That is no true invitation, sir.'

'Nevertheless, I am here.' He grinned as he bowed before her. 'Lord Jasper at your service.'

She looked him up and down, seeing in him a genial face, a body neither exceptionally strong nor overly fat. Truthfully, to her eye, he looked harmless, almost kind. But there was a cruel joy in his eyes that spoke of arrogance and privilege. And her blood boiled even hotter.

'You have heard, have you not, that I meted out discipline on the ship where I served as navigator?'

'I know nothing of your heathen ways, Miss Richards, but I can already see how unnatural you are as a woman.'

He called her unnatural? When he had forced a naïve girl outside at her own ball?

'Aboard ship, if there was a crime against a woman I was

the one to administer justice. Do you claim that an English ballroom has less justice than a Chinese ship?'

He arched a brow. 'Again, *miss*.' He sneered that last word as if her very sex were suspect. 'I know nothing of your heathen ways.'

'Then let me enlighten you.'

She slammed a hand against his throat, cutting off his breath. And while he reeled from that she kicked him as hard as she could straight between his thighs. He could not scream. She had cut off his breath. But he could crumple to the ground, his eyes bulging and his body twitching in agony.

Good.

'I thought Englishmen were different,' she hissed. 'I thought that with your fancy clothes and your smooth manners I could expect more from you. How disgusted I was to learn that you are worse than a common sailor.'

She reared back and kicked him again, straight in the groin. She did not examine the fury that built inside her. She didn't restrain it. Instead, she let all the hatred flow from her as she kicked and kicked, until she prayed that organ he cherished so much was crushed to oblivion.

She had not meant to lose control. She had not meant to become ruled by her fury. But once she had begun hitting the man, she had not been able to stop. She saw Pheobe and so many other girls in her mind's eye. She saw their tears, felt their agony, and she knew the terror that had dogged her from her earliest memory. Women were often vicious to one another, but men were casual brutes. Men took their strength and their power, and they hurt women. This man—and so many others—deserved to die.

So she kicked him again, until strong arms wrapped around her. A powerful body lifted her up, dragged her away, and held her aloft as if she was a child.

She screamed her fury. She bellowed like an animal. But she was not released.

'Enough. Grace... Enough!'

It was the Duke's voice and the Duke's arms. It was his body that she railed against, and his arms that held her away. No, she belatedly realised. He held her safe. Safe from the man on the floor. And safe from descending into the mindless disaster of her fury.

It took her some time. Still she kicked the air and heard the Duke's grunt when her feet found him.

'Grace!' came another voice. Phoebe's. 'Grace, I'm all right. He only bruised me.'

That did not make it right, but it was enough to quiet her. Enough to make reason push to the fore. Enough for her to realise that she flailed like a wildcat in the Duke's arms.

'Are you all right?' the Duke asked her, his voice strong in her ear. 'Are you calm now?'

'He hurt her!' she rasped.

'And you have delivered justice.'

She doubted it. She suspected that Lord Jasper had abused many more innocents than Phoebe. But the message was delivered. She needed to gain control of herself.

And while she was quieting her pounding heart, the Duke turned to the people surrounding them. 'Isn't that right?' the Duke asked everyone, his voice raised to carry throughout the ballroom. 'Miss Richards did exactly what was needed, and Lord Jasper got exactly what he deserved.'

Silence greeted his words. Silence and an uncomfortable shifting of feet.

'If I hear one word different,' the Duke continued. 'If any whisper against these ladies reaches my ears, I will destroy the speaker. Do you understand me? Lord Jasper...' He paused to glower at the wheezing man. 'Got exactly what he deserved.'

Again there was no answer, just the gaping, dumbfounded looks of stunned people. No one spoke against the Duke. But then again, no one spoke to agree with him.

'Do I make myself clear?' he all but shouted.

As a group, every soul nodded his or her head. Every soul looked not at Lord Jasper but at the Duke. And every soul began to murmur.

'Yes, of course, Your Grace.'

'Completely agree, Your Grace.'

'Quite right.'

And there Grace saw true power. The Duke had not raised a fist. He had not beaten anyone bloody and he'd barely raised his voice. But the entire assemblage bowed to his wishes.

'You may put me down now,' she whispered, ashamed of her outburst but not regretting it. 'I am calm.'

'Are you hurt?' he asked her.

'Only because I could not save Phoebe beforehand.'

'Tonight or another night, it would have happened eventually. Her dowry is too large to prevent such things.'

Meanwhile, Phoebe's father stepped forward. 'I believe that is the end of this evening's entertainment.' He pointed to Lord Jasper's nearest compatriots. 'Take that rubbish away. And be sure that your names will be remembered. Bankers are in close community with barristers,' he drawled. 'Your families will find credit hard to come by. Not to mention legal assistance.'

Grace had no understanding of what that meant, but she could see satisfaction cross the Duke's face. Also a flinch as he looked at Phoebe and her mother.

'You should take her home,' the Duke said to Mrs Gray. 'I will see that the ballroom is managed.'

The lady agreed and started ushering Phoebe to the door. But then she stopped, turning back to face him. 'Grace is supposed to stay with us tonight.'

'I will see her safely home,' the Duke said.

Lord Domac stepped to her opposite side. 'That will not help her reputation any more than this has.'

'A maid,' Grace said, looking at the woman who had helped Phoebe. The woman stood at the edge of the ballroom with a satisfied smile on her lips. 'Do you mind?'

'Not at all, miss.'

And so it was decided. While Phoebe's parents took her home, the servants and the Duke supervised the clearing of the ballroom. Grace didn't see what became of Lord Jasper. Honestly, some part of her hoped he'd die from his injuries, though she feared that would bring further harm to her. The death of a nobleman, whether English or Chinese, always drew a penalty.

But she had no time to worry about that now. All her attention was occupied with learning how to end a ball. And once that was accomplished she settled beside the maid into a dark, intimate carriage with the Duke. She stretched out her feet and sighed. How lovely to finally sit.

But all too soon the darkness closed in, and she was deeply aware of the Duke seated across from her. Especially when he spoke gently into the darkness.

'Are you all right?' he asked. 'Are you hurt?'

'I was not hurt at all.'

'Was Miss Gray badly injured?'

Meaning was she raped?

'No. She was frightened, and it was a great disappointment for her come-out ball. She was so excited when the night began.'

'Large dowries always bring out the worst. Truly, I am ashamed of my fellow men.'

'I expect she will be better prepared in the future.'

He was silent for a long moment, and then he spoke again, his voice rough. 'I have never seen anyone fight as you did.'

She all but rolled her eyes. 'Your women need to learn how to defend themselves.'

'We have women who fight. Bare-knuckle punching, even, and people bet on the outcome.' He shook his head. 'What you did was different. That style of fighting…' There was awe in his voice. 'I have never seen the like before.'

That was not surprising. It was a style taught only by the monks to other monks. Except at her temple, where the children were allowed to learn it as a means of self-defence.

'The monk who taught me is the same one who believes a mixed-race child deserves a full life as much as anyone else. He said I was not worthless, but that I would need to defend my worth often.'

'That is a wise man.'

Did he sound surprised? 'Do you believe the Chinese are all savages?' Her face twisted into a grimace. 'I would not blame you. They believe you whites are all apes.'

'I believe that men do terrible things. We allow our worst impulses to rule. Lord Jasper is one terrible example, and Cedric gambles with people, using blackmail to meet his needs. And I have such feelings,' he said, his tone achingly hollow. 'It seems that every moment in my life is aimed at controlling my temper. Every choice, every breath, is governed by that need.'

She frowned. 'But I was the one who lost control tonight. You stopped me.'

He nodded. 'Righteous fury is understandable. And he deserved everything he got.'

Grace took a moment to think, seeing something she had not understood before. The Duke obviously damned himself for every display of temper, but he forgave her.

'How is what I did different from your fight with Cedric?' she asked. 'You thought he was hurting me.'

The Duke turned away, his gaze focused somewhere outside the carriage. 'I could have killed Cedric.'

'I could have killed Lord Jasper. We both needed each other to stop.'

He looked back at her, and when he spoke his voice was barely audible. 'You are astounding,' he said. 'How can you forgive me? I was a beast against Cedric.'

'How can you forgive *me*?'

He had no answer, and neither did she. It would seem they both had the same fault in an explosive temper. That might be disastrous. Or else they could be good checks, one upon the other, keeping each other in line.

'I think,' she said finally, 'that we are just people. Arrogant and small, powerful and weak, all thrown together in a very large world where we manage to hurt one another.'

'That is a very dark statement.'

'But,' she continued, 'we can choose to help each other. Stop the worst, encourage the best.'

'Some of us do. Some of us try very hard to be better.'

He was referring to himself, and she respected him for it.

'Have you taught your women to fight?' she asked.

He snorted. 'My mother doesn't need any more weapons. She's dangerous enough. And the others have never asked.'

She let that hang in the silence, uncertain how to respond until the maid sitting beside her spoke up.

'I should like to learn, miss. Unless I'm too old.'

Grace turned to her. 'All ages can learn.'

'I saw what you did to him. We all did. And I have a daughter, miss. A right pretty one. She needs to learn.'

'Yes,' Grace agreed. 'She does.'

But before she could say more, they had arrived at her father's home. The carriage stopped and the Duke's servant quickly opened the door, leaving no time to plan.

'I give you leave to contact me,' she said to the maid. 'My sister can teach you as well. If your daughter is pretty, then there is no time to waste.' She squeezed the woman's hand. 'And even if she is not.'

Then she allowed the Duke to help her out of the carriage. He walked her to the door, his steps slow.

'That is kind of you,' he said quietly. 'But it will not endear you to the *ton*.'

'Do you think that was ever a possibility? Even before tonight's events?'

He sighed. 'Probably not. But you are notorious now.'

She wondered what that meant, but there was no time to ask.

He squeezed her hand. 'Which room is yours?'

'What?'

'What bedroom is yours? Light a candle in it so that I know you are safely within.'

'Do you fear I will be attacked in my own home?'

'No, but I wish to be sure.'

It made no sense. She was safe in her father's home. And yet she appreciated the sweetness of his worry.

'My room is at the back. You will not see it from the street. But I will light a candle in the parlour there, before I see my father.' She pointed to the parlour window.

He nodded, then lifted her hand to his lips. It was a courtly gesture, one that was foreign to her eyes, and yet it thrilled her nonetheless. That glow was in his eyes, luminescent in the moonlight as he bent over her hand. He did not look down even as he kissed her glove.

She gazed at him, feeling a tightness in her belly. Was that yearning? Desire? She didn't have a word for this feeling. In a life dominated by fear, this was something altogether different and she relished it.

He straightened from his bow, but he did not break the connection of their gazes. And so they looked at one another, saying nothing, and yet she felt so much. A tingle in her breasts. A dryness on her lips. An ache between her thighs.

This was desire, and it felt wonderful. Sharp, hungry, and so exciting. She understood now why people sought it so fiercely. And when he straightened up she abruptly twisted her hand, gripping his wrist.

He froze, his eyes dark in the shadow, but the air was filled with need. Hers? His? She didn't know. But her heart was fluttering, and her body ached for him.

'Grace,' he whispered.

'Yes.'

She didn't say it as a question. It was an answer to the question he hadn't asked and the desire she couldn't voice.

He leaned closer, without touching her, his body large and the shadows dark. He was shielding her from view while his breath grew short.

'A kiss?' he asked.

She could barely hear him over the beating of her heart.

'Yes, please.'

How bold she was. She had run all her life from sex, knowing it was dangerous. And yet here she was, begging him for it. She was begging him. And he was not going to refuse.

He didn't take the kiss. Instead, he touched her cheek, his glove warm and soft as he caressed her. A finger slipped below her jaw, and she lifted her face to his. Already her lips were parted. Already they tingled with awareness.

His thumb brushed across her lower lip and she felt heat in its wake. Was it always like this? Did his body tingle as hers did? Did he feel as if he would die if their mouths didn't touch?

He leaned forward, the air between them narrowing until their breath mingled. His was sweet. Hers was hot.

Then it happened. He touched his lips to hers.

They were clever as they moved across hers. That was what she thought. What a clever mouth he had, teasing hers as she stretched for him, nipping against her flesh before soothing it with his tongue. How clever of him to delight so easily. Just his mouth and his tongue, and she was desperate for more.

She stepped forward, pushed up against his chest and angled her head. She wanted more. She needed to feel more. He matched her, wrapping an arm around her back as he tugged her high against him. She arched her back and he thrust his tongue inside.

The dance they shared now was overwhelming. Tongues parrying as they stroked across and around each other. And all the while he thrust in and out of her mouth while she clutched at his coat. She wanted to climb higher on his body, she wanted to surrender completely to his kiss, but she knew that it was too dangerous to continue.

Too much! Too fast! And altogether too exciting for her to stop.

Thank Heaven that he did. Thank the Divine that he ended it with a slow withdrawal. She had not the strength. Indeed, as he set her back onto her feet she wondered if her knees would support her.

'This is dangerous,' he whispered.

'I know.'

'I do not regret it,' he confessed.

'Neither do I.'

They stood there, slowly disentangling their bodies. They were on her front step. It might be in shadow, but it was not safe.

She stepped back, banging into the front door. He stepped back too, a proper gentleman once again. And then they heard footsteps.

By the time the door was opened they stood in proper distance from one another.

'Miss Grace!' the footman said. Then his eyes widened. 'Your Grace!' he said as he fumbled with a bow.

'Good evening, Samuel,' she said as she turned away from the Duke. 'How is my father?'

'Resting comfortably, miss.'

'Thank you.'

She didn't look back, though her whole body tingled with awareness of where the Duke stood. She entered the house, taking the candle from the footman's hand. And then, finally, she turned around.

'Goodnight, Your Grace.' She kept her tone level, or she tried to, but there was a hesitancy in her voice. Or perhaps it was a yearning that seemed to echo in his gaze. 'Thank you for escorting me home.'

'It was my pleasure,' he said as he bowed.

How could words be felt physically? As if he were caressing her with his voice? Madness… And yet she relished every sensation even as she dipped into a shallow curtsey and firmly shut the door.

Meanwhile, Samuel stifled a yawn. 'The house is abed, miss. Your father said you wouldn't come back tonight.'

'There was an incident at the ball,' she said as she crossed into the parlour. 'I had to come home.'

She set a candle in the window, pausing as she watched the Duke return to his carriage. Such a large man. Normally, she disliked men of such imposing size. She was often frightened of someone so physically powerful. But not of him. Instead of fear, she felt longing. She wanted to be surrounded by him, protected by him, and…and more.

She waited there at the parlour window until the Duke's carriage pulled away. It was as though her body strained to be with him, lingered over the thought of him, wanted…

Well, what she wanted was obvious. She understood carnal desire. There had been a time when she had been fascinated by it, talking to older girls about what they did and why. She'd even spent time with the prostitutes who had come to the temple. She'd wanted to understand, and they had wanted to explain.

But it hadn't been long before she'd decided to forego that nonsense, to learn navigation from the old sailor with milky white eyes. She'd thought the whole business of copulation something too fraught with danger for her to pursue. Even when she'd developed breasts and begun to feel attraction, she'd ruthlessly suppressed the urge.

Too dangerous. Too tricky. She would not risk her survival on something as unmanageable as passion.

Until now, when her place in her father's affection was secure, and when an English mandarin—of all people—spoke to her with respect while hunger burned in his eyes. Now she thought about it. Now she *yearned* for it.

Could she risk it? What folly! And yet as she headed for her bed he remained in her thoughts and in the tingles that still teased her body.

Chapter Eighteen

Declan had ample time to think as he returned the maid to her home. Naturally he had known that women were often abused in one way or another, but he'd always made sure those in his household were protected. And certainly he disliked those men who abused their physical and societal power to exploit ladies who should be under their protection.

It had never occurred to him to teach the women around him how to fight. That wasn't ladylike. And yet Grace had fought, and she had never seemed more powerful or more attractive to him.

That she had so obviously lost control of herself only increased her allure. Here was a woman who understood his struggle to maintain his composure. That turned her into a Valkyrie in his mind. She was a warrior woman, to be respected if not revered.

He said nothing to the maid. He was not in the habit of conversing with other people's servants. But before they stopped, he did venture a comment.

'If you or your daughter feel unsafe in your current employment, you may apply to my housekeeper. I am sure she can find a place for you both.'

The woman's eyes widened with shock. 'Your Grace?'

'What name should I give Mrs Williams? In case you choose to communicate with her?'

'I am quite happy, Your Grace, but my daughter...her name is Molly Smithee.'

'Molly Smithee,' he repeated, committing it to memory.

'She wants to be a lady's maid, Your Grace, but will be happy in whatever capacity is available.'

'I'll let Mrs Williams know, though I cannot promise advancement. I am a bachelor without need of a lady's maid.'

'I will trust to your good judgement, Your Grace. And that of Mrs Williams.'

And with that she curtsied as best she could in the carriage and stepped out. Once he had seen her into her home, the Duke stared into the space where Grace had sat. He stared at it and thought about the evening. He thought of her and he lusted. He thought of her and he...

'Home, Your Grace?'

'What?'

'Should we head for—?'

'No.' He quickly thought about the London streets. The Richards lived not so far from a few of the better-quality gaming hells. He grinned. 'Drop me off at the Lady's Delight,' he said.

'Your Grace?'

His coachman was shocked, and well he might be. It had been years since he'd stepped into that infamous gaming hell, but he was not averse to pretending.

'The Lady's Delight,' he repeated forcefully.

And then he sat back and allowed his mind to wander. It went to her, of course, and he let it. He had no exact plan as to what he would do, and he didn't want to examine his thoughts too closely. So he let his mind wander to the lascivious and the carnal. And when he stepped down from his carriage his gait was a bit stiff.

'Go home,' he said to his coachman. 'I shall take a hackney back.'

'Aye, Your Grace.'

The man eyed him for a long moment. He was twice Declan's age and had known him since he was boy. He no doubt had guessed what might happen, but he didn't say anything before he left.

Soon Declan was whistling as he walked not into the gaming hell but down the street, towards where Grace lived.

He wanted to see her again, he thought, without prying eyes or shocked gossipmongers. He wanted to speak to her as a man might to a fellow soul who had piqued his interest.

His thoughts were a lot less clear when he walked by the dark house and then wandered, oh-so-casually, behind it. There was a small alley, no light except for the waxing moon, and not even a tree to ease the sight of dirty bricks and rubbish. Then he looked up at her window and wondered what he was doing.

She was likely abed, her face freshly washed and her legs stretched naked beneath the sheets. She wore a nightrail, he imagined, made of soft cotton or sensuous silk. But beneath that simple gown would be her plump breasts and her narrow waist. He imagined he could feel the muscles in the strength of her arms and the grip of her legs. He thought of her kisses and her sighs. And he wished—

'What are you doing here?' she hissed.

He was jolted out of his fantasy only to see her for real, wrapped in colourful silk as she peeked out from behind the back door.

'Grace?'

'Why are you standing there, Your Grace?'

'Call me Declan.' He wanted to hear his name on her lips.

'That's not proper.'

'I won't tell.'

She stared at him, and then she jumped as a dog barked in the distance.

'This isn't proper,' she repeated, but then she waved him in.

He grinned as he moved inside. They were in the dark kitchen, quiet and still, without even a cat to hunt for mice.

'How did you know I was out there?' he asked. 'Why aren't you in bed?'

She sighed and lifted her hands in a gesture of futility. 'I have a temper, too,' she whispered. 'And it doesn't let me sleep.'

He understood. 'I applaud what you did to Lord Jasper.'

'Will he survive?' she asked.

'Probably. Either way, I've made it clear that it was what he deserved.'

Grace folded her arms across her chest. It was a gesture of anger or fear, he wasn't sure which.

'What will your mother say when she hears?' she pressed. 'Will she blame Lord Jasper? Or will she say that the heathen has shown her true colours?'

There was a wealth of disgust and self-recrimination in her tone. He touched her shoulder and pulled her gently to face him.

'Do not blame yourself. He deserved—'

'I don't,' she interrupted. 'But I know that the lower caste always shoulders the blame.'

'That's not true.' He lifted her chin until she was looking at him. There was very little light here, but he could see her eyes widen in her pale face. 'That's not *always* true,' he hedged.

And then he did what had been burning in his thoughts all night long, even before they had reached her front door.

He kissed her.

He cupped her cheeks, tilted her mouth to his, and kissed her more thoroughly than he had managed before.

He went slowly. He could tell that she was not experienced. Her mouth was soft, her lips only slightly parted. She was willing, but unschooled, and the roar in his blood nearly overcame him.

He brushed his lips across hers, then gently teased his tongue against her lips. She stretched up towards him and he felt the brush of silk against his legs as her dressing gown fell open.

He slipped his tongue inside her mouth, tangling with hers and then withdrawing before plunging in again. He felt her breath catch as her body moved towards him. Or maybe he had simply pulled her tightly, such that he could feel the swell of her breasts and the length of her thighs. So hot. So sweet. So very much *his*.

He felt her hands press flat against his chest. Did she mean to push him away? He felt her palms skim across his chest, restless and uncertain.

He drew back, looking into her dark eyes. 'Have you never been kissed before tonight?'

'Yes. By sailors and others.'

'Kissed like that?'

Kissed in a way that had made her breath stop and her heart thunder?

As he spoke, he brushed his thumb across her swollen lips while he slipped his other hand beneath her dressing gown.

She wore simple cotton beneath, the fabric soft and without restriction. He outlined the curve of her waist, the strength of her ribs and the swell of her breast. He had not meant to be so free with her, but he could not stop himself.

'Have you ever felt pleasure, Grace?'

He was speaking obliquely, but she understood.

'Not as you mean.' She curved her fingers around his waistcoat. 'I have never wanted it before. The risk was too great.'

His hand trembled beneath her breast. How he wanted to go further. It was taking all his willpower to hold himself back.

'Do you want me to touch you?'

She nodded, the movement of her chin jerky. 'Yes,' she whispered. 'Just…a little.'

Could he do it? Could he pleasure her 'just a little'?

He curved his hand up until he palmed her breast. He felt the sharp point of her nipple and the full weight of her. She was small compared to many women he had known, but her shape was exquisite. And even better was the way her breath caught as he held her.

Her eyes widened and her mouth parted on a pant. Then he rubbed his thumb back and forth across her peak and she trembled as she swayed towards him.

'Has anyone ever touched you like this?' he asked.

'Just you.'

He dropped his head to her neck, nuzzling beneath her ear and rubbing his teeth along the curve of her jaw. Her dark hair fell from its coil, spreading out across her shoulder. It was still short, but the feel of it made his knees weaken. Dark hair, golden skin, and the scent of sandalwood and honey.

He untied the ribbon of her nightrail. He used his mouth to brush apart the flap of cotton that shielded her breast.

'Declan…?' she whispered.

Her hands were tight on his waistcoat, and he idly wondered if she would tear the fabric. He didn't care if she ripped it apart.

'I want to show you pleasure,' he said. 'I want to teach you.'

So saying, he tried to tongue her nipple, but the cotton

shift did not open far enough. So he adjusted. He lifted her breast with his hand and set his mouth above the fabric. It was thin enough that he could use his teeth to bite her nipple, then suck it far into his mouth.

She cried out at that. A soft mew of delight. He caught her hips then, steadying her as she arched beneath him. Tightening his grip, he lifted her up and set her onto the table in the centre of the kitchen. It was sturdy wood and the right height. He could touch her this way, but not take her. The table was too high.

'I want to show you,' he murmured against her skin. 'I want to feel your first time.'

He set his hands to her knees, gently spreading them. The length of her nightrail prevented him opening her as he wished, but it was enough. He felt the heat between her thighs and smelled her musky scent.

But before he could touch her she gripped his arm. 'Even I know this is wrong.'

'I won't take you. I swear.'

'This is allowed?'

No, not exactly.

'This is something women teach each other,' he said. At least he had been told so. 'Where to touch. How it feels.' He shifted, pulling his hand away while setting hers on her own body. 'I won't do more,' he swore. 'But I will tell you what to do.'

And he would watch.

She bit her lip, clearly tempted.

'Can you be silent?' he asked.

She nodded, her eyes lighting with hunger.

'Is everyone asleep?'

'Yes,' she whispered.

'Then let me tell you what to do.'

He backed to the other side of the room until he was well out of reach.

'Has no one ever spoken of this to you before?'

'I have heard about when it can be good, but...'

'You didn't believe?'

'I didn't want to be tempted. I had other things to learn. How to navigate. How to fight.'

He nodded, awed again by her intelligence. But now she was tempted. *He* tempted her. And the thought surged heat through his body.

'I will tell you, and then you can learn on your own.' He gripped the back of a chair rather than reach for her. 'Widen your legs and lean back.'

She did as he bade. Slowly, carefully, and with a shyness that had the lust pounding through him. What a sight! Her muscular legs spread until her gown strained. She didn't mean to be seductive, but nothing was more enthralling to him than her inexpert motions as she pulled her nightrail up and up.

She stopped just short of giving him the full view. All he saw was shadow, though her scent tantalised.

'Set your fingers between your nether lips.'

'What?'

'There are folds between your legs.'

Her fingers began to explore.

'Move around until—'

She gasped, and he knew she had found it.

'Feel how wet you are?'

She nodded.

'Dip inside. Take that sweetness and stroke it up and down. Up and down. You'll find what you want.'

What an exquisite pleasure to watch her explore. Her one candle barely lighted her, but he could see her face, hear the sounds she made and see the changes in her body.

'Adjust how you touch, move your fingers in different ways. Discover yourself.' His voice rasped and his body pulsed with need, but he didn't move.

She looked at him, doubt in her eyes.

He did not know what the Chinese believed, but he knew what the priests here said about women pleasuring themselves.

'This isn't wrong,' he said, to himself as much as her. 'This is what you should learn about your own body.'

He said nothing more. Let her choose what she wanted. And he gloried in seeing her intimate explorations. He felt her every gasp like a gong in his body. He knew when her speed increased how wonderful she would be feeling. And he watched with his breath held because she was beautiful in her bliss.

Soon she was moving faster.

Soon her breath became soft gasps.

And then...

A single cry.

Her body shuddered. Her head dropped back.

'Yes,' he whispered. 'Oh, yes.'

He was ready to catch her if she fell. He was ready to kiss her into silence if need be. He was ready for any excuse to touch her, but she kept herself apart from him. Her body, even in the midst of bliss, was wholly her own. And he couldn't have been more impressed.

When she was spent, she sagged back against the table. She let her hand slip away and her legs fall together.

He dared come close then. He gently resettled her nightrail around her knees. Then he took the hand that she had used to pleasure herself and kissed it. Indeed, he drew the scent into his lungs and the taste into his mouth. He kissed her hand as he'd wanted to kiss her most intimate places.

And she returned the favour by touching his face, his hair, and the long stretch of his jaw.

'All Englishwomen know this?' she asked.

'No. But they should.'

'Then how do you?'

'There are women who teach men like me. Women who introduce us to pleasure.'

She nodded. 'Prostitutes.' There was no condemnation in her tone.

'Usually.'

'They offered to teach me.'

He winced that she had been in such close quarters with such women. The dangers they faced were myriad and often lethal.

'I chose to become China's greatest navigator instead.'

'A wise choice.' He pressed another kiss into her palm. 'And now you know their secrets.'

She shook her head, her gaze still languid. 'I bet there are many more to learn.'

He grinned. 'There are.'

'And you want to teach me.'

'Oh, yes.'

'No.'

The bluntness of her word jolted him. After what he had just witnessed, he had not expected such a final response. And into his confusion she smiled. It was a sweet expression, but it did not hide the determination beneath her words.

'I wanted to learn this,' she said, her voice a low whisper. 'I wanted you to teach me.'

His body jerked with hunger at that, but he knew better than to act on it.

'But this was improper.' It wasn't a question. 'And you said—'

'That women teach each other.'

'Because it's improper for a man to do it outside of marriage. Yes?'

He swallowed. 'Yes.'

She straightened and pulled the silk dressing gown about her shoulders. 'I wanted to learn this,' she said. 'I do not say you are at fault.'

Now he understood. 'But you will not risk more with me?'

'With anyone.'

That was something at least.

'It is time for you to leave,' she said.

Long past time. But he couldn't depart without asking one more thing. Why it was so important to him, he had no idea, but it had brought him to her door in the middle of the night just to see if she would answer.

'Will you tell me…?' His voice faded away. What an awkward question to ask.

'Yes?'

'What is your name in Chinese?'

She blinked, startled. 'Nayao. It means a person with grace or beauty. Enough that it is a unique quality that stands out.'

His brows rose. 'That is an excellent name for you.'

'What does your name mean?'

He frowned. 'Declan means that I am the Tenth Duke of Byrning.'

Her eyes widened. 'Your name is the same as your title?'

He shrugged. 'I suppose you could look at it that way.'

'Then you have no identity apart from that?'

'I—'

He clapped his mouth shut. He'd been about to claim that of course he was more than the title he'd been destined to inherit. Of course his identity was vastly more than his title.

And yet from his earliest days he had been reared to be the Duke of Byrning and all that entailed. Even his middle names were attributed to one ancestor or another, not to mention a saint thrown in there for good measure.

'I suppose my name is my heritage.'

'And I have no heritage except my name.'

Did that mean they were opposites? That there was a gulf between them that made them unsuitable?

Obviously not, given what they had just done. He couldn't think of a more suitable woman right now. And yet, despite what they had shared, she felt so far away from him. And exponentially more intriguing.

He opened his mouth to say something—he wasn't even sure what. Perhaps he just wanted to say her name again, to make it more familiar. But before he could form the syllables a thump sounded above them, then a series of weak coughs.

'Father,' she whispered.

Oh, dear. Lord Wenshire did not sound good.

'You must go!' she said, gesturing him out the door.

'Do I call a doctor?'

She shook his head. 'No. No, this is common.'

That was even worse. But as another thump sounded above stairs he knew his time was up. He had to leave without even a goodnight kiss. If he touched her even once now, he would not be able to tear himself away.

He gave her a last look. One that was filled with the desire for *more*. More conversation, more interaction, more touching. Instead, he gave her a quick bow and hurried away.

Chapter Nineteen

Declan barely slept that night. His thoughts kept returning to the sight of Grace—Nayao—bringing herself pleasure under his direction. What a sight! And he pleasured himself while remembering it.

But now it was morning, and he had a task to accomplish. He'd decided on this course several days ago, perhaps from the moment he'd first met Nayao. But last night's display required him to be more aggressive in his campaign. Which meant the mid-morning sun found him banging on his mother's door.

Once the haughty butler opened the door, he was tempted to barge straight upstairs into his mother's bedroom. After all, she'd done the same to him. But that was petty, so he opted for the manners appropriate to his title.

'Tell my mother that I await her in the library.'

His words and tone were abrupt. He preferred to be polite with his servants, but he knew that in this case Nagel approved of only the rudest manners from his superiors. It made no sense to him, but then the whims of polite society—even among their servants—rarely made rational sense.

Appropriately, Nagel bowed deeply to him and intoned, 'Yes, Your Grace. I have already sent for tea and a morning biscuit, if you'd like.'

'Yes, thank you.'

Damn it, he should have remembered not to thank him. He could hear the man's disapproving sigh as he headed for the library. His mother certainly did hire servants who reflected her attitudes.

He found his way to the library and seated himself at the desk there. It was his mother's desk, the drawers filled with her correspondence. As was normal for her, the top was pristine, the desk locked. He sat here merely for effect. This was his mother's seat of power, but he was the Duke. And he had every right to everything she owned.

She took her time coming downstairs. Long enough for him to enjoy several morning biscuits and a proper cup of tea, not to mention a good portion of the morning paper which Nagel had brought with breakfast.

'Have you lost all your money, Declan? Have you come to move in on my peace?'

'Good morning to you too, Mother.' His tone was rather cheerful, he thought. Must be the biscuits. They had put him in a good frame of mind.

'You're being overbearing. You're invading my library just because I woke you up on your birthday.'

He couldn't tell if she approved or if that was chastisement. Either way, she wasn't wrong. He leaned back in her chair and smiled at her.

'It was the day after my birthday, and you didn't remember it.'

'You're not a child who needs sweets.' She dropped down into the chair opposite the desk. 'What is it? Your aunt will be down at any moment and she'll want to know what Cedric is doing.'

'You already know what he's doing. He's trying to blackmail me into giving him ten thousand pounds.'

'It would be a loan.'

'It would not, and you know it, because he won't pay it back. And since when did you start defending Cedric?'

'When the alternative was him marrying that awful woman.'

Declan sighed. He really disliked going over the same ground with his mother. 'Miss Richards is not awful. Indeed, I find her rather compelling.'

The Duchess rolled her eyes at him. 'Every man enjoys watching a brawl, but that does not mean it belongs at a come-out ball.'

Ah. So she had heard about last night.

'Lord Jasper deserved punishment.'

'Then *you* should have given it to him outside of the ballroom. Ladies of the *ton* do not mete out justice like common ruffians.'

He didn't respond because he knew it was true. Gentlemen were supposed to keep each other in check, but the opposite was often true. They egged each other on into wilder acts all in the name of fun, and be damned to whoever got hurt in the process.

'Neither she nor I would have had to do anything had you not sent the worst of society to that ball. So I lay what happened at your feet, Mother.'

Far from being chastised, she smiled. 'I merely created a situation whereby everyone could see her true colours.' His mother lifted her chin to peer down her nose at him. 'Miss Richards will never be accepted in polite society now.'

'Really?'

'Really. Lord Jasper may never be able to have children. Did you know that?'

'I don't care.' Indeed, part of him hoped it was true.

'Well, his mother cares. And see how I was able to accomplish what I directed you to do without even being present?'

'And what do you think you have accomplished?'

'She's banned from society. Cedric can't marry her now.'

And there was his mother's greatest flaw. She seemed to think that the world was made up of the *haut ton* alone. All other people existed to serve. Ergo, if Miss Richards was not in society, Cedric could not marry her.

'You're wrong, Mother. Cedric will marry her for her dowry. He's never cared for society or its games. All you have done is play directly into his hands.'

'Don't be ridiculous. He has a great deal of pride. He will never marry someone so outré.'

He shook his head. 'You underestimate him, Mother. The only way to keep Cedric from marrying her is to get her married to someone else.'

'Just give him the money!' snapped a voice from the hallway.

It was his aunt.

As was appropriate, Declan rose from his seat and bowed to the Countess. But when he straightened, his expression and his voice were hard.

'No.'

'Why ever not?' His aunt dropped her hands to her hips. 'You don't spend it. Everyone else is buying houses and boats and whatnot. Cedric should get the same as everyone else.'

Declan sighed, looking at the drawn face of his aunt. He usually avoided the woman because she was so shrewish, but also because he knew he would be equally awful if he had to live her life. Her husband was an inveterate gambler who had charmed her when she was too young to know better. Now she lived on his mother's generosity and was pitied throughout the *ton*. Her only hope for salvation was in Cedric, whom she coddled as if he were a babe in the woods.

Except now he saw how his forbearance had damaged

the entire family. Cedric thought he could blackmail the duchy, Cedric's father was off gambling money he did not have, and now his mother stood here speaking to him as if he were her maid.

This could not continue, and so he set his own hands on his hips.

'Cedric gets what his parents give him.' Which, as everyone in this room knew, was nothing but debt. 'You get food, clothing, and a home because of my mother. And if you are very careful I will find a way to help your daughters, whom you seem to have abandoned.'

'Do not speak to me of my children!'

'Very well,' he said. 'I will not dower them.'

It was a lie. He already sent regular funds to his female cousins, and he definitely planned to help with their dowries when the time came.

'We are your family!' the woman cried.

'And I am the head of that family, so mind your tongue.'

His aunt tried to object. She puffed herself up to her largest height to glare down her nose at him, which was hard, given that he was taller than her. But such a position had no effect on him. Indeed, he was ready to throw her back to her country estate, where she could work the fields as his cousins sometimes did. Though, to be fair, his cousin Cora claimed she enjoyed farming.

In any event, he did not move except to slowly raise one eyebrow at her. That was enough for her to collapse sideways into a chair, where she began to weep with great drama.

'You see,' his mother said as she patted his aunt on the shoulder. 'We cannot accept that woman into our family. It would destroy everything.'

'No, Mother, it would not. And you are a fool to suggest such a thing.'

The Duchess's eyes widened in shock at his statement, and he honestly couldn't understand why. Then it came to him. He had not spoken in anger, and neither had he swallowed down his thoughts out of fear that he was overreacting. His words had been calm, rational, and implacable. And apparently she could not believe that he could be so controlled.

'Are you well, Declan? You are speaking like a mad man.' When his aunt set off on another wail, she squeezed the woman's shoulder. 'Leave us, Agatha. You're upsetting the Duke.'

Agatha gaped at the Duchess for a moment, but she quickly realised she was not helping her own cause. Burying her face in her handkerchief, she headed out of the room, though her sobs continued.

Meanwhile, his mother focused on him and continued her campaign.

'It's my fault,' she said as she claimed his aunt's chair. 'I was so terrified of your father's moods that I kept him away from you. He couldn't teach you the proper way to be a duke. If he were here now, he would tell you that a Chinese girl cannot marry Cedric. It's simply not proper.'

'Mother—'

'Think, Declan. Do you know anyone with a foreign wife?'

'Yes, I do.'

'Not *Chinese* foreign! Good God, even a Spanish wife is frowned upon. You know it is true.'

He did know. But it was true because women like his mother and aunt were leaders in society. They decided who was allowed and who was not. So what she was truly saying was that *she* would not accept a foreign girl, and she would make sure everyone else reviled her, too.

Thank God he was the head of the family. He now realised he had been too lax, choosing to ignore society, avoid his mother and aunt, and generally bury his head in his ledgers while he set the ducal estates to rights. But now he saw how arrogant his relatives had become, thinking they could dictate not only his actions, but society's as well.

This had to end now.

'Mother, I will not bandy words with you. You will repair the damage to Miss Richards' reputation.' He spoke calmly, but he could see that his mother wasn't receptive.

'No one could do that!' she exclaimed. 'The moment Miss Richards punched Lord Jasper, she put herself beyond the pale. No hostess will accept her now.'

'Nevertheless, you will do it. You will do as I ask because I am the Duke. You will do it because Cedric will marry her if she doesn't have another option.' Those words choked him, but he continued. 'And you will do it because I will no longer tolerate your ridiculous games. If you must meddle in people's lives, sponsor a charity. What you are doing here—setting yourself against a woman merely because she is Chinese—is beneath you. It is beneath the title you hold, and I will not allow it.'

'You will not allow it?' she cried, gaping at him.

'That is correct.' He tapped his chin, as if he hadn't already decided on what would happen now. 'I believe vouchers to Almack's will be a good start.'

'Almack's! Never!'

'And you must tell all your friends to invite her to their social events.'

'You have gone mad!'

'It is either find her a new husband or accept that Cedric will marry her.'

The words burned in his gut, but he kept his expression bored, as if he cared not one whit what she chose. It was a lie, of course. He was here championing Nayao's cause because he very much cared that Cedric did *not* marry her. Nor anyone else for that matter.

Somehow, during the night, he had decided that she would be his. He didn't know how he'd manage it. Indeed, he feared that she set off so many feelings inside him that it would be a terrible disaster. But he had now realised how much more of a disaster it would be if she went to anyone else.

He might very well go insane if that were the case.

Oblivious to his decision, his mother made a gesture of frustration. 'You cannot think she is remotely attractive. Perhaps as a mistress, but a wife?' She shook her head. 'No, even Cedric is not so reckless.'

'Mother, Miss Richards is strong, clever, and so much more than any woman I have ever met. Different, powerful, and capable of things I have never seen before.'

His admiration for her rang loudly in the suddenly quiet room. He could see that his mother was genuinely confused. She wasn't arguing his decree, necessarily, but trying to talk around his logic.

'Every man enjoys novelty, Declan. A cow is novel, too, but one doesn't marry it.'

A cow was one of the least novel things in England, and damn his mother for comparing Nayao to cattle! He sighed, trying to work out a path here. Yesterday had opened his eyes on so many levels. Ever since he'd met Nayao she'd quietly challenged his blind assumptions. His mind felt open for the first time in his life, open and willing to look at the world through new eyes. And not just the world, but his own family and their limitations.

'Miss Richards is like a wild rose, growing against all odds.'

'On a dung heap? Even you must admit the stench.'

No, he did not. To his mother, everything but a very tiny

corner of England was a dung heap. To him, there was a very large world out there, and Nayao tempted him as no one else.

'I think she is fascinating,' he said. 'And I am not the only one. So if you don't want her marrying Cedric, I suggest you make her appealing to respectable men.'

'Respectable! But then I would have to see her at parties. She would become part of the *ton,* if not the *haut ton.*'

He shrugged. 'Would you prefer her at the family Christmas dinner?'

His mother shuddered at the thought, but Declan smiled at the image. He would enjoy seeing Nayao lighting the yule log. And he would definitely enjoy kissing her under the mistletoe.

'Get her a voucher, Mother,' he instructed as he headed for the door. 'Immediately.'

'Or what?'

A very good question.

'Or I shall pay for Cedric's special licence myself.'

He walked out on her gasp of outrage and headed to his club. Or that was what he'd intended. Instead, he directed his coachman to take him home. He wanted a bath before he showed up on Miss Richards' doorstep and asked to take her riding in Hyde Park.

And bathe he did. He even allowed his valet to tie his cravat in a complicated affair that took twenty minutes to settle right. His boots were polished to a mirror shine, and his signet ring had a quick clean.

Which was why it was rather upsetting that when he finally presented himself at Miss Richards' home he found he was not the first to command her attention. Indeed, the parlour was filled with blackguards and fortune-hunters. And that included his cousin.

Chapter Twenty

Grace knew the moment the Duke entered the room. Of course she did. He was dressed to perfection, he carried himself as if he were the Emperor himself, and yet in his eyes she saw a clear hunger. She felt it across the room, she knew it every time their eyes met, and she burned with it whenever she heard his voice.

He burned for her. And she for him.

She could not forget his touch, his kiss, or the low rasp of his voice as he had instructed her. He had not touched her most intimate places, and yet last night she had felt as if every stroke had been made by him. She'd tried to recreate the experience alone, but it was not nearly as satisfying without him.

They exchanged the usual pleasantries. He was one of a throng of men who apparently wished to further their acquaintance with her. She knew it was because of her dowry, but that didn't stop her from appreciating the flattery. Never before had she been the subject of such approval—even if it was false. Even Lucy seemed to glow from the attention. She had been allowed to join the salon, and her normally composed demeanour was flushed pink.

This was heady stuff for two girls who had lived in constant danger of being killed just because they were neither white nor Chinese.

When the Duke's face tightened with anger whenever she smiled at someone other than him, she felt a surge of satisfaction. It was petty of her, but he had consumed her thoughts for so long there was a measure of satisfaction in seeing him think he was only one among many. It wasn't true, of course. She saw only him. She felt only him. But she pretended to be fascinated by all the others, including his cousin.

Her walk to Hyde Park later was uneventful, probably because the Duke did not join the crowd that went to promenade. And the ball she attended that night was equally boring.

The Duke arrived late, so she had no dances left for him. He arrived on time the next night and managed to write his name down twice on her card. But when he swept her into his arms for the waltz they said not one word to one another.

They didn't need to.

When his hands touched her body she was right back in the kitchen. She was touching herself as he told her what to do, what to feel. It all rushed back into her mind and body, such that their waltz left her breathless with need.

When the dance was done, he slowly released her body. His gaze roved over her, burning everything it touched, and then he spoke.

'I cannot stop thinking about you.'

'I am the same.'

Her words didn't make logical sense. But when he looked at her like that she became too lost to think clearly in another language.

And then the chance was over as her next partner claimed her.

He left soon after that.

The next night was an excursion to the theatre. At the Duke's invitation, both her father and Lucy were allowed to attend too. Grace had never seen a theatre before, and the experience enchanted her. Best of all was the way he walked with her during the interval. They went from box to box, with her on his arm. She was introduced to important people who greeted her kindly merely because he stood beside her. She exchanged pleasantries with powerful Englishmen and their haughty wives. Another time, she might have trembled at their reluctant acceptance. She knew how quickly that would change if ever she was away from the Duke.

But she was not apart from him, and so she stood tall and spoke clearly.

When the interval was over, the Duke patted her hand and smiled at her.

'You did very well,' he murmured as they headed back to his box. 'I'm impressed.'

'That was nothing to do with me,' she said. 'That was about your power here in England. They sought not to offend you.'

'And they found no fault with you.'

She doubted that. There would be whispers, but with him beside her she didn't care.

She cared even less when he abruptly ducked them into a side corridor. It was dark, and secluded, and she should have been terrified to be caught like that.

She wasn't.

She was thrilled as he pressed her against the wall.

'Grace... Nayao.' He spoke her name reverently as he caressed her cheek, framing her face with his hands. 'I dream of you every night.'

She nodded. He hadn't even asked her if she did the same, but she answered nonetheless. 'You are in my thoughts always.'

Then their lust overcame their senses as he slowly, inexorably, pressed his full body against hers.

She gasped at the feel of him on top of her. She could not

run, she could not escape, and all she wanted to do was raise her knee along his flank as he kissed her.

He lowered his mouth to her ear, the heat of his breath stirring the hair along her face and neck. He said nothing, though she was tensed for words. Instead, he stroked his tongue along her flesh, her jaw, her neck.

She felt his thickness against her groin. She knew when it pulsed with need. She didn't even realise she had pressed upwards against him until she heard his hiss.

'What am I to do?' he murmured.

As if she knew.

'I cannot stay away from you.'

He kissed her then, deep and hard, while his hands roved over her breasts. She arched into his touch. She ached to give him everything. And when they broke apart to breathe he continued to touch her everywhere, even as he whispered into her ear.

'You cannot marry any of those men. They want only your fortune.'

She knew that. 'No one wants me for myself.'

He pulled back. He looked her in the eyes. 'I do,' he said. 'I think this is love.'

He spoke the words as if they terrified him. As if loving her were a terrible thing.

'Why do you say it like that?' she asked. 'Why is love so awful?'

His head drooped then, setting gently against her forehead. 'Is love enough?' he asked, and the words sounded more for himself than for her. But then he raised his head up to look her in the eye. 'Do you want to be part of this world? Do you know how people will treat you when I am not by your side?'

She did. After all, she'd been to balls, teas, and musical

evenings. He hadn't been at all of them, and he certainly hadn't been at her side the whole time. Most people were polite to her. A few said mean things. Several wanted to further their acquaintance with her. But she didn't know if it was for herself or because they wanted the connection to him.

In his world, she had only him as a bulwark against hate. And yet that was still more than she'd ever had in her life. There'd been people who had supported her, else she never would have survived. But he was different. He loved her. She could feel it in his touch. She knew it in his desperation to be with her. And she felt in her thrumming heart.

She loved him.

The knowledge rolled through her with the force of a tidal wave, and she embraced the feeling as new and exciting.

But one look at him destroyed all her budding happiness.

He saw it as a disaster. For him, the truth was obvious.

'Love is not enough for you,' she said. It might be for her, but clearly it wasn't for him. 'You don't want a wife who detracts.'

'You don't *detract* from anything!'

And yet in his eyes she saw doubt and fear.

'I feel so much when I am with you,' he said. 'It's not you I fear,' he said. 'It's myself.'

She couldn't help him, then.

He had to resolve this in his own mind before they could have a future.

But still she couldn't resist touching his face, stroking his lips and whispering her own words into his mouth. As if she could make him say the words to her.

'I love you,' she said, but she didn't think he heard it.

He was too busy kissing her throat, stroking her breasts, making her insane with need. And then he plundered her mouth, twisting his tongue around hers, teasing the roof of her mouth and thrusting in and out as if they could make love right there in the theatre.

Her knees weakened and she gripped his shoulders to hold herself upright. He curled an arm around her back. He supported her as he thrust against her—above and below—over and over. Was it possible to attain bliss from just this? A kiss and a thrust through thick layers of fabric?

She thought it was.

Her heart was thundering, her body willing. He could have done it. He could have lifted her skirts right then and she would not have stopped him.

How he found the strength to resist, she didn't know.

But, with a growl that reverberated from his body into hers, he drew back. Then he slammed his palm down hard on the wall beside her body. He hung his head as his breath heaved in and out.

'I cannot,' he growled.

He could have. She would have allowed it. And what madness was that?

She didn't argue with him. What good would that do? But she could ask him what he meant by this. By kissing her in a dark corridor and then stopping.

'What do you want?' she whispered.

He lifted his head. His gaze roved over her face. His body trembled, still close enough to her that she knew he ached.

'What I cannot have.'

'Why not? Aren't you a great mandarin among your people? A leader? A duke? Every soul here bows to your presence.'

'Only to my face.' He snorted. 'I cannot explain the intricacies of English politics to you.'

'I could learn.'

His head tilted as he looked to her. 'I suppose you could… But why ever would you want to descend into that madness?'

For him.

'You say you are afraid of yourself with me. That makes no sense. What do I do to you?'

'You make me feel!' he all but shouted. Then he sighed. 'And when I feel, I am afraid of what I will do.'

He meant his rages. He meant beating up his cousin in Hyde Park. He meant his legacy of destruction.

'But I am not afraid of you,' she said. 'Even at your worst I was never afraid.'

It was the truth, and she saw her words hit him full force. His body jolted, his eyes widened, and hunger burned hot in his eyes. But she still saw doubt in his face, and knew he held himself back from her, as he held himself away from everything.

He was a man so controlled that he denied himself everything, she realised. Even love.

And then they were out of time. She heard a noise from down the corridor. People. Whispers. A couple no doubt doing exactly as they were. It was enough to make the Duke jerk back from her.

'Do you know where my box is?' he asked.

'What?'

'Do you know how to return to my box?'

She nodded. They were barely ten steps from it.

'Apologise to your father for me. I shall leave my carriage for your use.'

'What? Why?'

He stroked his thumb across her lower lip. And as he did so he wet his own. She lifted her hand to his face, but it never arrived there. He grasped it quickly, then slowly, inexorably, lowered it down his body. While her breath caught, he pressed her hand to his organ.

She felt heat and thickness. The thrum of a heartbeat, or perhaps it was the rumble of her own. Either way, he thrust into her palm. His eyes fluttered closed and he dropped his head back.

She began to grip him. How could she not?

But he pulled her hand away.

'I cannot be seen like this. And I cannot stay near you without it.'

'But—'

He kissed her again. His tongue nearly undid her. But then he pulled away.

He scanned her quickly, then twisted to open a side door.

'It's empty,' he whispered. 'Go quickly.'

'But—'

He gave her no time to speak. He pushed her firmly through the door, then closed it behind her. What could she do but exactly as he wanted?

She went back to his box, she made apologies for him, and then she sat down next to her sister while her entire body throbbed with need.

That was bad enough.

But then it happened again in a secluded alcove at the next night's ball. And again in the instrument room during a musical evening. It was crazy. They would get caught eventually. But she could not seem to stop herself. Or him.

Which was why, when the summons came, she went immediately to see his mother. If anyone understood the Duke's intentions, then it would be the Dowager Duchess. Didn't English men revere their mothers? If she could get through the lady's arrogant disdain, she might finally understand what he wanted.

Chapter Twenty-One

Grace tried not to be impressed by the London abode of the Dowager Duchess of Byrning. She'd been there before, for that first disastrous tea, but she hadn't understood things as well as she did now. Now she knew that this place was owned by the Duchess alone and housed herself and her sister. The large staff supported only two souls, and that made it a grand palace.

Certainly there were such edifices in China, but she'd been a half-white orphan who could only look at them from afar. Today she was walking into one by invitation. And, though she'd attended balls in other private residences, she had been one of many attending a party. Today she entered alone except for her maid, who was immediately swept away below stairs.

That left her feeling small behind a sour-looking butler as he escorted her past footmen to a different parlour from the one she had been in before. This one was called 'intimate', and it was larger than some boats.

The butler left her one step inside the door. It took her a moment to survey the room and see—fully at the opposite end—the Duchess of Byrning and the Countess of Hillburn, sitting on ornate chairs as if they were thrones. They were, of course, the mothers of Declan and Cedric, and they did not look friendly, for all that they smiled and gestured for her to sit.

She could already tell this was not going to be easy, but she also knew that they wouldn't beat her or whip her.

'I'm so glad you could join us, Miss Richards,' intoned the Duchess. 'I assume you know who we are?'

She did, and she curtseyed to each in turn, with her head bowed and her legs steady. 'Your Grace, my lady,' she said. 'I am pleased to renew our acquaintance.'

They will not beat me. They will not beat me.

She repeated that over and over, to give herself perspective. No matter how intimidating the circumstances, these women would not physically harm her. It wasn't done in England—at least not between women who shared tea with one another—so she was safe. And, even more important, if her physical body was not in danger, what harm could a few words do? Worst case, she would be insulted, and that had been so common in her life that it felt no more substantial than air.

She sat down in a chair placed opposite them. The tea tray arrived without use of a bell or any kind of signal. There was also a display of sandwiches and tarts, which no one touched.

'How do you take your tea, Miss Richards?' the Duchess asked.

'Strong,' she answered, 'and without addition.'

It wasn't meant to be a challenge. It was merely the truth. To her, sugar and milk were luxuries, and she was not used to such things.

'Ah,' the Duchess said as she set the pot down. 'Then we shall allow it to sit a while longer.'

'Pray do not wait on my account,' she said with a smile. 'There is no reason to deny yourself your preference.' She meant it as a courtesy, but the Countess sniffed in an expression of disapproval.

'That is not the way it is done,' the lady intoned. 'If the guest waits, then we all wait.'

What was she to say to that? If the women wanted to drink tea they disliked, she was in no position to stop them. She dipped her chin and waited. After a dozen breaths, she finally spoke.

'I'm sure the tea is fine now. I should be very grateful for a cup.'

The Duchess poured. She served Grace first, then the Countess, before pouring her own. And when the beverage was adjusted to their liking, they both lifted their cups in a single co-ordinated movement. With their gazes fixed on Grace, they sipped their tea.

She scrambled to drink as well. She didn't know the exact timing. Was she to delay drinking while they sipped? Were they all to drink at once? Surely she should know this by now? And wasn't that a measure of how rattled she was, that she couldn't remember even so simple a thing as the English tea ceremony?

The tea wasn't bracing enough. But then, no tea could be strong enough to combat the sheer intimidation of these two women. The contrast to her first cup of tea in this house was marked. Where the Countess had been mean and petty, the Duchess was reserved, careful with the niceties, and appeared every inch an empress.

They will not beat me.

They would, however, make her sit in uncomfortable silence as they drank and stared at her. Until now, she had not realised how a long stare would be so much more effective when given in exquisite timing with another. These two women had perfected it to the point that she was beginning to sweat.

'I suppose you are wondering why you have been asked to tea,' the Duchess intoned.

'I do not ask such questions, Your Grace,' she said, in full honesty.

'Wise of you,' the woman said. 'Nevertheless, we shall alleviate your curiosity.'

Grace set her teacup down into its saucer. She waited. And she waited even longer. Oddly enough, this game of pauses was having a calming effect on her. Only women with nothing else to do could spend so much time in pauses. She had been trained at the temple in meditative silences. So she sat, she breathed, and she waited. Eventually they would come to their point.

Besides, this was the worst they could do to her. There was nothing to fear.

Eventually Cedric's mother spoke, her voice stiff and her expression one of extreme distaste. 'It has come to our attention that our sons have behaved with an extraordinary lack of kindness.'

What?

The Duchess set down her teacup. 'To you, Miss Richards. They have been unkind towards you.'

What was she supposed to say to that? 'I don't know—'

'Don't interrupt,' the Countess chided. 'They are men, and therefore unaware that their games can have a profound effect upon the fairer sex.'

'We taught them better,' said the Duchess.

'Most assuredly so,' said the Countess.

'But men play games and never think twice about us.'

The Countess nodded, and they both looked to her as if it were her turn to speak.

'About us?' Grace asked.

'Yes. Us women,' the Countess stressed. 'They don't think about us.'

'About *you*, Miss Richards,' inserted the Duchess. 'They don't think about how their game might affect you, and for that we have brought you here to explain.'

'Explain?' Grace asked.

'Yes, Miss Richards. Pay attention,' the Countess huffed. 'My son Cedric—Lord Domac to you—needs ten thousand pounds to buy a boat and cargo. Some business about selling things to the Chinese?'

Grace nodded. She already knew this. He'd been very open about how he would spend her dowry.

'It is difficult,' said the Duchess, 'to admit that one's nephew is a fortune-hunter, but there it is. He was courting you for your dowry.'

'That's not true,' said the Countess, and she turned away from Grace to address the Duchess directly. 'He had no plan to actually marry her. He was just using her to get the family to invest with him.' She turned back to Grace. 'You're unsuitable, you see. You must know that. He's to be an earl one day, and he must marry a woman of appropriate breeding. It was just one of his games. A way to get money from the family because they'd rather that than see him marry someone unsuitable.' She paused for a long moment, then curled her lip. 'You.'

Grace held her tongue. She already knew this, and yet they were speaking as if it was the deepest secret.

'It's all very distasteful,' the Duchess fumed. 'Lord Domac threatened to marry you if the family did not give him ten thousand pounds.' She shook her head. 'I knew I had to intervene, and I went straight to Declan.' She pointed her fan at Grace. 'The Duke of Byrning to you.'

Yes, she knew who Declan was.

'You did the sensible thing, my dear,' the Countess said with a fond smile. Then she turned back to Grace. 'She asked her son to intervene and put an end to Cedric's nonsense.'

'I meant him to speak to Cedric,' the Duchess huffed. 'Instead, he thought he would have some fun—'

'Fun!' the Countess sniffed.

'Fun—the idiot boy.' The Duchess shook her head. 'He set about gathering the funds, of course, but he had to delay your growing infatuation with Lord Domac. I did not think he'd make such a spectacle of himself by courting you.'

'To be fair,' the Countess said, '*she* is the spectacle, not him. Nevertheless, Miss Richards, it was cruel of him to engage your affections.'

'Most cruel…' said the Duchess.

'And so you have been brought to tea so that we can explain the way of things.'

'So you will understand.' The Duchess leaned forward. 'You do understand, do you not?'

She did, she supposed. These ladies were explaining the shallowest aspects of what was happening between herself and their sons as if she could not understand them on her own.

'It is a boy's game,' the Duchess emphasised.

'It isn't real. None of it,' the Countess continued.

'And you are telling me this because it's cruel?' She didn't elaborate on who was being cruel—these ladies or their sons.

The Countess pursed her lips. 'We are telling you this so you will not put any thought to marriage with either of our sons.'

The Duchess tapped her fan into her palm several times before she spoke again. 'Pray, let me be blunt. You are a foreigner, not versed in our ways. We fear that you do not understand that there are expectations of a duke's wife—'

'And an earl's!'

'—that a foreigner is simply not able to fulfil.'

Now they were getting to the point. But she needed them to put it more plainly. 'What kind of expectations?'

'Duties. Tasks. They're quite significant,' said the Duchess.

'Exhausting and unending,' echoed the Countess.

That wasn't specific enough.

'I am a hard worker, my ladies,' Grace said. 'And a quick study. Both your sons have expressed awe at my accomplishments.'

The Duchess waved her fan in the air. 'But they would, you see. That was all part of their game.'

The Countess released a heavy sigh. 'She doesn't understand. Look at her. She hasn't the wits to comprehend.'

If anyone was lacking in wits, it was them, for underestimating her so thoroughly. She'd known from the beginning that it wasn't likely that the English would accept her any more than the Chinese had. Both countries saw her as half of a whole rather than a full person. But her father had told her his status would change things. No one had protected her in China, he'd argued, but he would protect her in England. His name would keep her from being discarded.

And she now saw it was true. After all, she'd known from the first moment that his status would prevent her from being beaten by these women. She would not be whipped for daring to speak to their sons. She would not be poisoned or stabbed or in any way physically damaged for her audacity.

What she hadn't realised until this very moment was that lies could hurt so much more than a beating. She knew that every moment she had spent with Declan had been more than a game. She felt it in her heart. But her head questioned it.

Could a man reared by such women truly feel love for

her? Or had she simply believed what her heart wanted her to? Was it likely that most English gentlemen were like her very unusual and generous father? Or was it more likely that her father was unique and that the men of his country were like the men everywhere else in the world? They play with lives—with *her* life—as a game with each other?

And while she struggled with her doubts she heard the door behind her burst open. The next sound was loud, the heavy tread of boot heels echoing in the large chamber. She knew who it was before she heard his voice. But even so, she braced herself from the sheer impact of his tones. They were heavy with fury, for all that his words sounded polite.

'Mother! Aunt!' said the Duke. 'What tales are you spreading today?'

Chapter Twenty-Two

Information came to Declan in a variety of ways. Rarely, however, did it come from his valet in the middle of the afternoon, and in his library, no less. Turner had walked right in, held up a cravat, and offered to help him put it on before tea at his mother's.

Declan hadn't intended to go anywhere near his mother, but at his valet's significant look he'd agreed.

Which was when he had learned that Turner had heard that a maid had overheard the footman saying to someone else... He couldn't follow it all. But the main point was that Grace was set to have tea with his mother and his aunt, and that could not be good.

He'd headed straight for his mother's house, to discover that everything Turner had said was correct. There sat his mother and aunt, as if in judgement over Grace, who was looking pale but seemingly composed.

Not a good sign. Grace became animated when happy, and right now a statue would show more signs of life.

'Mother! Aunt! What tales are you spreading today?' he asked.

When all three women looked at him with shocked expressions, he turned his question into a joke. 'I hope you're not telling that silly tale of me running out of the house naked when I was four.'

'You were five,' his mother said as she lifted her face for a kiss, 'and you were protesting the need for a bath.'

'Good thing Nanny caught me before I became lost.' He turned and greeted his aunt, then finally was able to bow over Miss Richards' hand. 'You must share what stories they have been telling. Allow me to defend my honour.'

He kept his tone light, but the words were meant with his whole heart. He knew his mother and aunt could be intimidating, especially to a woman only recently thrust into the social whirl. Which was why he had rushed over here. He did not like the idea of them anywhere around her, much less alone with her and in such a setting.

'They told me the tale of my dowry,' Grace said, her voice flat. 'And that neither you nor Cedric will ever marry me. Indeed, they said it was all a game from Cedric to extort ten thousand pounds.' She waved her hand vaguely in the air. 'I don't quite understand the details. Only that you and Lord Domac have been courting me in a game and I was the…' She winced as the word left her mouth. 'Toy.'

He shot an angry glare at his relations, but he didn't bother with them. Instead, he touched her hand. 'You know that's not true.'

She arched a brow at him. 'I know it *is* true. At least in part. I have known Cedric's purpose from the beginning.'

'But not mine.'

She met his gaze, her feelings completely unreadable.

'No,' she agreed, 'not yours.'

He swallowed. This was not something he wished to discuss with his mother and aunt watching. So he squeezed her fingers. 'Let us go for a walk. We can discuss this in private.'

He watched her eyes flicker, and he read so many conflicting emotions in them. But none had a chance to settle because his mother refused to be ignored.

'Step away from her, Declan. You've been cruel,' she said, her voice as cold as the arctic. 'It is heinous to raise a woman's hopes when you have no intention—when you *never* had any intention—of fulfilling them.'

'What hopes?'

'Marriage, you idiot boy!' his mother snapped. 'You let her believe you'd wed her!'

He straightened up to his full height, the familiar tide of fury burning dark in his vision. In that one moment he remembered all the times his father had raged at his mother. All the reasons why his cold, calculating mother deserved the hatred that burned in him.

'She thinks she is protecting you,' Grace said, her voice low.

When he looked down at her, he watched her gaze turn troubled.

'Is she?' she asked.

'What?'

'Protecting you from your feelings for me? Protecting you from a disastrous choice in marriage?'

'That is not her concern!' he snapped.

Grace had the audacity to roll her eyes. 'She is your mother. You are her son and heir. Your choices affect her profoundly. Of course she is concerned.'

He gaped at her, but not for the reason she likely suspected. He was shocked that the rage in his blood had cooled. A few simple words from Grace, and the black tide receded.

That had never happened before.

Meanwhile, Grace slowly stood to her full height, matching him in dignity. 'Is she right?'

He blinked, trying to shift his thoughts from his rationality to what he was being asked. It was true, his mother was indeed worried about exactly the same things he was.

Marriage to a mixed-race woman would damage his power in politics, his influence in social circles, and it would definitely carry down to his children.

He now saw how ridiculous that thought was. Indeed, he'd spent the entire night thinking about just what she meant to him, and how little he cared about everything else. Political and social influence ruled his mother's mind, but meant little to him. Whatever sway they'd once had over him was now dwarfed by what Grace gave to him.

Around her, he felt alive. She calmed his rages and brought new thoughts into his world.

That was worth everything to him!

Meanwhile, his mother snorted in satisfaction. She thought that his silence was an admission.

'I believe we have made our point, Miss Richards.' She held up a large engraved envelope. And while she waited for Grace's attention, she spread her fingers to show that there were actually three envelopes. 'I have in my hand a voucher to Almack's. Not just one, but three—one for you, one for your sister, and one for that chit Miss Phoebe Gray. I have invitations for them all—'

'Mother,' he interrupted. 'You cannot buy her off—'

His mother continued as if he hadn't spoken. 'You aren't aware of it, but admission there—especially at my invitation—will establish all three of you with the *haut ton*. You will become respectable, and every man in attendance will also be respectable. No more of those fortune-hunters and card sharps.'

'You forget that Cedric is one of those fortune-hunters,' he growled.

His aunt sent him a caustic look before she stepped in. 'We shall give you our support. We shall make each of you a viable flower on the Marriage Mart—'

'Provided,' continued his mother, 'that you do not look to our sons.'

Declan folded his arms. 'You will give her the vouchers and support them either way, or I shall make life very unpleasant for you both.'

Grace sighed. 'Do not threaten them. It only makes them more afraid.'

He turned to her. 'But what does it mean for you?' He gestured to his relations. 'They are not unique. They will never accept you, no matter what you do. Not as I do, Nayao.'

He used her Chinese name deliberately, so she knew he referred to all of her. But in his mind she was always Grace—not as a name, but as an attribute. For all that she had suffered in life, she was the epitome of poise and refinement.

He watched her eyes grow sharp. They hopped between him and the ladies.

'And what of your children?' she asked. 'Would they accept them?'

He flinched. He already knew the answer. His mother would decry the blood in her grandchildren. Their every fault would be laid at Grace's door. Their every gain declared due to his blue blood.

The light in Grace's eyes died out. 'I know what it is to be without family. It is a terrible thing.' Tears welled in her eyes, but she blinked them back. 'I will not do that to your children.'

They had never talked about children before this moment, but at her words he saw them in his mind's eye. Bright, inquisitive, exploring the world in ways he'd never managed.

'Our children will be raised in a way we never were,' he said. He touched her hand. 'You will be an incredible mother. And I will do everything to guide our children.'

He would make sure that the legacy of rage ended with him.

'But you said it yesterday,' she pressed. 'You said that love was not enough.'

'You said that,' he corrected. 'And I think you are wrong.'

She looked at him, then back at his mother and aunt.

'Don't look at them. They don't matter. Talk to me,' he said as he gently drew her face back to his.

'Yesterday you said you cannot have me. Now you are here telling me to ignore them and their fears. What has changed?'

How did he explain the extraordinary changes she had wrought in him? How did he tell her that the things he'd once valued seemed unimportant now? That there were emotions beyond rage and intellectual curiosity, feelings that he wanted to experience with her?

These were not easy things to say, and certainly not in front of his mother, but he'd try his best.

'I heard you,' he whispered. 'I heard you say you love me.'

He saw her wince, as if her love was painful for her. And apparently it was, because she stepped away from him.

'Love does not solve everything,' she said. Then she looked to his mother and aunt. 'I had love growing up. The monk who raised me, the navigator who taught me and the captain who protected me—they were each like a parent to me. They showed me love and taught me things that fill me even now.' Her voice broke as she looked back to Declan. 'You have never known that kind of love. One that is generous and supportive. So when you finally experience it, you grab it with both hands.'

She looked down at her own hands as she spoke and slowly curled them into fists.

'But it is not enough,' she said loudly. 'Love, no matter how strong, cannot fill your emptiness when an entire society reviles you. Better never to have children than to watch them suffer when their own grandmother despises them.' She lifted her chin to look directly at Declan. 'And I hope I may not be here when you realise my love is not enough for you.'

'Nayao, of course it is—' he began, but he never got the chance to say more.

Her gaze had swept back to his mother. 'I accept your vouchers and their conditions. I shall enjoy meeting the best of English society. And then I shall happily turn my back on all of you. My father and I will live in Italy without any of you.'

She turned to leave, but he caught her arm. 'Please, Grace. You were never my toy. And this has never been a game to me.'

'I know,' she said, her voice barely audible. 'But it is for them. And I can never be a winner in it. Which means you will always be the loser, and your children even more so. Eventually you will realise that, and whatever is between us will end.'

He shook his head. 'That's not true. That doesn't even make sense!'

'Maybe not to you, but your children will know. And I will know. It is a terrible life.'

And with that, she swept forward. His mother was ready, holding the vouchers out. Grace took them and departed.

He didn't stop her. He knew now was not the time to confront her. But what pain seared through him, watching her leave!

More than he'd expected, more than he thought rational. More, indeed, than he had ever experienced before.

What was this agony? Why did rage burst through him as the door shut behind her? Rage directed at his mother and his aunt. Rage at the pain Grace had suffered. Rage at anyone and anything that would set a wedge between himself and her.

He knew the answer even as he stood frozen in shock at the realisation.

He was in love with Nayao.

He loved everything about her.

Her strength, her beauty, even her determination to protect their children. Especially that!

Never had he thought anything could feel as strong as his rage, but he felt it now.

Love.

Such love that it tamed his fury. The anger wasn't gone, but it was tempered. It didn't rule him. And that was yet another shock.

He had been such a fool! He'd been afraid of his legacy of rage, afraid to risk hurting anyone, so he had hidden away from society and allowed his relatives to run roughshod over him. He'd never had an inkling of how powerful love could be. He'd never guessed that there was any woman who could tame his rage and show him how love changed everything!

He now knew he would up-end his entire life for her. She was everything he needed, everything he wanted, and everything he loved. But before he could claim her he had to make his world as safe as possible for her and for their children.

While the thud of the door behind Grace still echoed in the chamber, Declan turned to his mother and aunt. He spoke calmly. He would not have them blame this on the Byrning legacy. He didn't want to frighten them with his anger. He meant to impress his decision upon them.

'I did not realise until this very moment how poisonous you both are,' he said. 'I thought my anger was a curse, but I think the real curses are your narrow minds, your bitter manipulations and how very small your world is.'

His mother snorted. 'Do not cut up at me. We have solved

the problem. We said nothing but the truth, and now her reputation is assured. Just as you ordered.'

Perhaps that was true. She had obeyed the letter of his command, but not the meaning. And he saw now that he could not force her to change. Therefore, he must look to protecting those who would be harmed by them.

'Hear me well, both of you. You shall have no knowledge of my children. You are wrong. Your judgement is flawed because your minds are closed. You cannot imagine that anyone could have value but yourselves.' He shook his head as he finally saw how small they were. 'I will not allow your poison to damage the next generation.'

And with that he departed. He had a great deal to do before tomorrow night's dance at Almack's. Much to do before he apologised to Grace in the only way possible.

Chapter Twenty-Three

Grace dressed slowly for Almack's. She knew what a triumph it was for her to get not one but three vouchers. Indeed, Phoebe and Lucy were chattering like old friends, giggling about one thing or another. But she couldn't share their excitement. Perhaps they would find their future husbands tonight. Perhaps they would find love. But she knew her future was set. There would be no grand experience tonight. There would be nothing but the certainty of a life spent alone.

Because she had already found her love. She had already fallen for Declan. No other man saw her so clearly. He called her by her Chinese name, he defended her reputation, and even fought his own mother on her behalf. She tried to find an exact moment when she'd tumbled into love, but it had been a gradual thing. The way he had looked at her in the crow's nest. The way he had appeared beneath the burned pagoda. She relived his kiss. She felt his need. And she ached whenever she saw him.

But that wasn't love. She knew that. That was lust and desire. What had made her realise that it was love was the devastation she'd felt at the idea that her foreign blood would taint him and his children. He was the epitome of English perfection, and she would only poison his power and his position.

She would not do that to him. And that willingness to sacrifice her feelings for him told her as clearly as a full sail where the wind blew. She loved him. She loved his children, who didn't even exist yet. She loved his seeking mind and his open heart.

And so she would leave for Italy, or Africa, or wherever the wind took her, rather than poison Declan with her tainted heritage.

Her sister took her hand, jolting her out of her dark thoughts. 'You can always sail again,' she said softly.

Grace nodded, knowing it was true. But it wouldn't be the answer she wanted. She'd sailed as a way to find a safety that hadn't existed in China. She'd become an excellent navigator as a way to create value for herself. And when she had no longer been protected aboard ship, and no longer allowed at the temple because of her age, she'd found safety with Lord Wenshire as he sailed for England.

Everything she had ever done had been to find a safe space where she could live and thrive. She'd never expected to find it with an English mandarin. But Declan had proved himself strong, respectful, and generous. And she loved him.

'I am tired of sailing,' she said honestly. 'Perhaps Father and I will find a place in Italy.'

'No!' Phoebe exclaimed as she came to Grace's side. 'You will find true love tonight. We all will!'

Grace exchanged a knowing look with her sister. Phoebe had a generous heart, but also a naïve one. She still believed in fairy tales and Grace found that charming.

'Maybe I will,' she finally said. 'Who knows where the wind will blow?'

'Exactly!' Phoebe declared.

And then she all but dragged the two girls downstairs, where Lord Wenshire was waiting with Phoebe's parents.

'My goodness. I cannot credit such loveliness,' he said. 'You three astound me.'

'You are the best of fathers,' Grace said, feeling every word.

And Lucy echoed it a thousandfold.

In the end, the three girls climbed into a single carriage with Lord Wenshire. Phoebe's parents weren't allowed in Almack's without vouchers, whereas Grace's father had a title and would not be turned aside. Grace counted it a mistake that she hadn't thought to demand vouchers for Phoebe's parents, but everyone assured her they were well pleased with the situation.

After all, Pheobe would not have got a voucher at all without her.

They entered Almack's amid the usual crowds of debutantes. There were whispers, of course, and pointed stares, but Grace was used to them. Lucy seemed unnerved, but Phoebe shone brighter than them both. She heard the sneers. None of them could avoid it. But the girl simply grinned brightly and talked with excitement about how wonderful it was that the Duchess had sponsored them all.

It wouldn't have worked if the Duchess and Countess hadn't played their part. But they were there, right by the front entrance, when Grace presented their vouchers. The ladies exclaimed at their beauty, applauded their curtsies, and immediately introduced all three of them to an entire line of gentlemen.

Clearly they were working very hard to make all three of them acceptable to any man who wasn't one of their sons. And the girls did their best to charm, enchant, and otherwise dazzle the men who bowed before them.

But Grace's heart wasn't in it.

That was until Declan strode in.

He looked every inch the Duke he was. He wore black, with a red ruby in his white cravat. His boots gleamed, but not as brightly as his eyes as he scanned the crowd until his gaze landed on her. Then he smiled, and her heart tripped in her chest.

How she loved that man. Just looking at him made her feel safe. She knew, despite everything to the contrary, that he would make sure nothing harmed her in his presence. Not even his mother, who was just then coming to his side with a furious expression.

'Declan,' the woman said. 'What are you doing here?' Her voice wasn't loud enough for people to hear clearly, but the question was there on her face for all to see.

'I am here,' he said, 'to make my choice.'

And with those words he disentangled his mother's hand from his forearm and walked straight into the pattern of the dance.

It was incredibly disruptive. Dancers scattered before him, and the music faltered until everything was in disarray. But of course the dance had already been disrupted, because Grace hadn't been able to move from the moment he'd entered the hall.

It had been one thing to see him, to talk to him, to do such secret things with him when she hadn't been aware of her feelings. It was desire, it was distraction, it was excitement. But now she knew it was love. She was in love with him. And he was stepping through the crowd of people like a warrior of old, coming to stand directly before her.

'Your Grace,' she murmured as she dipped into a curtsey.

'Miss Richards,' he said as he pulled her up.

And he kept drawing her hand up, higher and higher, as he pressed his mouth to the back of her glove.

Somewhere in the distant part of her mind she was aware

of people staring at them. She heard outraged murmurs, and the Duchess saying something sharp to someone. She didn't care. All that mattered was that he was looking into her eyes as if she were the wind in his sails after a long stillness.

'Marry me.'

She read the words from his lips because she could not hear over the roaring in her ears.

'What?'

His lips curved and he stepped forward. 'I'm such an idiot. You kept saying that love was not enough. It's not enough if it's yours alone. That's what you meant. You love me, but that's not enough.'

She swallowed, tears destroying her vision. 'Your Grace—' she began, but her words were choked off as he dropped down to one knee before her.

'I love you. That's what I forgot to say. I love you. I want to marry you.'

She stared at him, not knowing what to do.

'I am the best that England has to offer. I am clever, educated, and titled. I lay all that at your feet, Miss Grace Nayao Richards. And I want more than the best of England at my side. I want the best of China.'

She blinked. 'But I am not the best of China or of anywhere.'

'You are beautiful and clever. You question things and learn. And you have taught me so much that I never even thought to wonder about.' He pressed his lips to her hands. 'There is a whole wide world beyond England, and I want to share every bit of it with you.'

'Have you lost your mind?'

A male voice cut through the crowd. She didn't even know who it was until Cedric grabbed Declan's arm.

'You can't marry her any more than I could!'

Declan didn't rise from where he still knelt on one knee. Instead, he rolled his eyes. 'Cousin, you are a boor.'

'And she's a thief and a liar.'

Her head jerked round. She heard the condemnation in Cedric's voice but did not understand it. Both men knew she had stolen to survive and lied to escape danger. But she had only done such out of necessity. Why would Cedric condemn her for that now?

'She's not really Lord Wenshire's daughter,' Cedric continued, his voice echoing loudly in the silent room. 'She lied about it in China and she's still lying to him. She is not his child.'

Grace's mouth dropped open. How could he know this? Then she remembered. Lucy had told him and had sworn him to secrecy. And now he had betrayed them both.

A slap rang out, loud and sharp. Grace had not seen her sister step forward, but the sound was clear as it echoed through the room. Not to mention the sight of Lucy's bright red handprint on Lord Domac's cheek.

'I did not think you could stoop any lower,' Lucy cried. 'And to think I once thought you clever. Safe, clever, and kind.' She shook her head. 'You have fooled me just as your father fooled your mother. You are a villain worse than Lord Jasper.'

Cedric reared up, his expression changing to one of horror as he looked at Lucy. Then he looked around at the crowd, and he flushed a dark red. 'Lucy, I didn't mean—'

'Step away, Cedric. Or I swear to God I will put you into the ground.'

That was Declan, his voice cold and hard as he stood to face his cousin.

'Not a penny, Cedric. Not a penny to you or your sisters.

You know that is how they survive now. It is upon my charity. But I will end it.'

'You can't—' Cedric began.

But it all was forestalled by Grace's father. He began swinging his cane as he cleared a path forward.

'Stop it!' he bellowed as he whipped the cane up and down between the men. 'Good God, I am ashamed to be English. Stop it!'

Both men had no choice but to back away, and in that space Grace looked to her father. She had tried so many times to tell him the truth, but it had always seemed too dangerous. And now she was exposed.

'I'm so sorry,' she said. 'I didn't speak English. I didn't know why you had chosen me. I didn't realise what you believed.'

She truly hadn't known he thought her his daughter. All she'd been told by the monks was that he was taking her away from China. And that was exactly where she'd wanted to be—away and safe.

'Hush…hush, child,' her father said as he set his cane on the floor. 'I knew the truth from the beginning. The woman I loved and our child died years before. I knew that long before I went to the temple.'

Grace gasped in surprise.

Lucy did as well, her hands clasped tight in front of her.

'You knew?' Lucy whispered.

'I did.' He touched Lucy's cheek, and then he smiled at Grace. 'I could not save my child, but I could save you. I could bring you here and give you a life such as I would have given my own flesh and blood.' He looked disdainfully about them. 'But I can see that was foolish. My own people are as ignorant and cruel as yours.' He lifted his chin. 'If you wish, we can leave at once for Italy, or Morocco, or any other land. We can try again to live without such idiocy.'

This was too much. Grace could not understand it. She stood there, looking at her sister, looking too at her father, who offered her a safe place far away from here.

What was she to do?

'Forget them,' Declan said. 'Forget them all. Look at me.'

She turned to him and felt her face heat with embarrassment. He was back on one knee before her.

'You should not be on the floor,' she whispered.

'It is our custom. I will stay here until you answer.'

'But you cannot want me,' she whispered. 'I am...'

'What?' he pressed. 'What are you? A by-blow of mixed blood? I don't care. A woman who has survived on her wit and her skills? Absolutely. A woman who can choose her future. A future with her father, who loves her, or...' He gathered her hands and tugged her closer to him. 'Or a future with me. You are the woman I love, Nayao. Stay with me.'

He loved her? Not possible.

And yet she saw it in his eyes. She felt it in his hands where he held her. And she knew it in her heart. He did love her.

'But your mother...' she whispered.

'Do you know why I have proposed this way? Here in front of the *haut ton*? Because it will be a huge scandal. It will be spoken of from this day on, long after we are dead and buried. I want everyone to know that you are exquisite and that I love you. That I will defend you and honour you until the end of my days. And any who speak against you will have to answer to me.'

How his words filled her. Everything she wanted, everything she hadn't dared dream of, was right here before her.

On one knee before her.

'And our children?'

'I adore them already.' He drew her forward. 'Don't be afraid. Remember the people who loved and protected you. Our children will have us. They will know more than this tiny corner of England. They will thrive, no matter what others say, because we will love them.'

Would that be enough? She didn't know.

'I never want them to be alone.'

'Neither do I,' he said. 'I will never abandon them, and I will never abandon you. I love you.'

She didn't have an answer. Not one that came from her lips. And yet she heard herself gasp. She felt her knees buckle as he steadied her coming down to the floor. Soon they were face to face, both on their knees, and he braced her even as he touched her face.

'Could you love me?' he whispered.

She nodded, unable to force the words out. But then other words came. 'How can you love me?'

'How can I not? You are everything I want.'

Then he kissed her. Right in front of his mother, his aunt, and all the *haut ton*. He pressed his lips to her mouth and wrapped an arm around her shoulders until she was deep in his embrace. And from that position she opened to him. She gripped him tight as he supported her. And when they separated to draw breath, he whispered into her ear.

'Will you marry me?'

What could she say? He was her safety. He was her love. 'Yes.'

'I have a special licence. We can be wed tonight.'

'What?'

'I will not let you change your mind.'

Or perhaps he would not let his mother or those around him force his hand.

Her gaze flickered to the people who surrounded them, all with their mouths agape.

'No,' he whispered. 'Don't doubt me. I will wait until you are ready or I will marry you this very night. Nothing will change my mind.'

'What of our children? What of your political power?'

'Both stronger for my being with you.' He touched her cheek. 'Do you not feel it? How we teach each other? How we make each other better?'

She did. She knew it because with him she felt free enough to do anything.

'Now,' she said. 'Tonight.'

'An excellent choice, Your Grace!' he cried as he pushed to his feet.

She didn't realise he was carrying her until she began to rise with him. Somehow he'd slipped his arm under her, and now he settled her against his solid chest.

'Your Grace!' she cried, alarmed.

'Declan,' he corrected. 'Call me by my given name.'

She smiled. 'I love you, Declan.'

'I love you.'

Chapter Twenty-Four

They were married by special licence that evening. Her father gave her away. Her sister and Phoebe stood radiantly by her side. They were her support.

The Duchess and her sister also attended, as did Lord Domac, using every possible moment to dissuade Declan.

Grace said nothing, waiting to see if he would allow their constant interference.

He did not.

After his mother's first interruption—just as the priest entered the church—he told them all to be silent or to be gone. And by gone, he continued, he meant that they would be gone from his life and his support.

Such was the power of his statement that they all stood silent.

Then he turned to her.

'I love you,' he said. 'But if they are too much for you—'

'Will you always defend me? Against them? Against others?'

'I vow it before them and before God.'

She smiled. 'I vow it as well. I will stand by you, aid you, and love you until my last breath. As I will our children.'

His smile was radiant. His kiss was passionate. And for her, that was the promise that sealed their marriage bond well before the priest spoke his words or either of them said, 'I do.'

Twenty minutes later it was done. They were married.

And that night, as he brought her to his home, she knew all would be well.

Except for one small, but enormous detail.

The marriage bed.

The English and the Chinese alike prized virgins. And though she had never had relations with a man, she could not prove her virginity. She understood better than most what men looked for to prove virginity. They wanted blood on their marriage sheets. They wanted pain during the coupling. She didn't know if such a thing was possible for her. So many men had told her that she was unnatural. What if she could not prove what she knew to be true?

She did not say anything about her concerns as they travelled to his home. She did not say anything as he introduced the staff. Nor did she say anything when her new maid was presented to her. It was Molly Smithee, the daughter of the servant at her come-out ball, come to be her abigail.

The girl was indeed pretty, but she was also smart and capable, ready with soothing words as she helped Grace into the bath already prepared for her. There hadn't been time since her come-out for Grace to teach the girl how to defend herself, but there would be plenty now, she supposed.

'I've set a salve for your use by the bedside,' Molly said, her voice low as she pointed. 'Mama says it will help with the ache.'

Grace nodded. She had heard of such things as well. Molly said other things, but Grace couldn't think. So much had happened this night. She could not believe she was married.

It wasn't until she was dried, and dressed in a gown of sheer silk, that she thought to grab the girl's hand.

'What will he do?' she asked. 'What will he do if he thinks I am not a virgin?'

The girl's eyes widened with shock, then she shook her head. 'He can have the marriage annulled.'

'Annulled?' She did not know this word.

'Ended as if it had never happened.'

No. *No!* He would not take it away now, would he? Not after their vows, not after all he had said.

'I cannot prove it,' she whispered. 'I have climbed ratlines, fought with sails in storms. I have whipped men and done things no woman has done before.' She swallowed. 'I have been told many times that because of that there will be no blood when I am married. That I will not be able to prove whether this is my first time or not.'

Molly nodded, but had no answer.

Every girl heard such things growing up. *Do not do these things. It will take away your virginity, whether or not you have been with a man.*

'In China,' Grace whispered, 'a woman can be killed for this.'

'Would the Duke do that?' Molly asked.

Grace bit her lip, trying to think rationally. She could not believe a man who had just vowed to love her for ever would do such a thing. But men were not always rational when it came to the marriage bed. And by his own admission his Byrning blood was prone to rages.

'He won't kill me,' she said, her voice strengthening. 'He will believe me.' She wrapped her arms tight around her belly. 'He will believe me,' she repeated.

And then there was no more time. There was a knock at the door that joined their rooms and Declan entered. He, too, had bathed, and his hair was still damp. His eyes gleamed in the firelight, and he walked with a predatory kind of grace. Not as a man who lived on a sailing ship, but as a creature who was wholly sure of himself in his domain.

Grace adored the sight of him.

But he paused when he saw her, and his steps slowed. 'You are afraid,' he said.

She didn't answer.

'That's natural. In the span of a few hours, everything has changed for you. For me as well.'

'I am not a natural woman,' she said, meaning that she was an orphan of mixed blood who had navigated ships and only just come to England. Nothing about that was normal or natural.

He touched her cheek, stroking it gently with his fingers. 'You seem completely natural to me.' He caressed the edge of her jaw before trailing his hand down the length of her neck. 'Exquisitely beautiful.' He grinned. 'And now you are mine.'

She had no time to search his face for subtle meanings. For all that he seemed a gentle man, she did not like his words of ownership. And yet, perversely, she thrilled to the mastery in his kiss. She enjoyed surrendering to him.

She opened her mouth to his. She felt his fingers slide across the ribbon of her gown and she trembled when she felt him pull it free. The silk gaped open across her chest, and his mouth followed the trail set by his fingers. Her body heated, her knees weakened, and her breath caught with each scrape of his teeth across her flesh. She gripped his shoulders to stay upright, but he clearly had no desire to stay standing.

He scooped her up in his arms and laid her gently on the bed. She pushed herself up, supporting herself on her elbows—not because she wanted to stand, but because she wanted a better view of her husband as he stripped out of his dressing gown.

She had never seen him naked before. She knew the shapes of men's bodies, knew how to evaluate them for strength against the sails or nimbleness in the rigging. He was neither bulky nor wiry. He was tall and powerful, his muscles reddish gold in the firelight. And his power seemed to ripple across his whole body as he came forward.

'What do you see,' he whispered, 'when you look at me like that?'

'A fortress,' she said as she skimmed her hand across his shoulder. 'And a sail,' she went on as she stroked the breadth of his chest.

He arched a brow at her. 'Those don't usually go together.'

'No, they don't…'

But she saw it in him. Strong shoulders to protect her, and the power to take her wherever they might need to go, even if it was nowhere but right here.

She shook her head. 'My head is muddled.'

He grinned. 'Good.'

Then he kissed her again, gently pressing her back into the bed. He thrust his tongue inside her mouth, he duelled with hers and he used his hands to push away her gown. First off her shoulders, then down to her waist. Her arms were pinned then, caught by the fabric. She knew she could rip her hands free if she wanted to. She knew she could fight if she needed to. But she didn't want to.

Instead, she let herself arch into the stroke of his hands on her breasts. Her head pressed back as his mouth trailed across her body. Such attention he gave to her breasts. His hands shaped her, his fingers pinched her nipples, and then his mouth suckled until she was writhing beneath him.

Then she felt the weight on the bed shift. While she lay panting, he stroked his hands across her feet and up her calves. His fingers were strong as they kneaded her flesh, and he moved steadily upward, bringing her gown with him until it lay tangled across her hips while he knelt between her knees.

She was open before him, and it was nothing like what had happened in the kitchen. This time it was his hands on her legs, his thumbs stroking her wetness. He spread her open, and when she thought to tense he leaned forward and blew air across her wet nipple.

The experience was so shocking—the cold on the wet—that she gasped. And then he captured her nipple between his lips while his fingers did wonderful things between her thighs.

She cried out as pleasure shot between her breast and her groin. And then her breath caught again as he rolled over the spot between her thighs. That wonderful place he had taught her. Over and over he stroked her, while her legs trembled.

Then he bit her nipple. Not hard, but sharp. Enough to shock her. And as she arched from the sensation he entered her. One hard thrust.

She felt the intrusion like a bolt of lightning. One that stretched her wide and filled her to bursting. It was too much, and it was wonderful.

She lifted her knees, not even knowing what she wanted. But he did.

He began to move and she revelled in it. Harder, faster.

She gripped him with her knees. She clung to his shoulders. She arched down against each thrust.

She heard his breath, harsh against her ear. Or was that hers?

Again and again he drove into her.

Climbing.

Building.

Bursting!

She flew on waves of bliss.

She had no idea how long she floated, but when she returned to herself she realised he had collapsed beside her, and she was snuggled into his side. She heard his breath steady. Hers, too. And she smiled for a while.

Until she remembered.

'It didn't hurt,' she whispered.

Her body stiffened when she realised she'd said that aloud. Afraid, she opened her eyes. Then she panicked when she saw him watching her.

'Grace?'

She swallowed, then adjusted herself on the bed. If there wasn't blood, she'd cut herself to make sure there was. But how would she do it without him seeing? Oh, heaven, she was flustered.

'Grace, what's wrong?'

'I...um... I need...'

She needed to fool him. He couldn't know. But—

He grabbed her arm, stilling her with the strength in his grip. It wasn't bruising, but it was firm.

'What do you need?'

His voice was calm, no sign of his fury, but there was a tightness in his face. If she'd thought ahead she could have had a convenient lie ready. But she'd never expected... She'd never thought...

'It didn't hurt,' she said.

'That's good.'

'I know I'm not a natural woman,' she said, her voice low. 'I know—'

'You are natural to me.'

'I have never been with a man before. Never before you. I swear. But—'

His expression abruptly softened. 'It doesn't always hurt for a virgin.' He flashed her a quick grin. 'Not if it's done right.'

'Oh.' No one had ever told her that. 'But there should be blood, yes?'

She moved to lift the coverlet, but he held her still.

'I don't need to see any blood. I know you were a virgin.'

'But—'

'I know.'

She blinked. 'How?'

He chuckled. 'Because you know nothing of sex. Because you haven't the wiles of a courtesan. No woman could lie so effectively.' He pressed a kiss to her lips. 'And besides, I don't care. So long as there is no one else after me, I am well content.'

'After you?' She didn't understand what he meant. 'I will not service your friends!'

He nodded, pulling her in tight. 'Damn right, you won't.'

He used his weight to gently settle her down against him. She curled tighter into his body. She smelled his scent, and immediately felt her body begin to relax. It took a while, but in time she felt her tension slide away.

'Is that why you were afraid?' he asked. 'Because you thought I was worried about your virginity?'

She shrugged. 'Yes and no. I think I was afraid about many things. This is very new.'

He was silent as he held her more securely against him. 'Were you afraid I would rage at you?'

She thought of his legacy and shook her head. 'I can defend myself. You are large, but I am quick.'

She felt him grin. 'Good.'

Then he pressed a kiss to her temple. He was silent for a long time. Long enough for her to think he had fallen asleep. She was nearly there herself.

And then he spoke again, his words barely above a whisper. 'Do you know why I love you?'

She was wide awake now. 'Why?'

'Because you make my world new. Before I met you, I had endless days and nights of the same damn thing. Certainly there were happy times, and there were bad times, but all in all the same thing. And every day I grew duller, emptier and colder.'

'So I am…' She searched for the right word. 'I am a novelty?'

'No!' He pressed a kiss to her temple. 'You have shown me that there is more to life than England. There is a whole world out there. And I want to share it with you.' He smiled as he looked at her. 'I told you this at Almack's. Did you not believe me?'

She had. She did. But hearing it now, like this, naked and enfolded in his arms, it came to her why she loved him back.

'You are a novelty to me,' she said. 'You have offered me a world that I never knew was possible. A life where I can be safe and new.' She pressed a kiss to his lips. 'I would not change that for anything. I love you.'

'And I love you.'

This time when they made love it was slow and sweet. And since she knew what was coming she could enjoy it more. And he could teach her more.

When it was done, she stretched out beside him. She was fully sated, fully delighted. And together they slept.

Chapter Twenty-Five

Reality didn't intrude until the next morning. They'd awoken late, eaten lazily, and spoken of things they could do another day. Tomorrow or the next. They were still at the breakfast table when the butler arrived with the mail. On one of the letters Grace read the name of her father's solicitor.

'What is that?' she asked as Declan slit open the letter.

'Your dowry.'

'The boat? Now it is yours.'

'Yes.'

He was quiet, his expression relaxed, and she wasn't sure what that meant.

'What are you going to do with it?'

He smiled at her, the letter in his hand. And then he set it on the table near her. 'What do you want to do with it?'

'Me?'

'Yes, you. Whatever you want, I'll see it done.'

She thought long and hard about that. She toyed with her teacup and she traced the letters on the linen paper.

'Your cousin did everything so that he could have the boat,' she said.

'Yes.'

'So let him have it.'

Her husband reared back. 'What? Reward him for everything—?'

'We would not be married were it not for him.'

Declan frowned, clearly thinking. 'I do not like giving Cedric what he wants. He needs to earn his keep.'

She agreed. 'He will.' She grinned at him. 'I may have sailed the ship, but it was my sister who advised on the cargo, who balanced the accounts, and handled the money. We had many ports of call along the way. She barely spoke English at first, but she knew what to sell and what to buy.'

He frowned at her. 'How could she know such a thing?'

'While I spent my days learning how to navigate, she spent her days with the merchants. She learned a very great deal.' She leaned forward. 'She is more clever than I am.'

He snorted. 'I doubt that.'

'I don't.'

'So, do you think she should have the management of *The Integrity*?'

Her husband was quick. He understood exactly. 'I think she should. And let Cedric work on it.'

'As a sailor? He'd never agree.'

She shrugged. 'Then he cannot have it. But it is what he wants more than anything. He told me so himself.'

'He would work as a sailor, completely under her control?'

'Not exactly. There are a few improvements to the boat that Captain Banakos wants, and selecting a cargo can take months. We shall give Lucy control during that time and see how it goes.'

'Then we shall give it to Cedric?'

She shrugged. 'Then we will ask Lucy what she recommends.'

He pursed his lips, considering. 'Cedric, supervised by your sister? Will Lucy agree?'

'Lucy will be thrilled.'

Epilogue

One month later, Grace was sharing tea with her sister. Lucy had found some Chinese tea at an apothecary, and they both relished the taste. But what Grace relished more was the moment when her new husband sauntered in. He'd been closeted in his library with his steward for hours, but now he strode into the parlour with an excited grin on his face.

'What has you so happy?' she asked as he came for a kiss.

'I have finished with my solicitor, my banker, and my steward, not to mention my valet and your maid.'

She blinked. 'Why ever would you be talking to my maid?'

'Because we must go. Now.'

He tugged her upright. She went willingly, but stopped when she was fully upright. 'Let me say goodbye to my sister—'

'No, no. She is coming with us.' He turned to Lucy. 'If you will join us, please?'

Lucy frowned, but nodded. In truth, her eyes were dancing. She enjoyed surprises much more than Grace ever had.

Soon enough they were all in a carriage, headed towards... the docks? Grace could smell the air and knew that terrible, wonderful scent from far away.

'What have you up your sleeve?' she asked her husband.

'Only what we have already discussed.'

She couldn't think of it. This last month of their marriage had been a delight. Nights of passion coupled with long hours of learning about one another. They had discussed boats and crops, Parliament and royalty, and every other topic under the sun. Too much to give her a hint as to what was coming and why it involved Lucy.

Until they arrived at *The Integrity*.

Captain Banakos was there, a broad grin on his weathered face, as was…

'Why is Lord Domac here?' Lucy whispered. 'I will not—'

'Oh, I remember now!' Grace exclaimed. And then she squeezed her sister's arm. 'Don't worry. You shall love this.'

Meanwhile, Declan rushed ahead, leaping with joy onto the deck of the large merchant ship. He greeted the captain with a warm embrace, and then arched a brow at his cousin, who was looking daggers at all of them.

'I'll make this quick, shall I?' Declan said as everyone made it on board. 'Miss Lucy Richards, your father and I have discussed things and come to an arrangement. The repairs on *The Integrity* are underway. It will take another month at least, but then she will be ready to set sail with a new cargo.' He leaned forward. 'Would you like to choose it?'

The girl's eyes widened as her hands flew to her mouth. It appeared she could not speak.

'Damn it!' Cedric snapped.

But he did not have a chance to continue as Declan turned to address him.

'I'm willing to give you a portion of that cargo, cousin. I'll let you supervise it, sail with it, and sell it in China as you initially planned. Any profit will be allotted to you and your sisters' dowries evenly.'

'What?' The man gaped at him.

'One condition, though.' He grinned as he turned to Lucy.

'She will be the one deciding on the cargo. She will be the one to set the price. And you will work under her and Captain Banakos. Prove your mettle and we can discuss the next sailing.'

'I'm to be her lackey?' Cedric asked, bristling.

'Yes,' Declan said cheerfully. 'For the next two months. If you want the boat.' He looked to Captain Banakos. 'I trust you will treat him as he deserves?'

The captain chuckled as he set his thumbs inside his waistband. 'That I will, Yer Grace. That I will.'

'Excellent,' Declan said as he grabbed Grace's hand. 'And now for your surprise.'

'What?' she said.

She'd been vastly entertained, watching her sister's reaction. Finally the girl was going to be able to put her skills to use. Few understood exactly how precious that was. Indeed, she'd been on the verge of asking if she could work on the crew as well. They'd need a navigator...

But she had no desire to leave Declan.

'Come along, my love,' he said as he tugged her down the gangplank.

They didn't go far, simply crossed to the bottom of the next gangplank. She frowned at the boat, seeing a sleek pleasure craft, large enough to weather turbulent seas, but not strong enough to carry a profitable cargo.

'What is this?' she asked.

'It's *The Duchess*,' he said as he gestured expansively at it. 'Or *The Duchess's Gift*. Or *The Duke's Pleasure*. I don't know. It's a yacht, and it's yours, my love.'

He scooped her up and began carrying her up the gangplank.

She squealed in surprise, but her eyes were on the sails, the lines, and everything else she could study.

'It's mine?' she whispered.

'It is,' he answered as he set her feet down. 'Will you teach me to sail, my love? Will you help me with the sails and the wheel and the...? I don't know what else?'

'But where are we going?'

He grinned as he spun her around. 'Wherever you want, so long as we are back within a month. Do you think I have been killing myself in my study these last weeks for no reason? It was to set everything in place so that we can sail to the Continent, or to Spain, or to wherever you choose, so long as we do it together. I want to see the world, and I want to do it with you.'

'The whole world?'

He shrugged. 'Or as much of it as we can see in a month. Possibly two the next time. But for now—'

'You must come back for Parliament.'

She had spent a great deal of time lately, learning the workings of his government.

He nodded, showing he was pleased, then shrugged. 'I must also be sure the crops are handled well.'

Farming. That was another thing she would need to study. Perhaps while they were sailing this beautiful boat.

'So we can play for a time now? We can sail—'

'Wherever you like for as long as it takes you to teach me everything.'

She laughed, knowing that would take a lifetime. 'I should like that very much,' she said.

'Good because we sail with the evening tide.'

She opened her mouth to argue, but he pressed a hand to her lips.

'I have a small crew who will help. Your bags are already on board, though I believe Molly was shocked by the clothes I have had made for you. And...' He waggled his eyebrows.

'We even have a crow's nest large enough for two. That took the longest time to arrange, but it's done now.'

He pointed up, so that she could see the double-sized barrel up top.

He had thought of everything, and she couldn't believe how happy she was. They would sail together! And even more than her own joy at the idea was seeing how absolutely thrilled he was. What a pleasure to see him so happy!

Then she looked at his clothes. 'Do you have equally scandalous attire?'

'I do.'

'Good. Then I believe we should both change, and I shall race you to the top.'

'Agreed.'

Then he dropped a kiss on her lips before dashing below decks. She was startled by how fast he moved. She had to jump to follow him.

It took longer than it should have for them to change. They were, after all, in the same stateroom together, and the bed was quite comfortable. But soon enough they were climbing the ratlines while she pointed out things that he needed to know. It wasn't until they were both settled one against the other in the crow's nest that she realised how incredibly happy she was.

'I never thought to be this lucky,' she whispered as she leaned back against him.

'Nor I,' he said. Then he pressed a kiss to her head. 'I love you, Nayao. I cannot imagine my life without you.'

'I love you,' she answered.

Then she twisted to kiss him. But just before her lips found his, he burst out laughing.

She pulled back, shocked and a little insulted, and then she looked to where he pointed.

There, still on the deck of *The Integrity*, stood Lucy and Cedric. They were nose to nose, both gesturing with hard, angry slashes.

'Oh, dear,' Grace said, fear skating up her spine. 'Maybe this wasn't a great idea.'

Cedric was much larger than her sister. He could hurt—

No, he couldn't.

While they watched, Captain Banakos grabbed Cedric in a casual headlock. Grace knew the position, knew as well how humiliating it was. And there he stood, holding Lord Domac in place, while Lucy leaned down and continued speaking. They couldn't hear the words, of course, but Grace knew her sister well.

Lucy was telling him exactly what cargo they would carry, and exactly what his responsibilities would be. Likely scrubbing the deck until his hands bled.

'She won't be too hard on him, will she?' Declan asked. 'He is a titled peer, or rather he will be eventually. I want him to learn what is needed on a boat, not—'

'She'll be fair with him…eventually. I trust Captain Banakos will keep them both in line.'

'Well, that will be an adventure for them, won't it?' Declan asked.

'That's their story,' she said as she twisted again to face her husband. 'I'm more interested in ours.'

'Me, too,' he said.

Then he pulled her into a kiss, one that they both knew would be repeated a hundred or more times up here. Because they had the time, now, and the freedom to be themselves. And the love to keep them afloat for the rest of their lives.

* * * * *

The Duke's Guide to Fake Courtship
*is Jade Lee's debut for
Harlequin Historical.
Be sure to look out for her next book in
the Daring Debutantes miniseries,
coming soon!*

HARLEQUIN
Reader Service

Enjoyed your book?

Try the perfect subscription for Romance readers and get more great books like this delivered right to your door.

See why over 10+ million readers have tried Harlequin Reader Service.

Start with a Free Welcome Collection with free books and a gift—valued over $20.

Choose any series in print or ebook.
See website for details and order today:

TryReaderService.com/subscriptions